WHERE ARE YOU LEOPOLD?

WHERE ARE YOU LEOPOLD?

HERO IN PLAIN SIGHT

BY SCHMITT & CAUT

BiG

Michel-Yves Schmitt
Writer

Vincent Caut
Artist

•

Miceal Beausang-O'Griafa
& Victoria Pierce
Translators

•

Amanda Lucido
& Victoria Pierce
US Edition Editors

Vincent Henry
Original Edition Editor

Jerry Frissen
Senior Art Director

Ryan Lewis
Junior Designer

Mark Waid
Publisher

Rights and Licensing - licensing@humanoids.com
Press and Social Media - pr@humanoids.com

WHERE ARE YOU, LEOPOLD?, BOOK 2: HERO IN PLAIN SIGHT. This title is a publication of Humanoids, Inc. 8033 Sunset Blvd. #628, Los Angeles, CA 90046. Copyright © 2021 Humanoids, Inc., Los Angeles (USA). All rights reserved. Humanoids and its logos are ® and © 2021 Humanoids, Inc. Library of Congress Control Number: 2020952031

 is an imprint of Humanoids, Inc.

First published in France under the title "Où es-tu Léopold ?" Copyright © 2013 La Boîte à Bulles & Michel-Yves Schmitt, Vincent Caut. All rights reserved. All characters, the distinctive likenesses thereof and all related indicia are trademarks of La Boîte à Bulles Sarl and / or of Michel-Yves Schmitt, Vincent Caut.

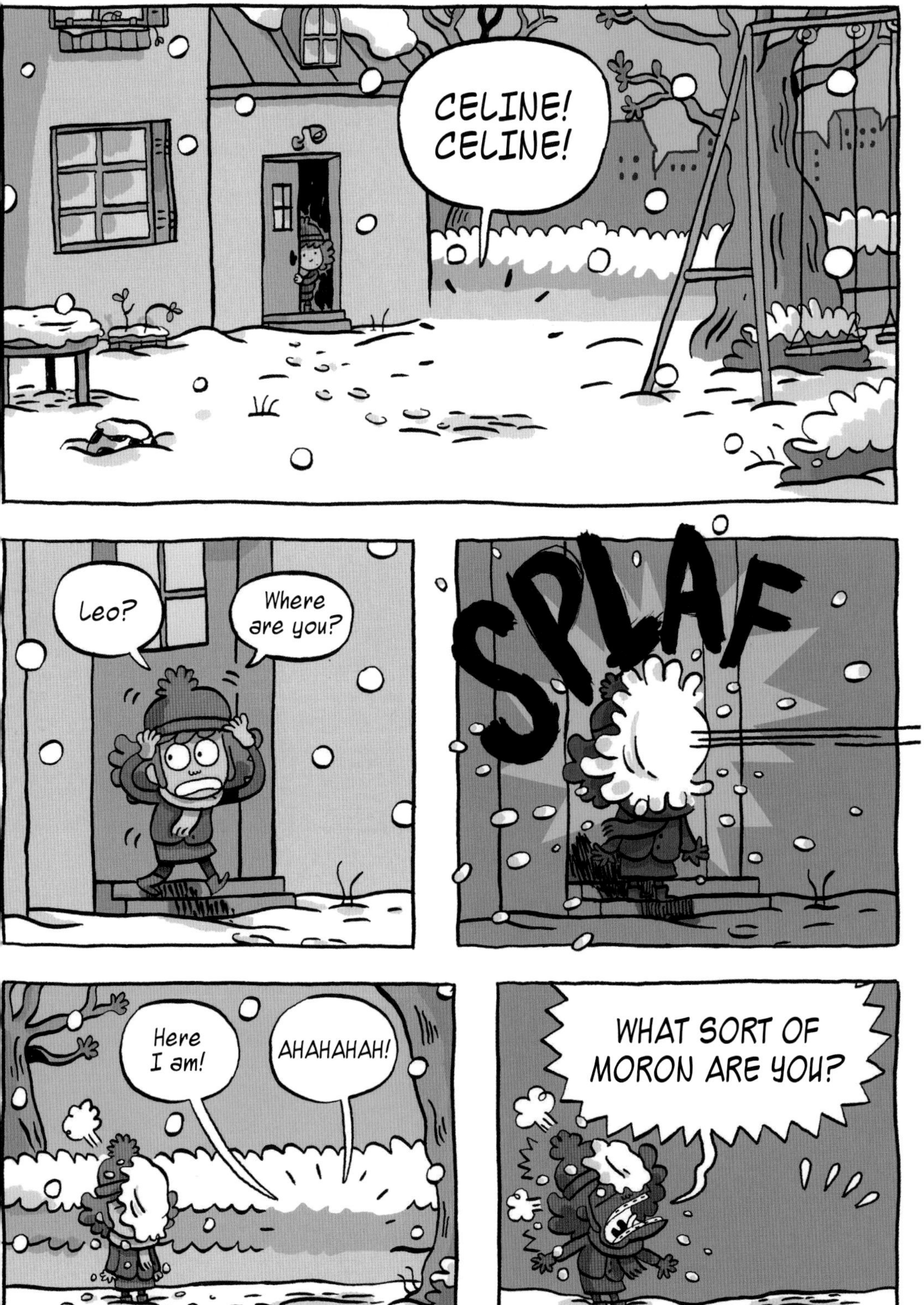
CELINE!
CELINE!
Leo?
Where are you?
SPLAF
Here I am!
AHAHAHAH!
WHAT SORT OF MORON ARE YOU?

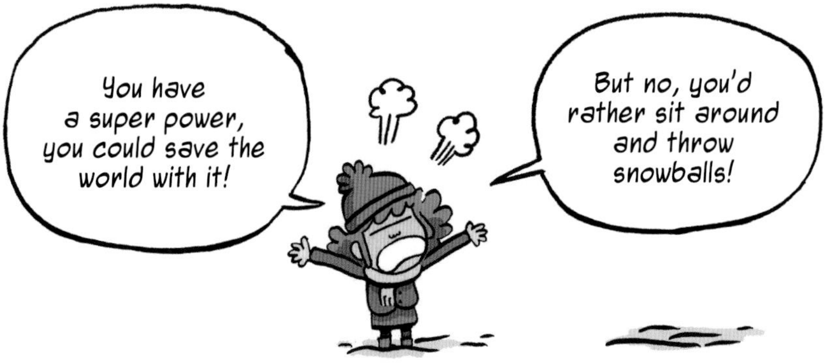
You have a super power, you could save the world with it!
But no, you'd rather sit around and throw snowballs!

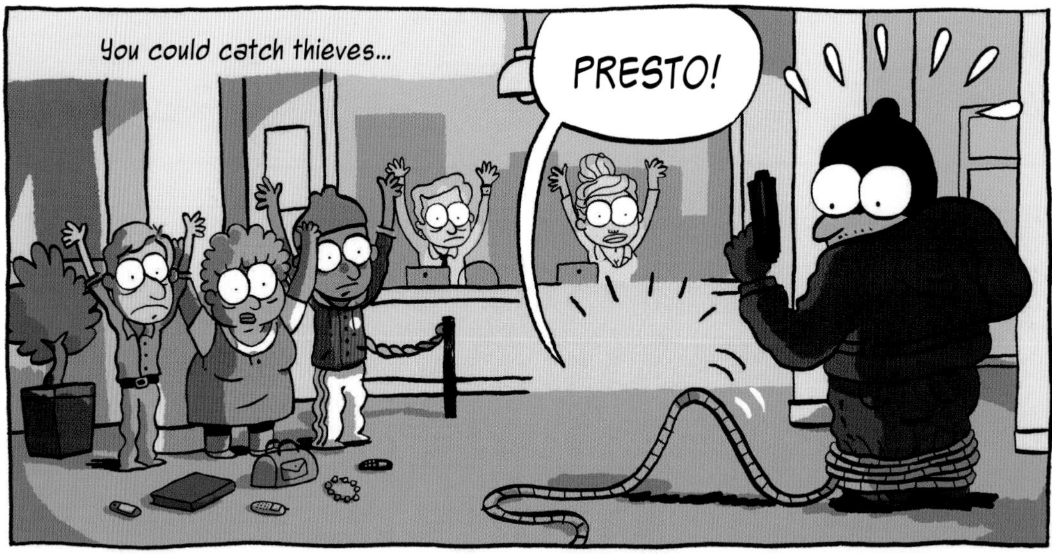
You could catch thieves...
PRESTO!

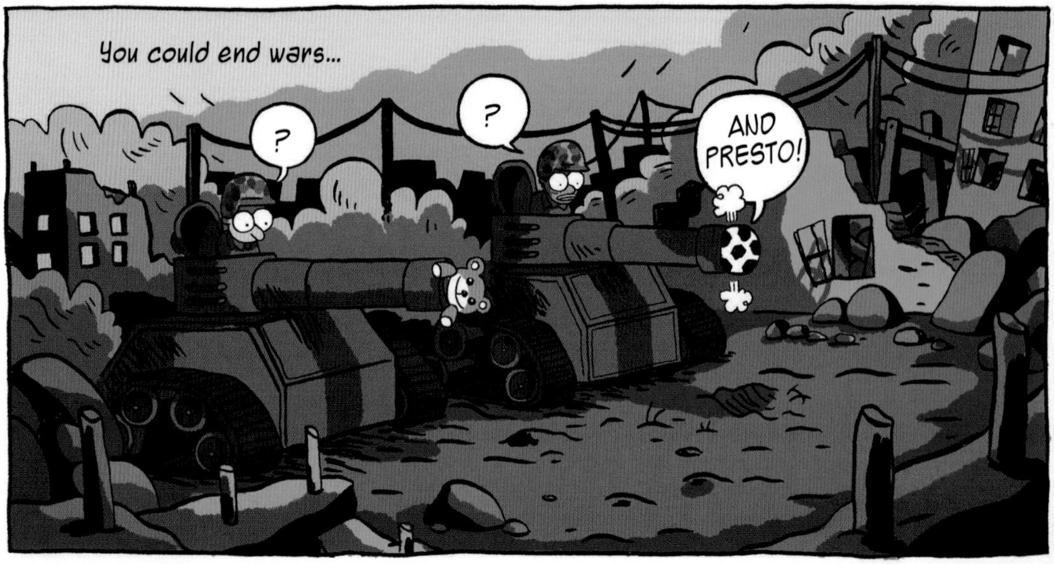
You could end wars...
?
?
AND PRESTO!

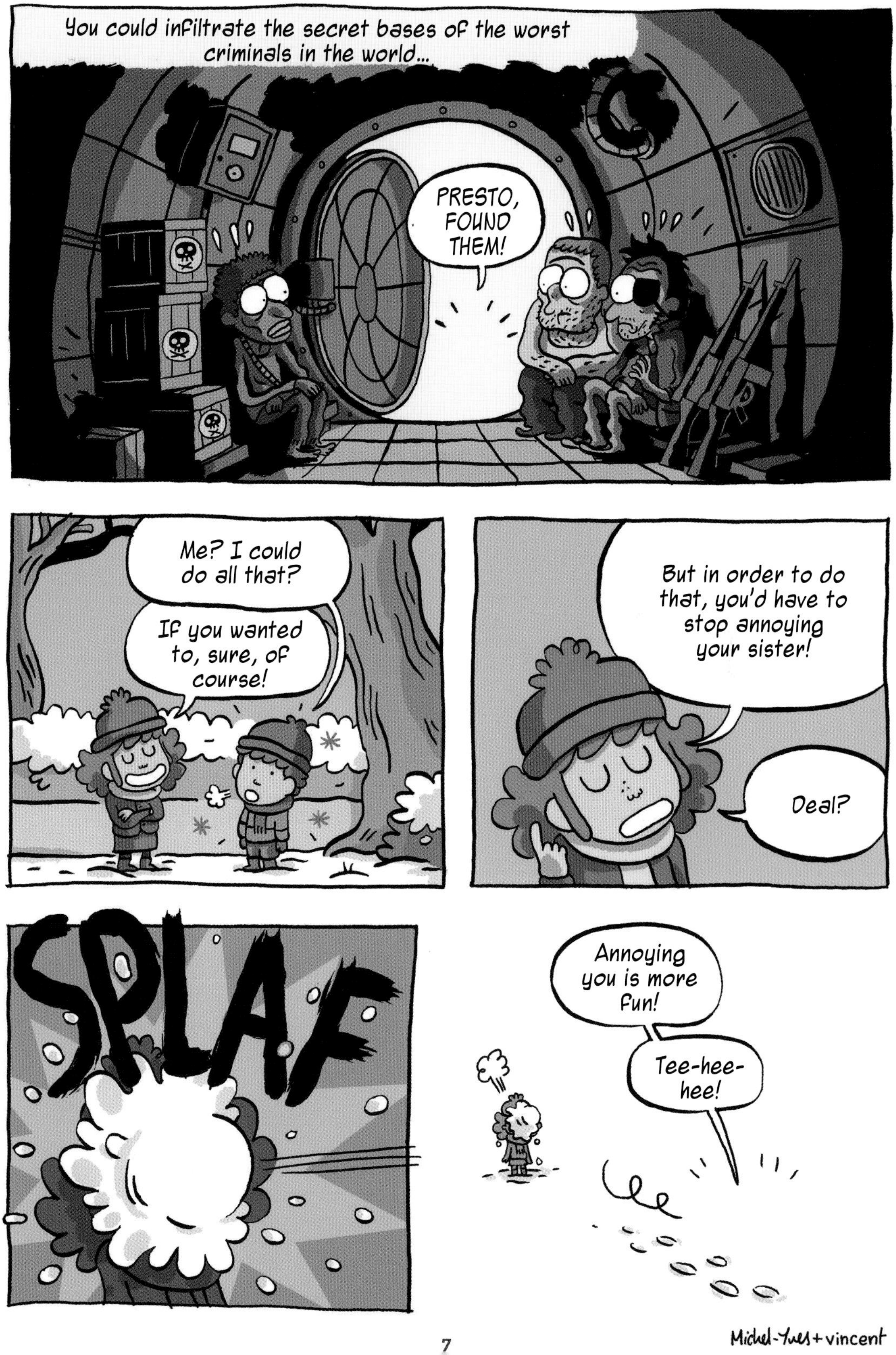
You could infiltrate the secret bases of the worst criminals in the world...
PRESTO, FOUND THEM!
Me? I could do all that?
If you wanted to, sure, of course!
But in order to do that, you'd have to stop annoying your sister!
Deal?
SPLAF
Annoying you is more fun!
Tee-hee-hee!
Michel-Yves + vincent

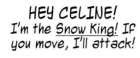

HEY CELINE! I'm the _Snow King!_ If you move, I'll attack!

AHAHAH! PATHETIC! I have an arsenal of a thousand snowballs! The entire bathtub is full of them!

Seriously?

HUH!

LET ME SEE!

Tee-hee-hee, tough luck!

They've all melted!

AH! LEOPOLD! Right on time for your bath!

Tee-hee-hee...

8

Michel-Yves + vincent

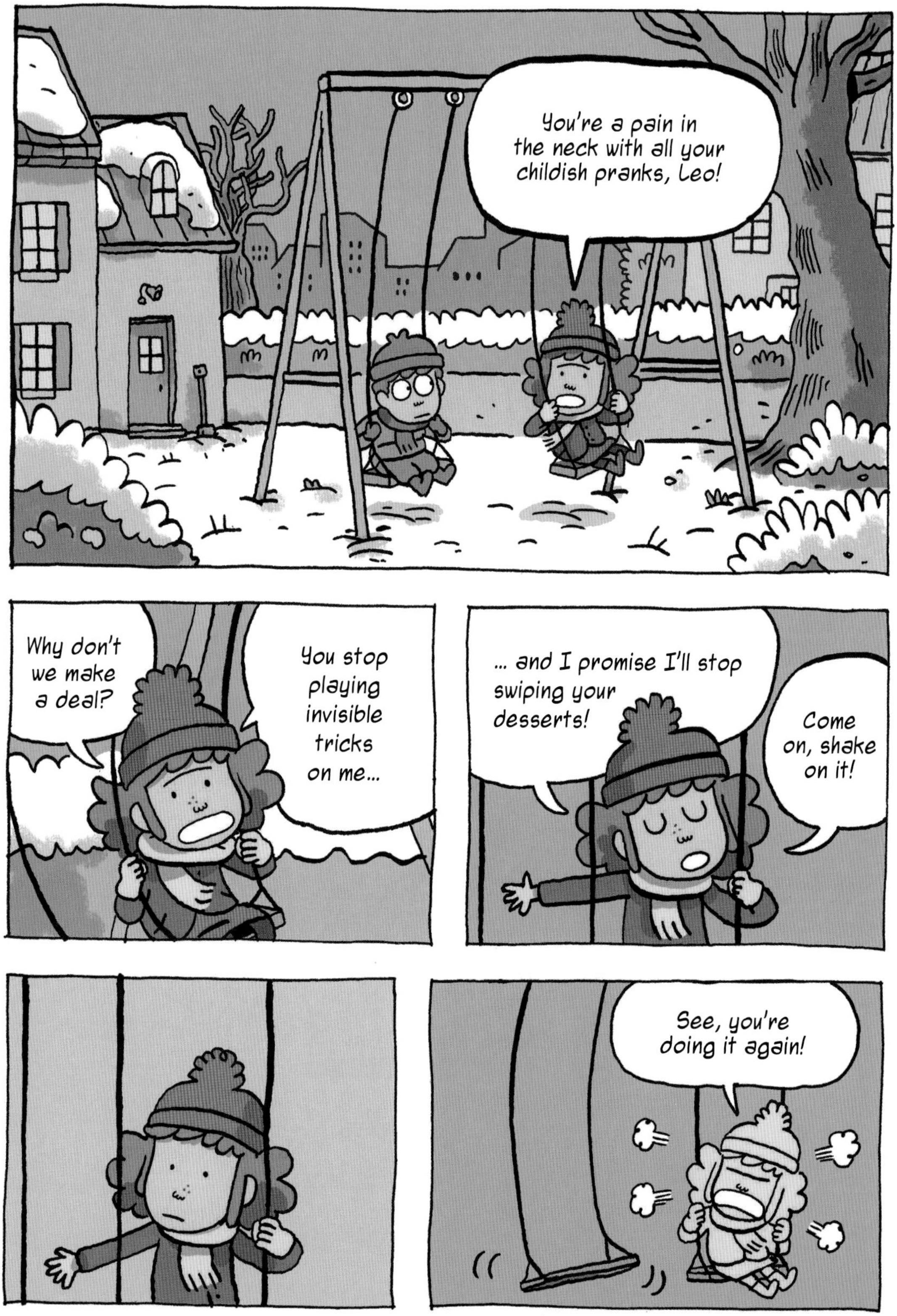
You're a pain in the neck with all your childish pranks, Leo!
Why don't we make a deal?
You stop playing invisible tricks on me...
... and I promise I'll stop swiping your desserts!
Come on, shake on it!
See, you're doing it again!

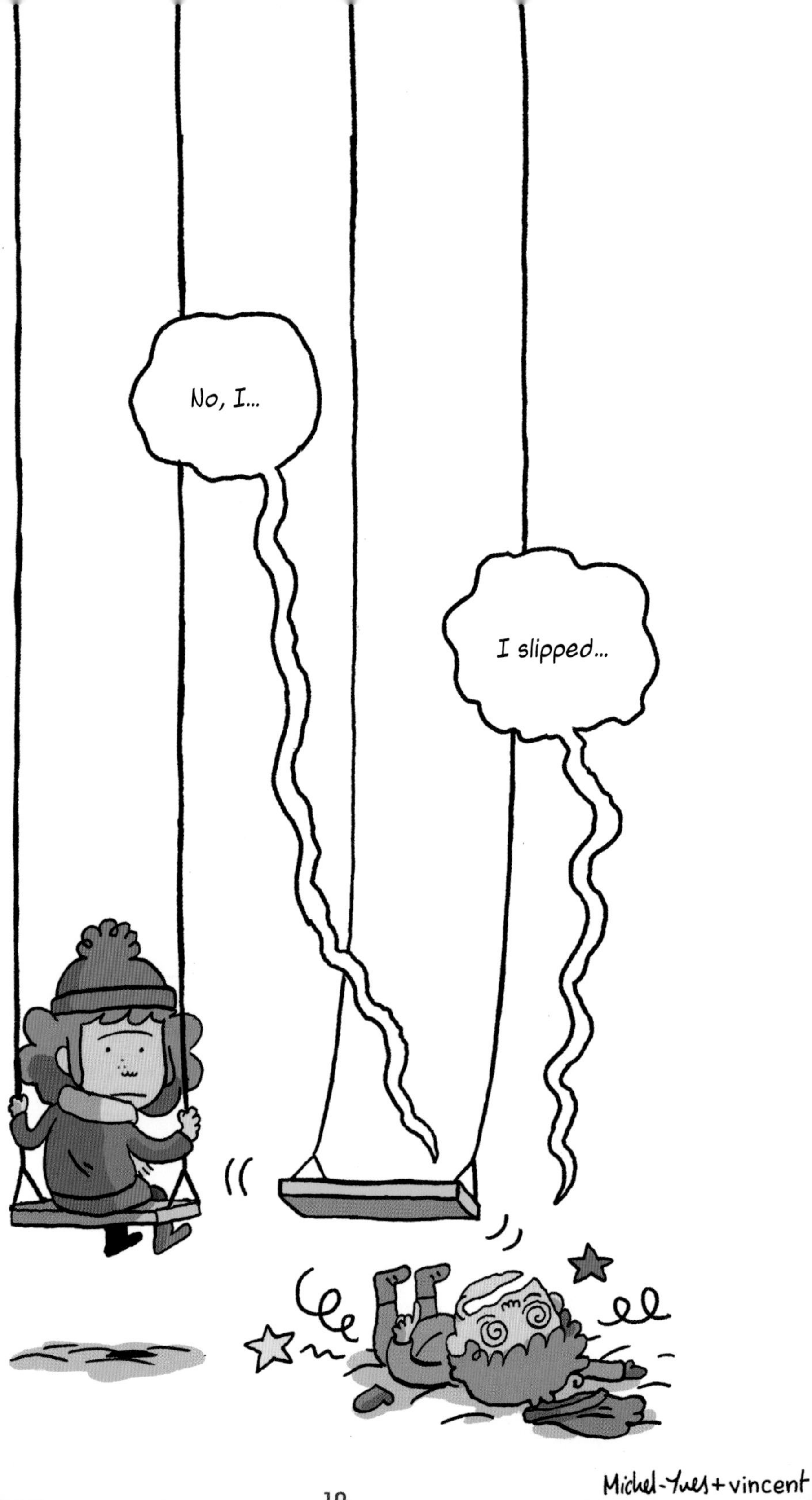
No, I...
I slipped...
Michel-Yves+vincent

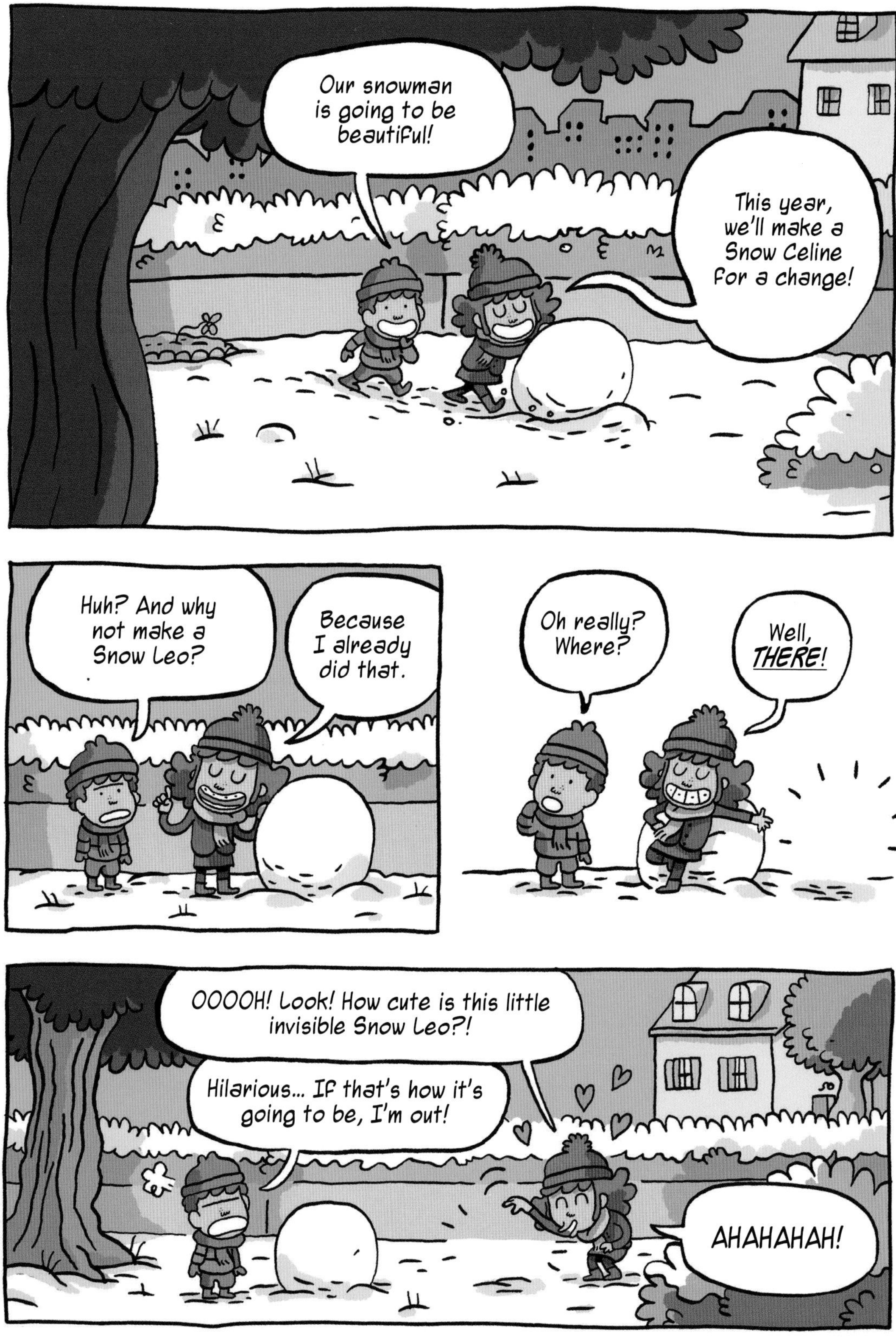
Our snowman is going to be beautiful!
This year, we'll make a Snow Celine for a change!
Huh? And why not make a Snow Leo?
Because I already did that.
Oh really? Where?
Well, ***THERE!***
OOOOH! Look! How cute is this little invisible Snow Leo?!
Hilarious... If that's how it's going to be, I'm out!
AHAHAHAH!

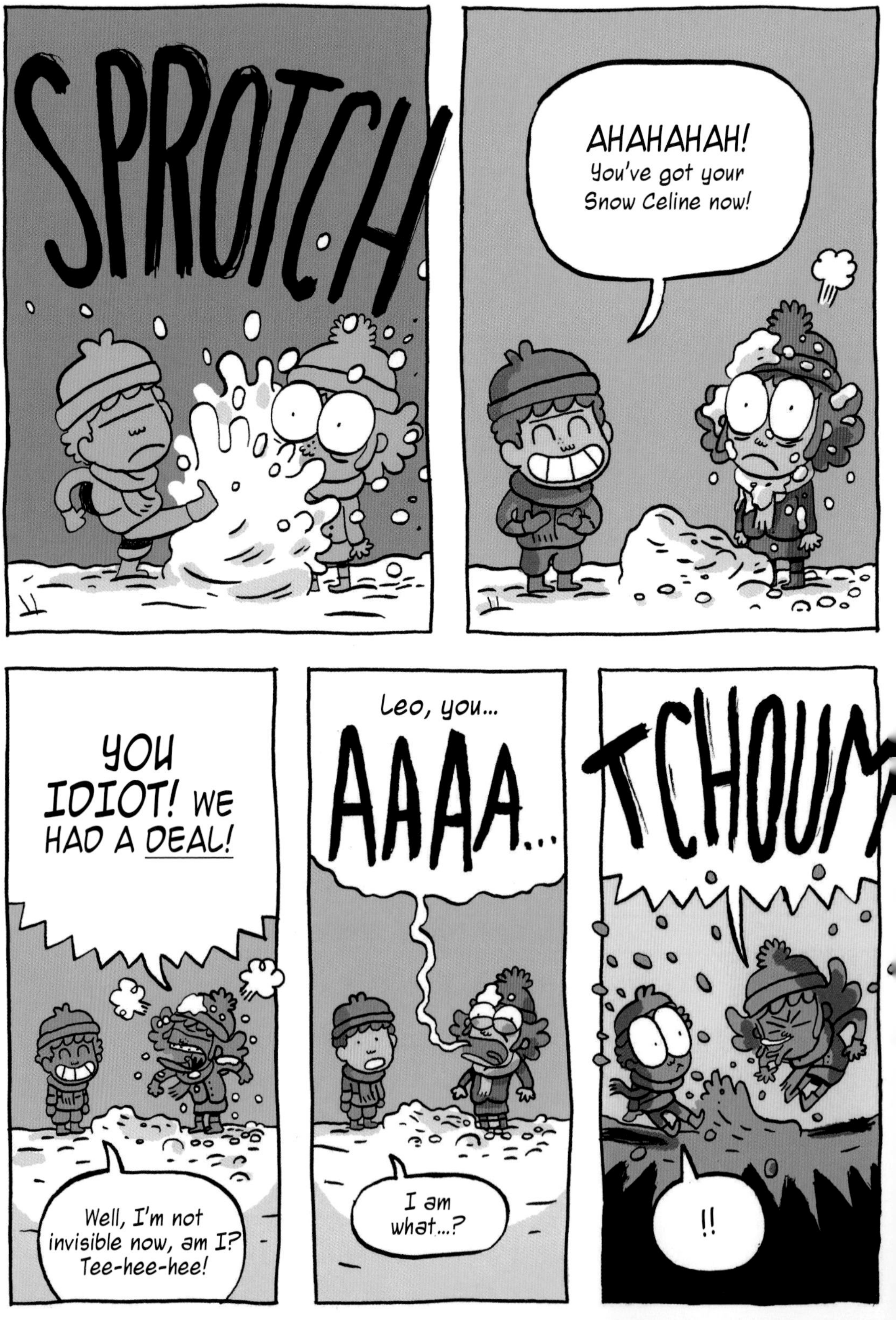
SPROTCH
AHAHAHAH! You've got your Snow Celine now!
YOU IDIOT! WE HAD A DEAL!
Well, I'm not invisible now, am I? Tee-hee-hee!
Leo, you...
AAAA...
I am what...?
TCHOUM
!!

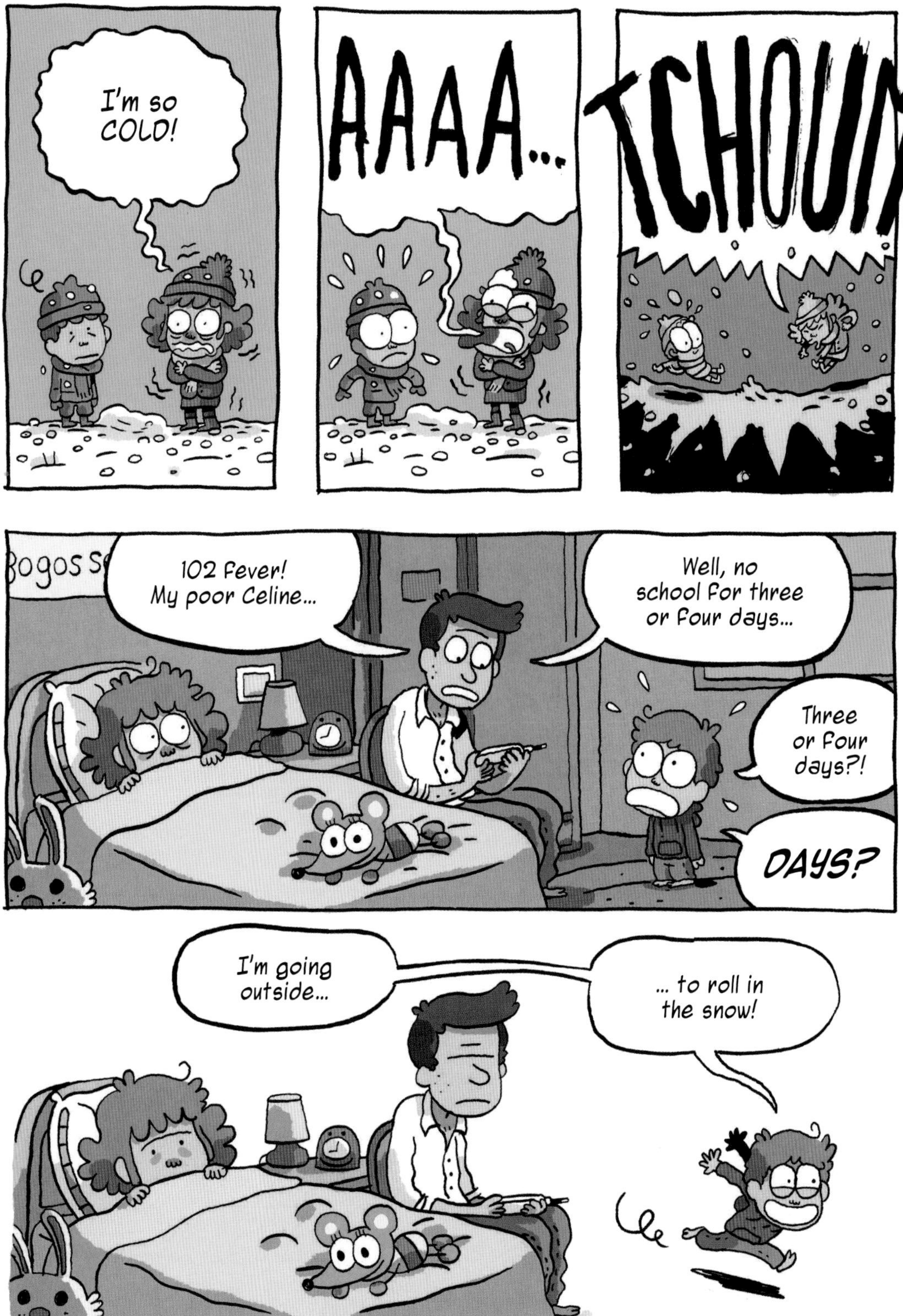
I'm so COLD!
AAAA...
TCHOUM
102 fever! My poor Celine...
Well, no school for three or four days...
Three or four days?!
DAYS?
I'm going outside...
... to roll in the snow!

Michel-Yves + vincent

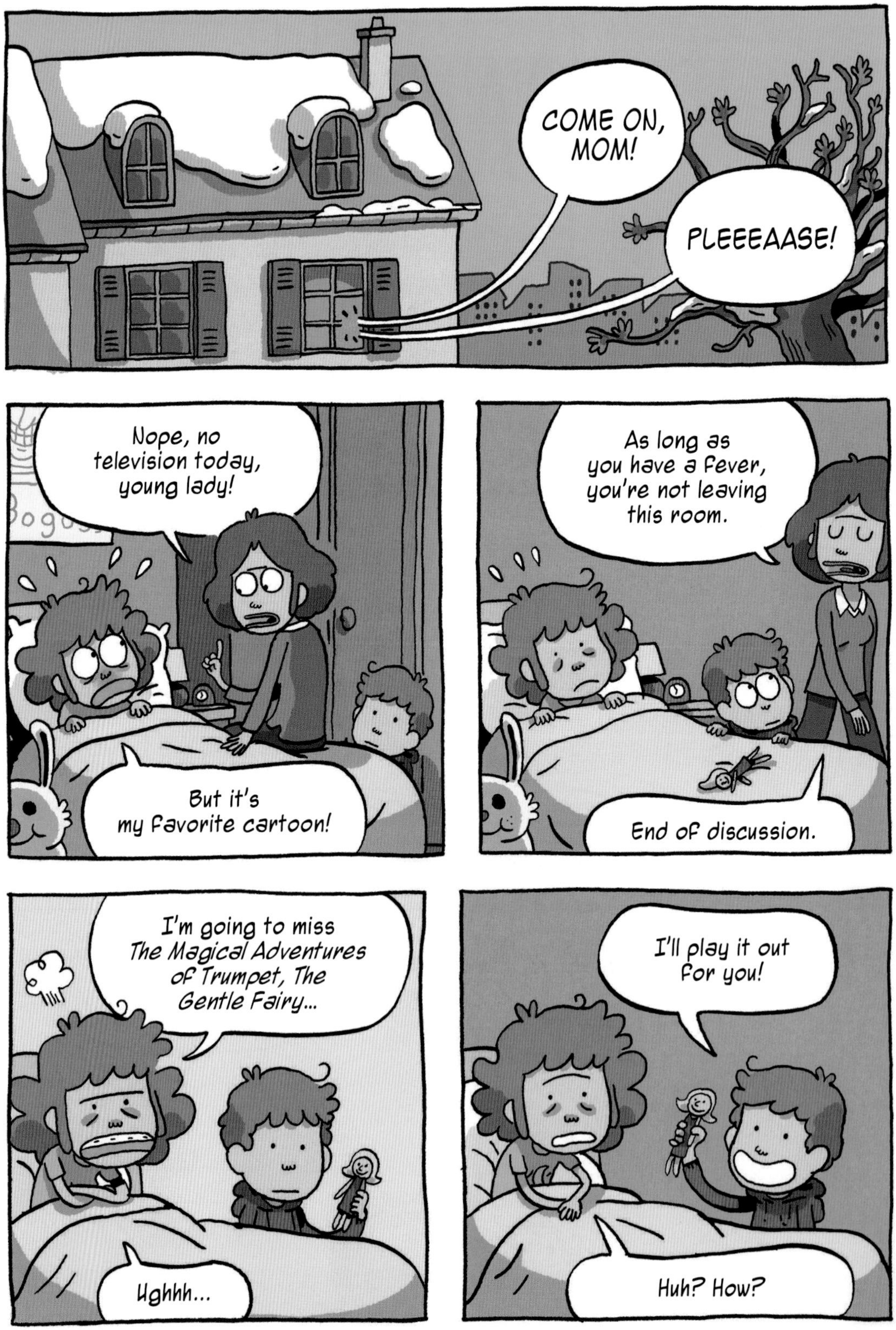
COME ON, MOM!
PLEEEAASE!
Nope, no television today, young lady!
But it's my favorite cartoon!
As long as you have a fever, you're not leaving this room.
End of discussion.
I'm going to miss *The Magical Adventures of Trumpet, The Gentle Fairy*...
Ughhh...
I'll play it out for you!
Huh? How?

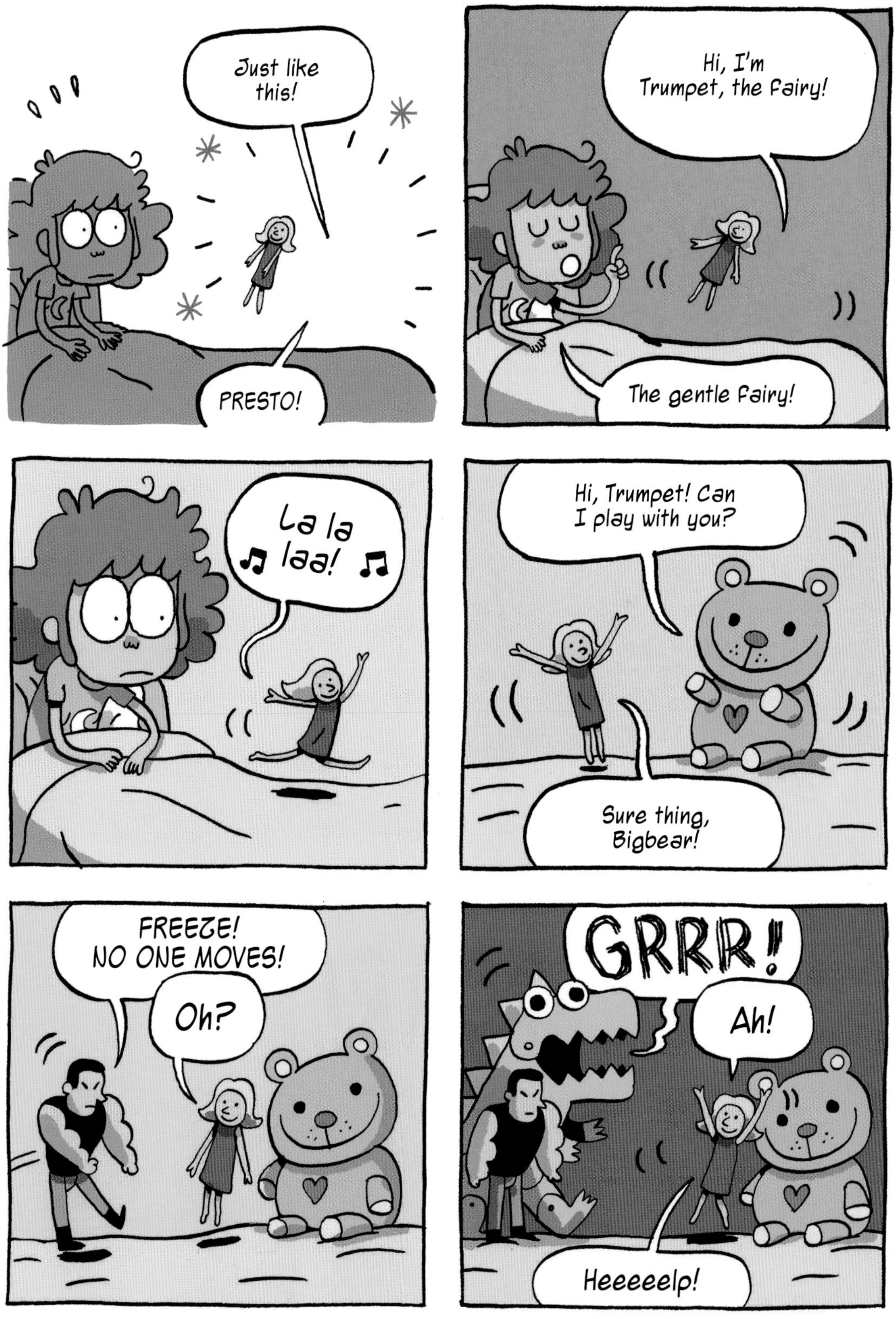

Just like this!
PRESTO!
Hi, I'm Trumpet, the fairy!
The gentle fairy!
La la laa!
Hi, Trumpet! Can I play with you?
Sure thing, Bigbear!
FREEZE! NO ONE MOVES!
Oh?
GRRR!
Ah!
Heeeeelp!

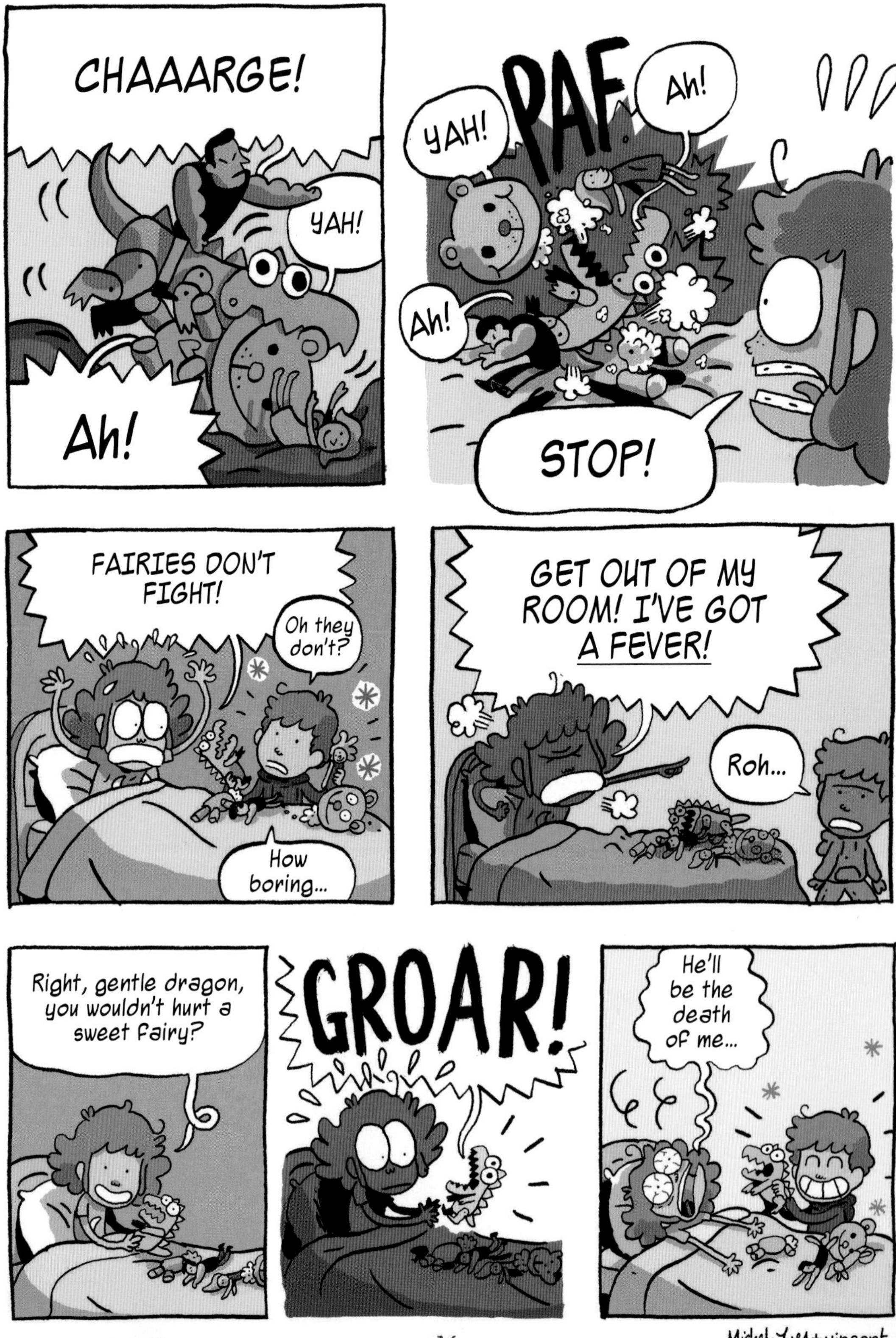
CHAAARGE!
YAH!
Ah!
PAF
YAH!
Ah!
Ah!
STOP!
FAIRIES DON'T FIGHT!
Oh they don't?
How boring...
GET OUT OF MY ROOM! I'VE GOT A FEVER!
Roh...
Right, gentle dragon, you wouldn't hurt a sweet fairy?
GROAR!
He'll be the death of me...
Michel-Yves+vincent

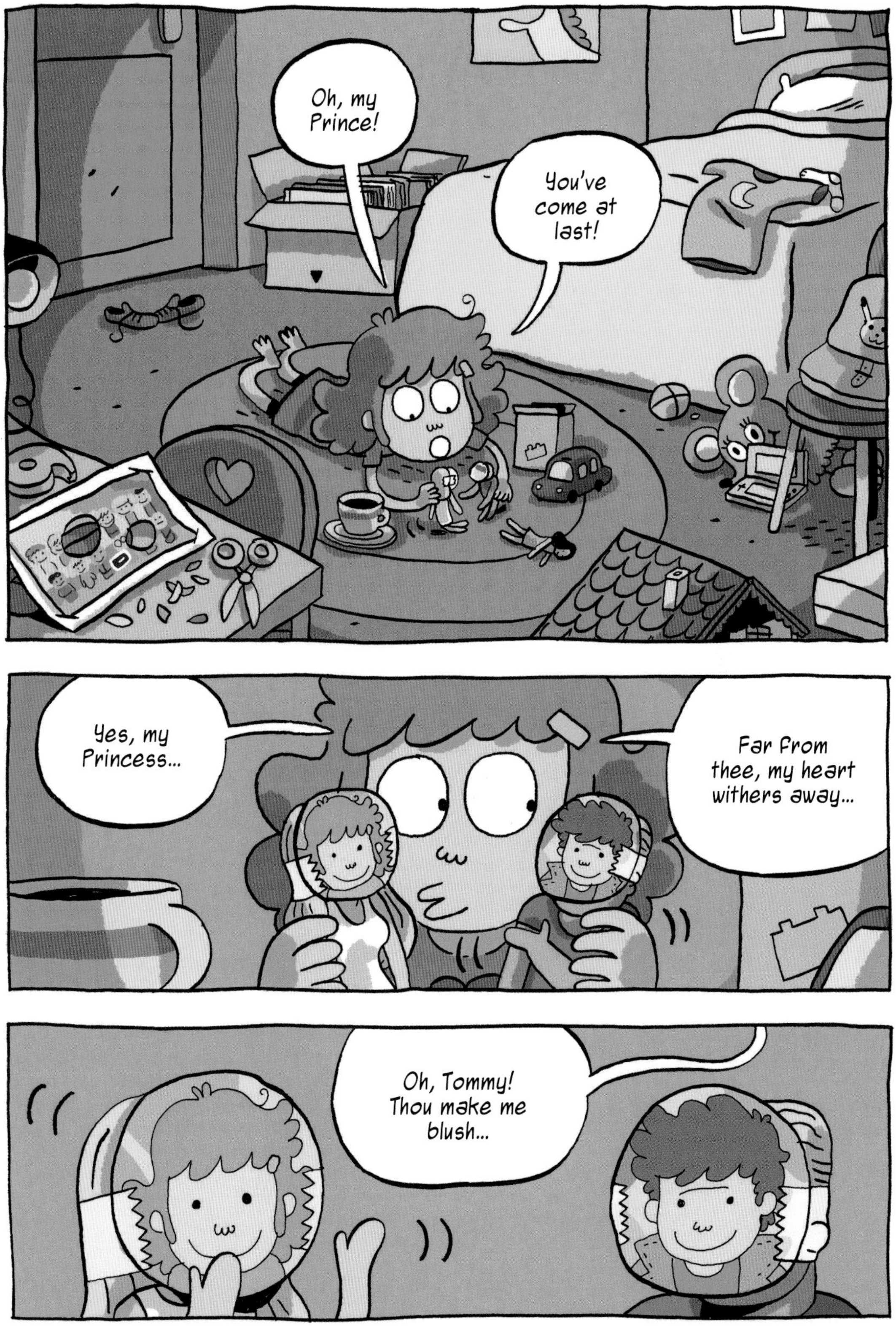
Oh, my Prince!
You've come at last!
Yes, my Princess...
Far from thee, my heart withers away...
Oh, Tommy! Thou make me blush...

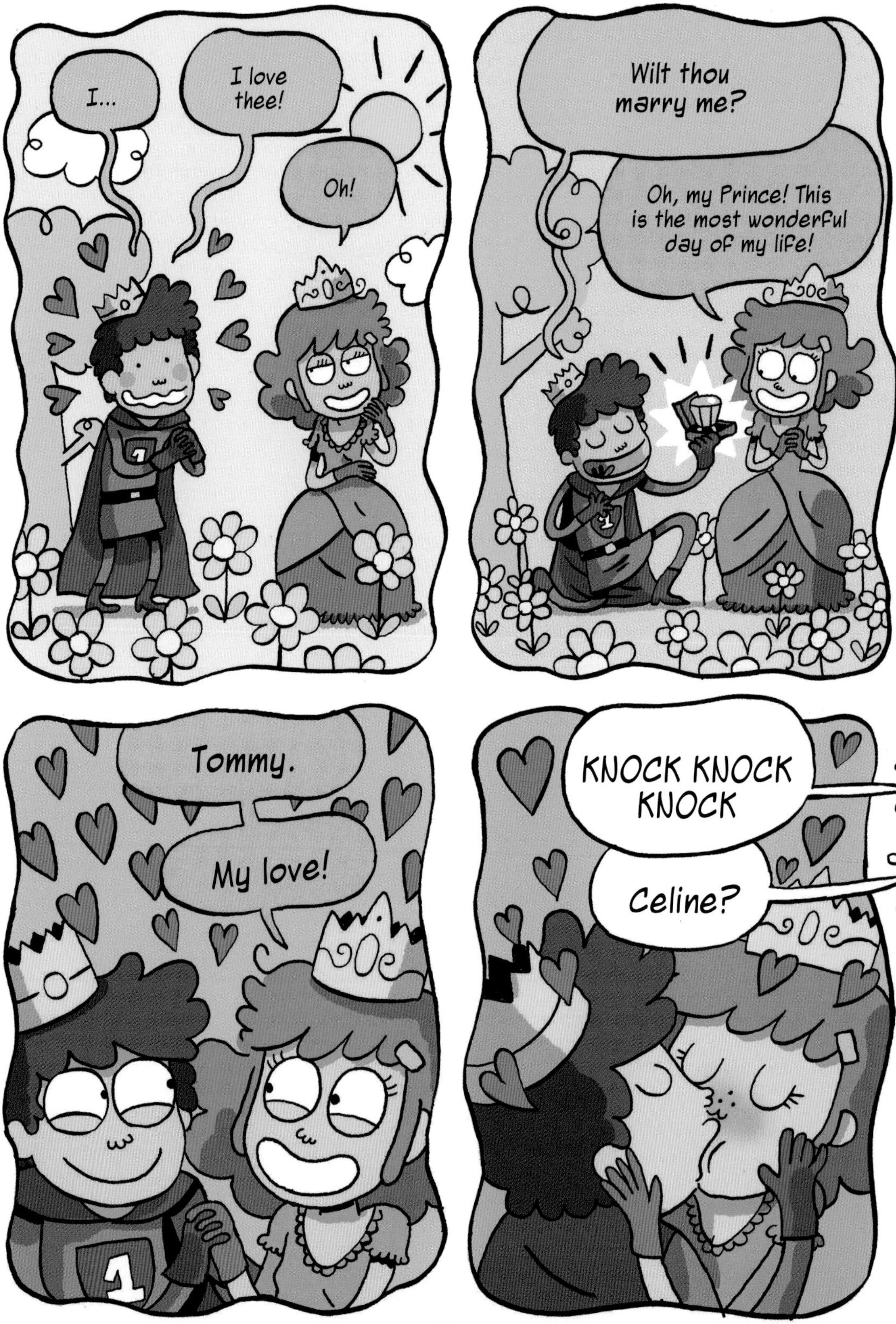
I...
I love thee!
Oh!
Wilt thou marry me?
Oh, my Prince! This is the most wonderful day of my life!
Tommy.
My love!
KNOCK KNOCK KNOCK
Celine?

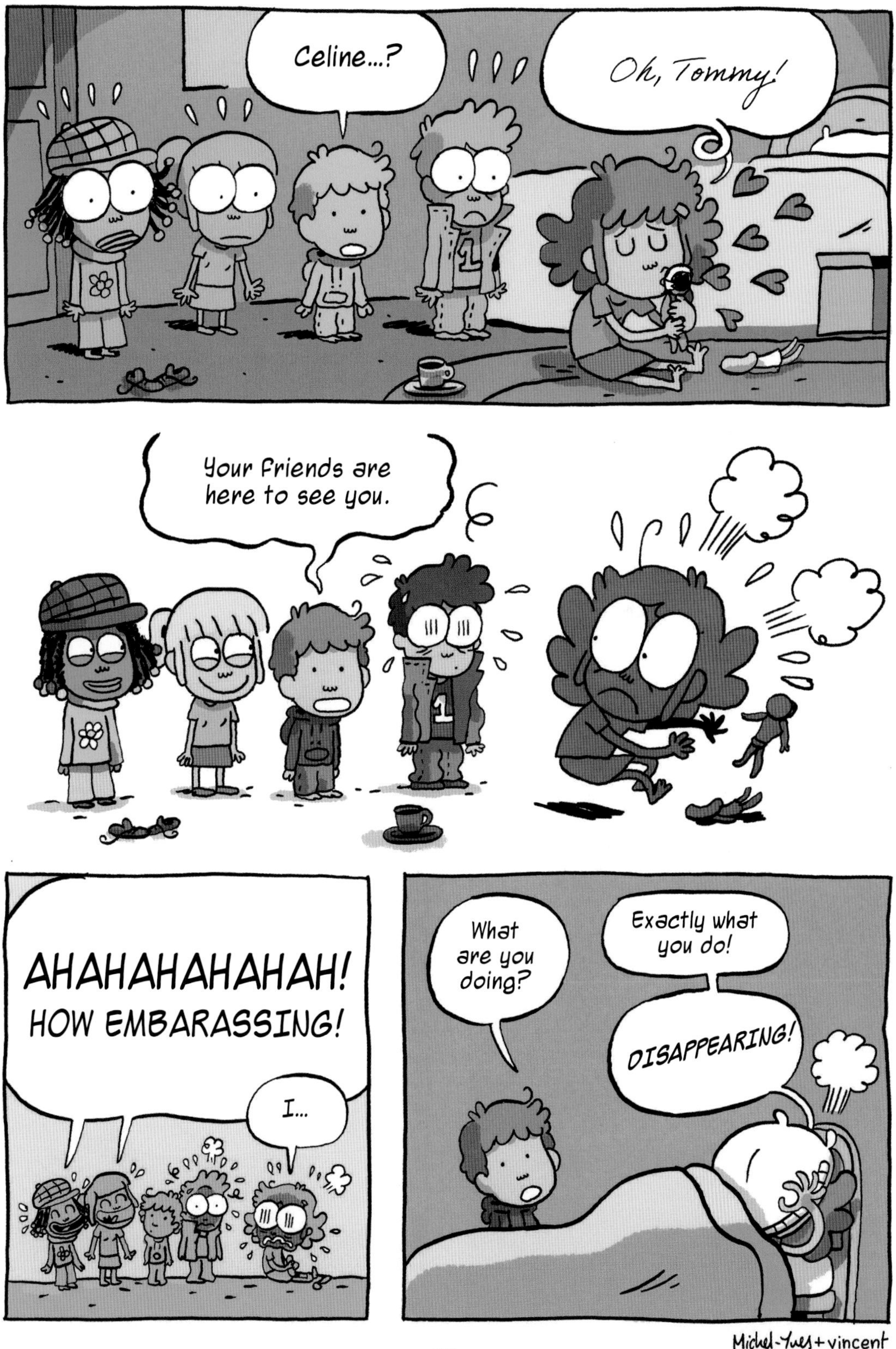
Celine...?
Oh, Tommy!
Your friends are here to see you.
AHAHAHAHAHAH! HOW EMBARASSING!
I...
What are you doing?
Exactly what you do!
DISAPPEARING!
Michel-Yves + vincent

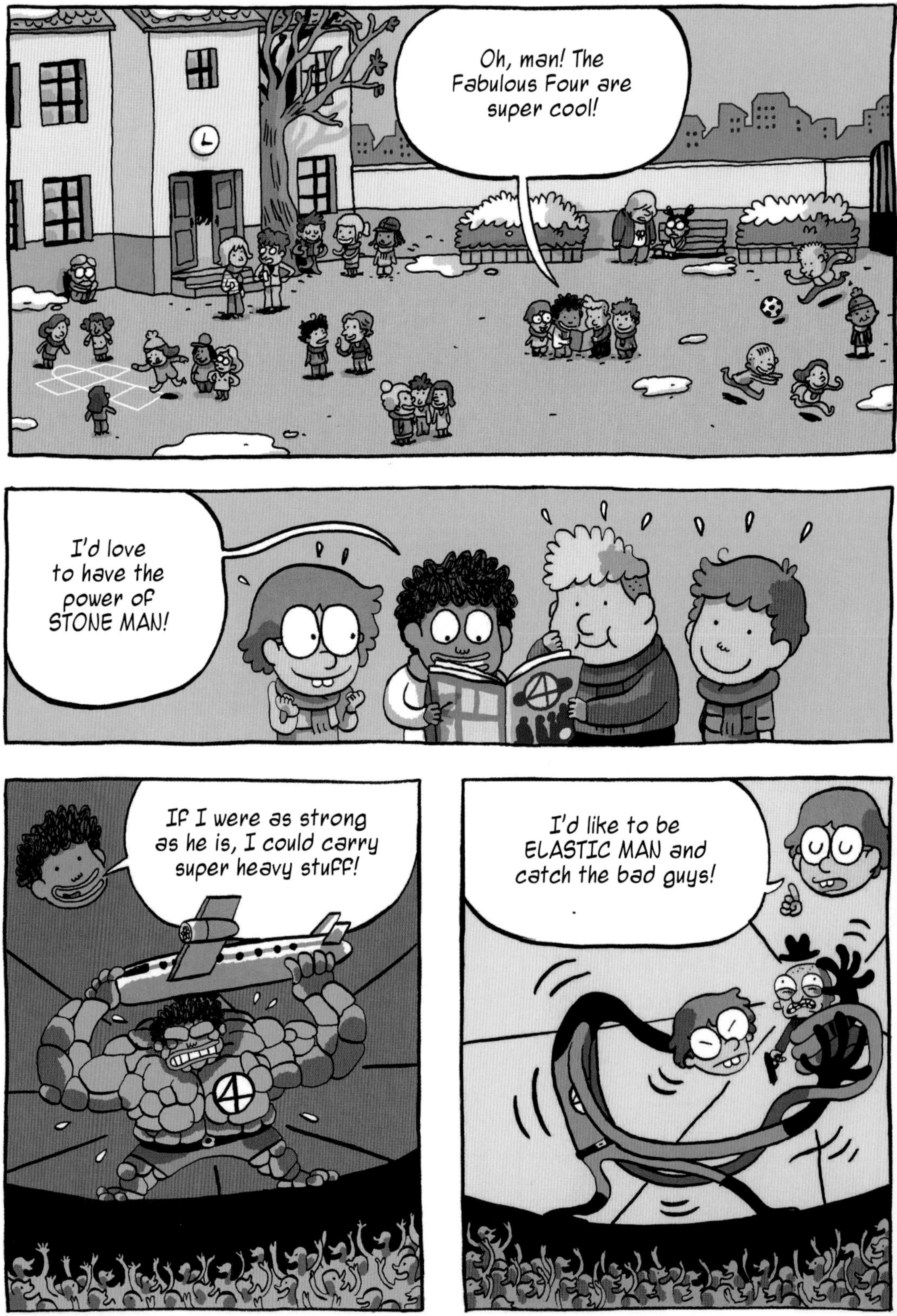
Oh, man! The Fabulous Four are super cool!
I'd love to have the power of STONE MAN!
If I were as strong as he is, I could carry super heavy stuff!
I'd like to be ELASTIC MAN and catch the bad guys!

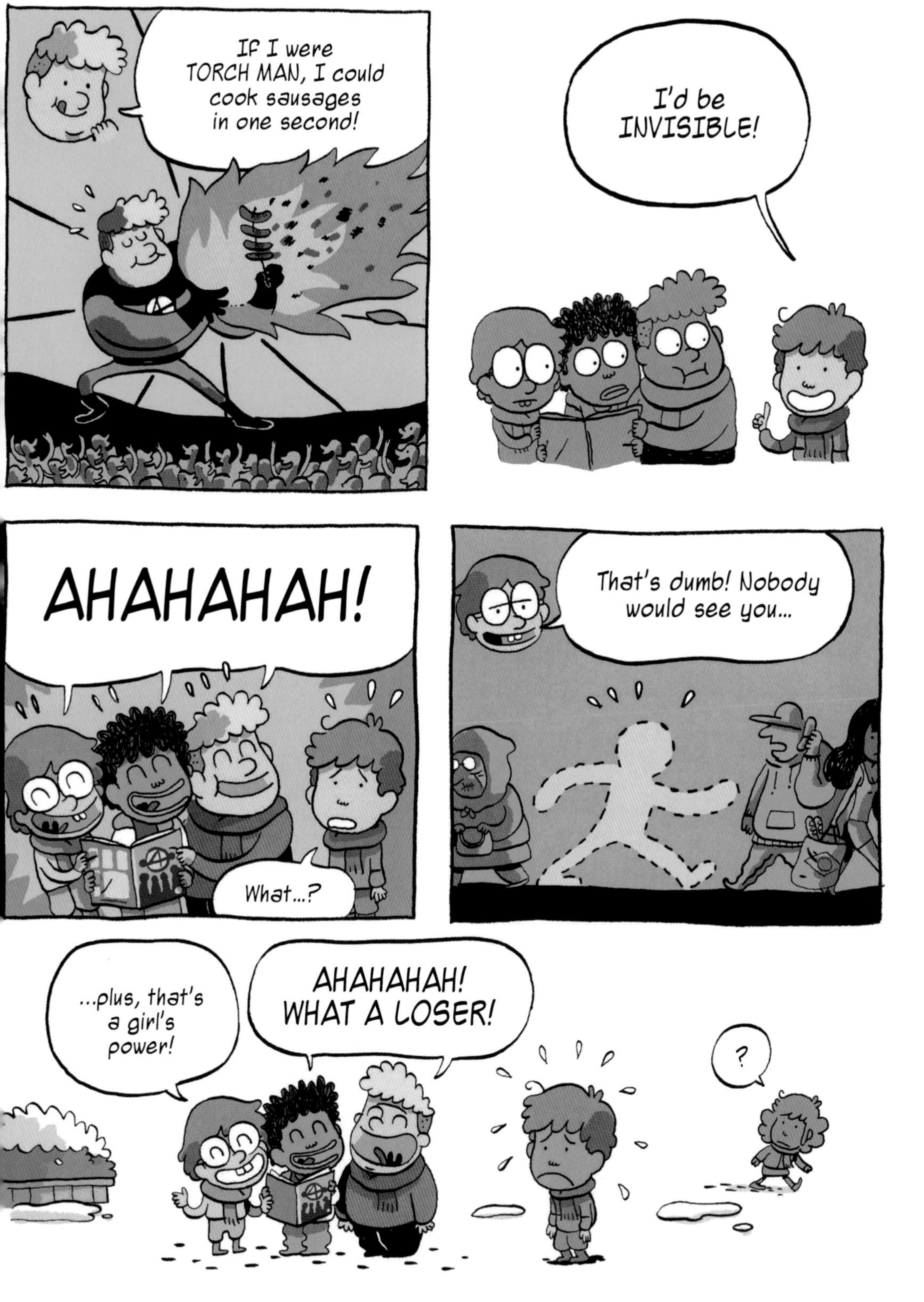
If I were TORCH MAN, I could cook sausages in one second!
I'd be INVISIBLE!
AHAHAHAH!
What...?
That's dumb! Nobody would see you...
...plus, that's a girl's power!
AHAHAHAH! WHAT A LOSER!
?

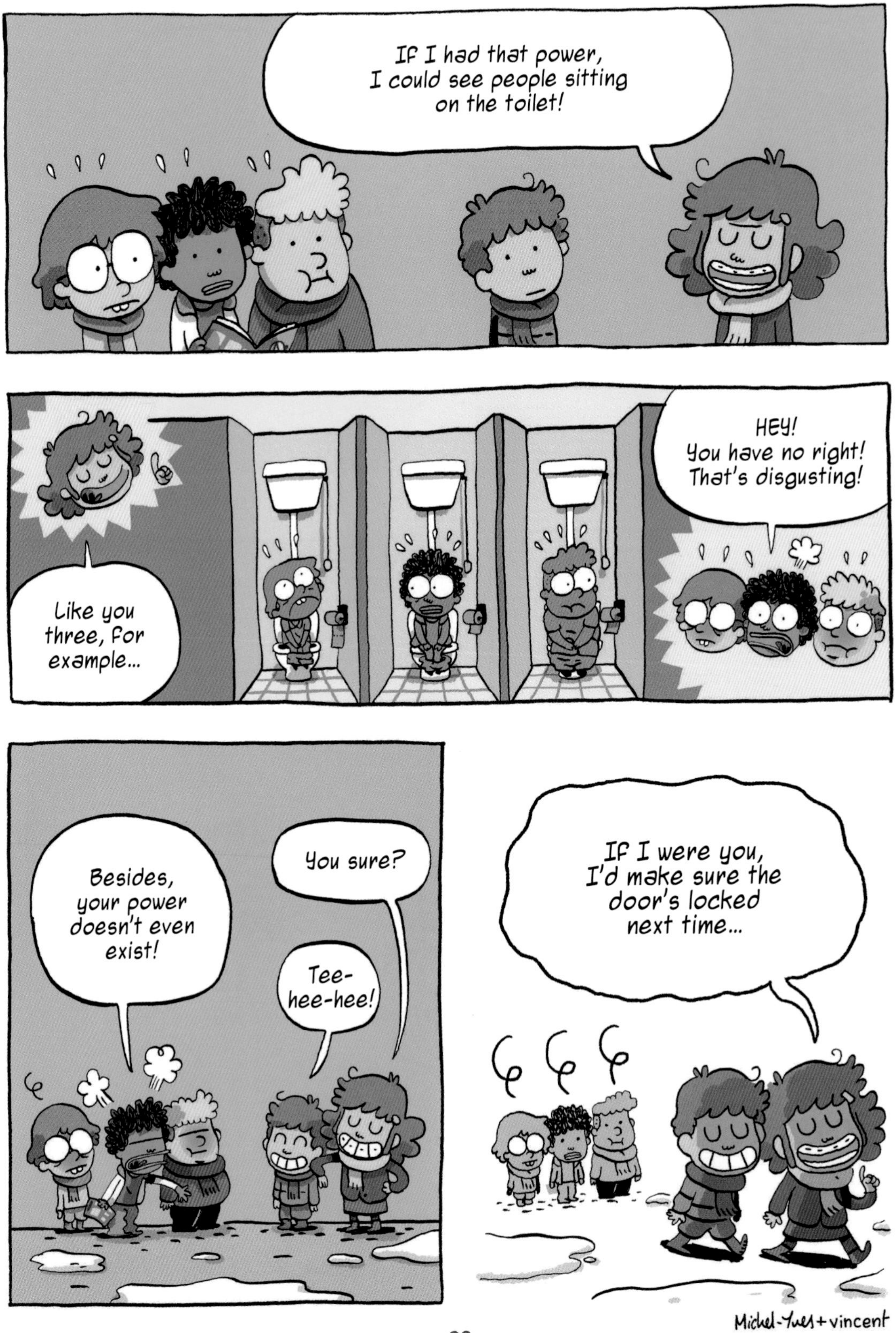

If I had that power, I could see people sitting on the toilet!
Like you three, for example...
HEY! You have no right! That's disgusting!
Besides, your power doesn't even exist!
You sure?
Tee-hee-hee!
If I were you, I'd make sure the door's locked next time...
Michel-Yves+vincent

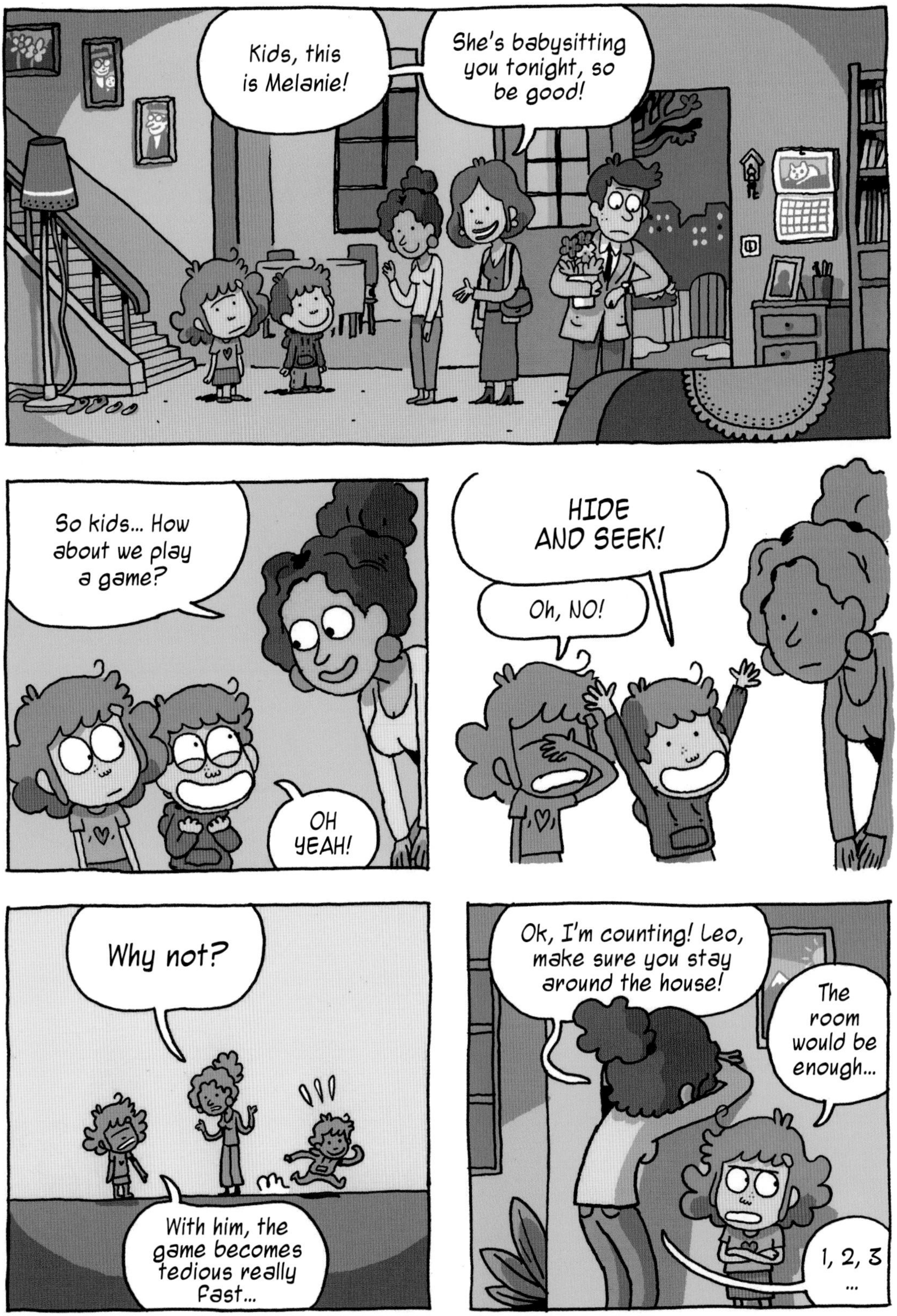
Kids, this is Melanie!
She's babysitting you tonight, so be good!
So kids... How about we play a game?
OH YEAH!
HIDE AND SEEK!
Oh, NO!
Why not?
With him, the game becomes tedious really fast...
Ok, I'm counting! Leo, make sure you stay around the house!
The room would be enough...
1, 2, 3 ...

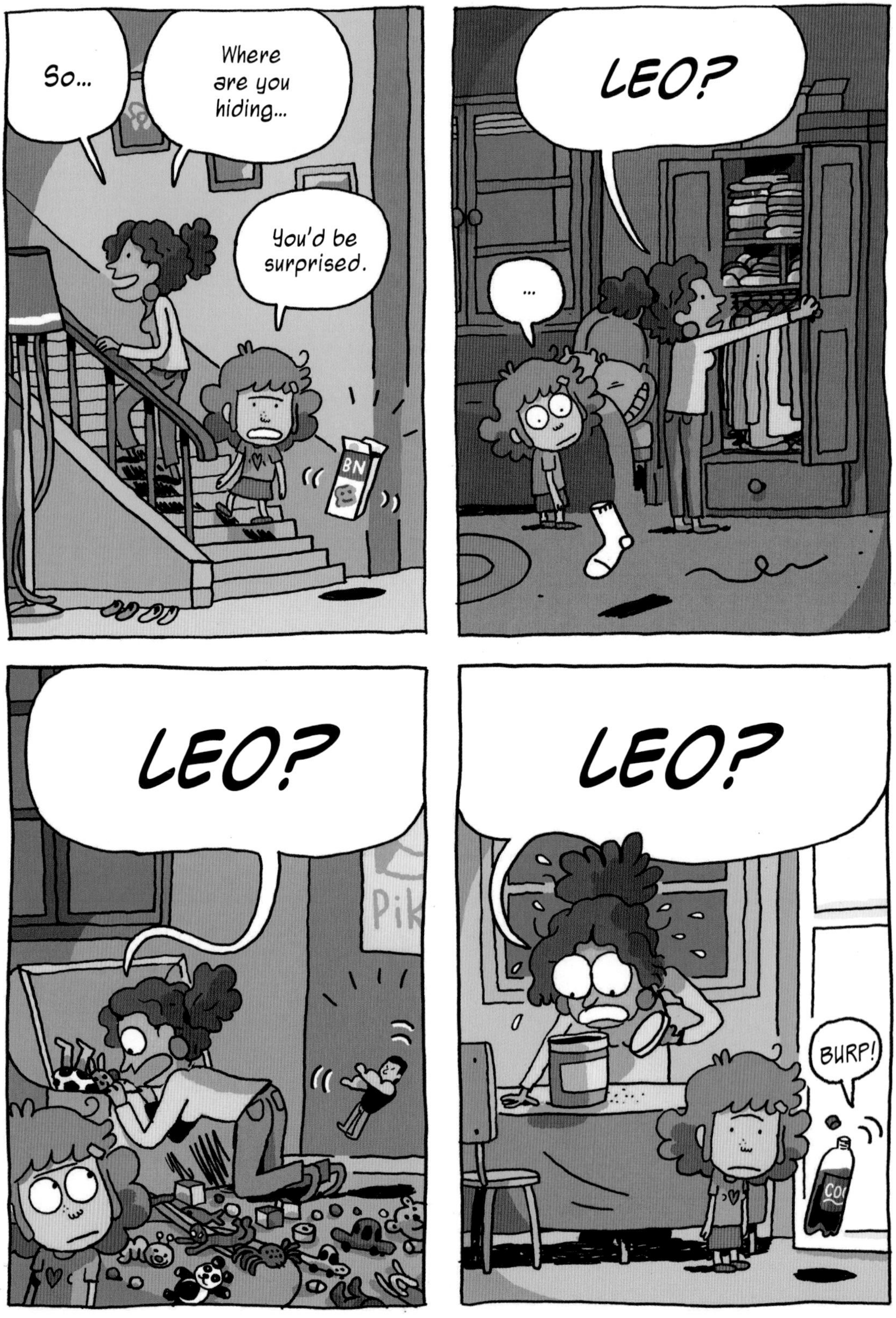

So...
Where are you hiding...
You'd be surprised.
BN
LEO?
...
LEO?
Pik
LEO?
BURP!

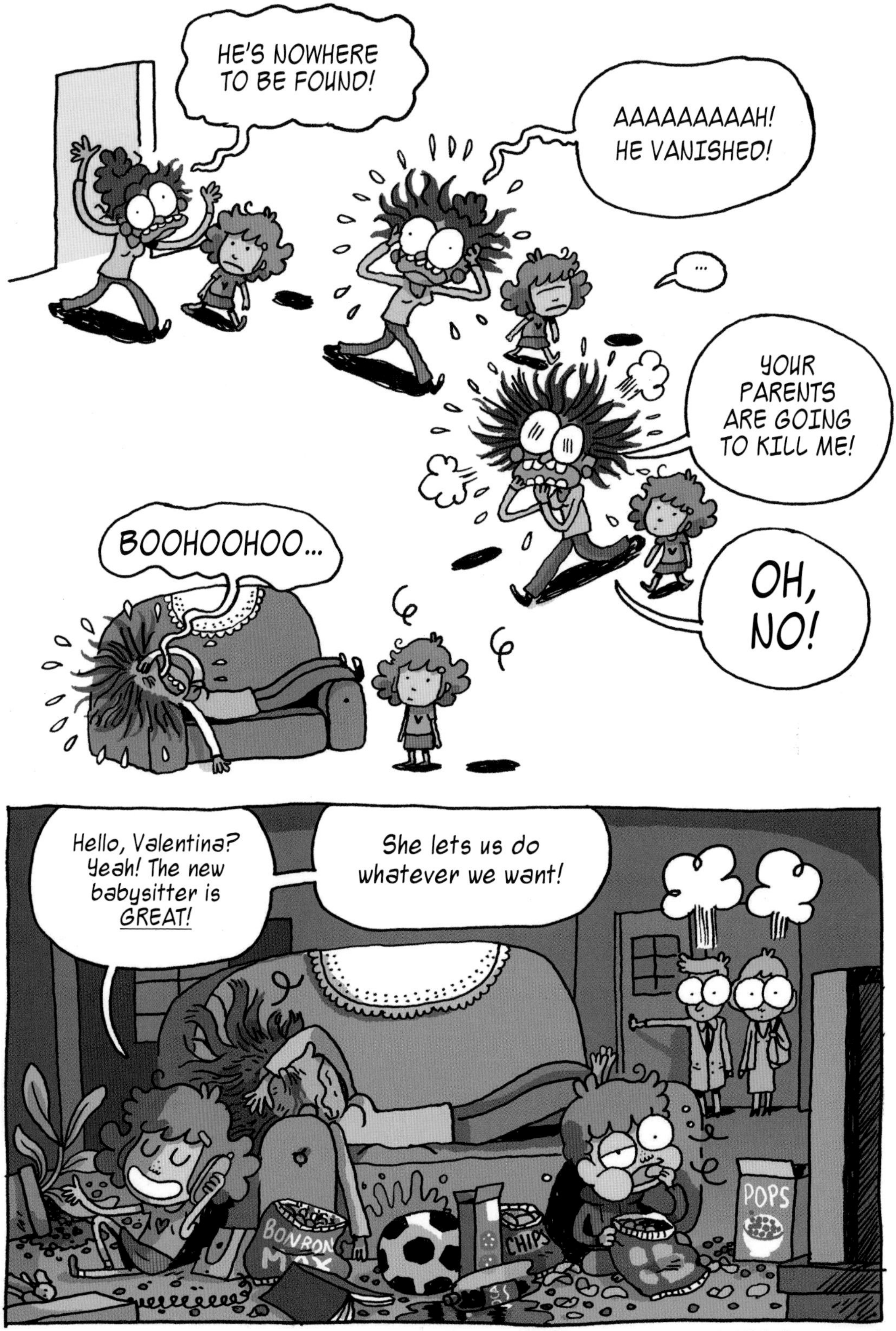
HE'S NOWHERE TO BE FOUND!
AAAAAAAAAAH! HE VANISHED!
...
YOUR PARENTS ARE GOING TO KILL ME!
OH, NO!
BOOHOOHOO...
Hello, Valentina? Yeah! The new babysitter is GREAT!
She lets us do whatever we want!
POPS
CHIPS
BONBON MAX

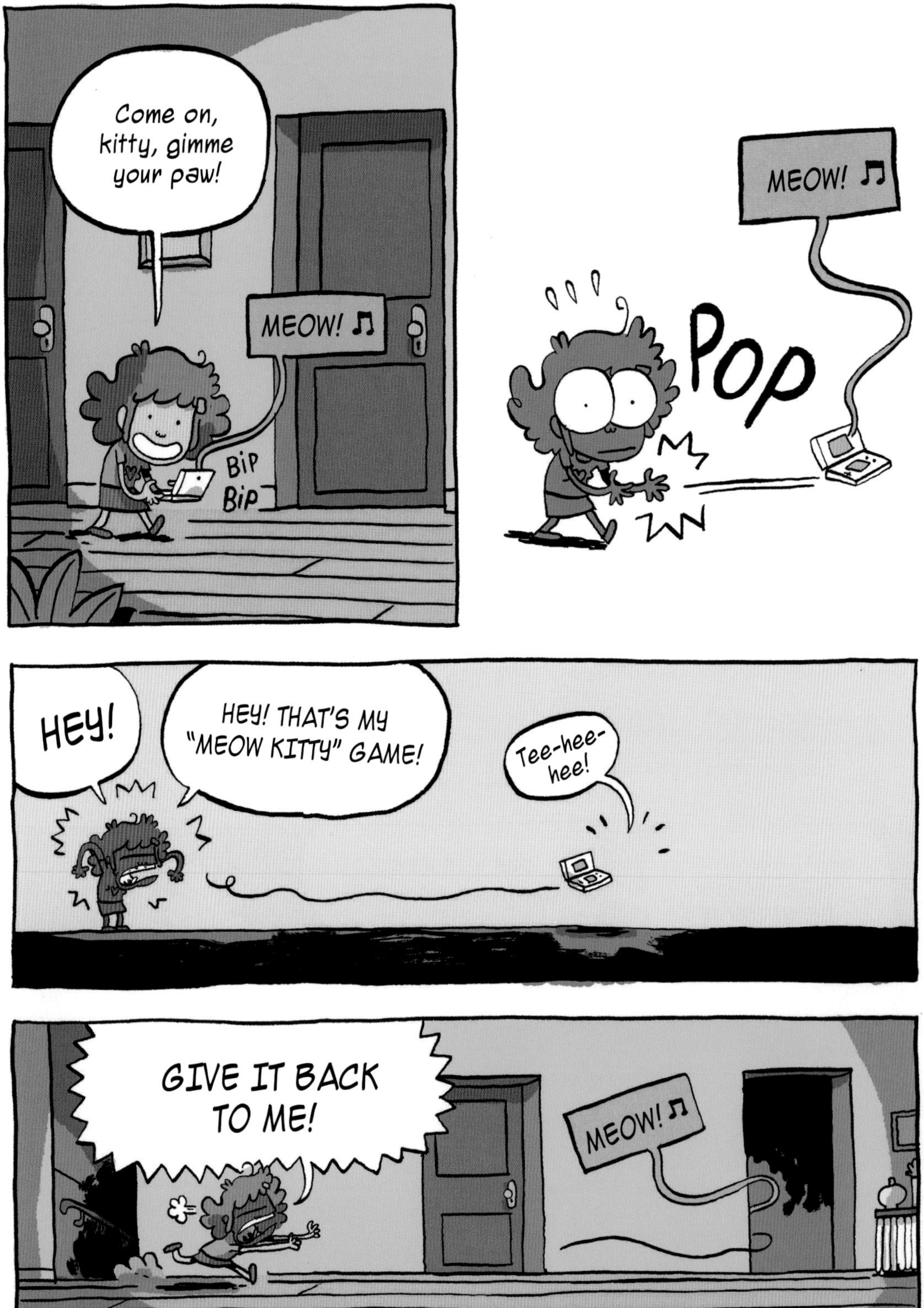
Come on, kitty, gimme your paw!
MEOW! ♫
Bip Bip
MEOW! ♫
POP
HEY!
HEY! THAT'S MY "MEOW KITTY" GAME!
Tee-hee-hee!
GIVE IT BACK TO ME!
MEOW! ♫

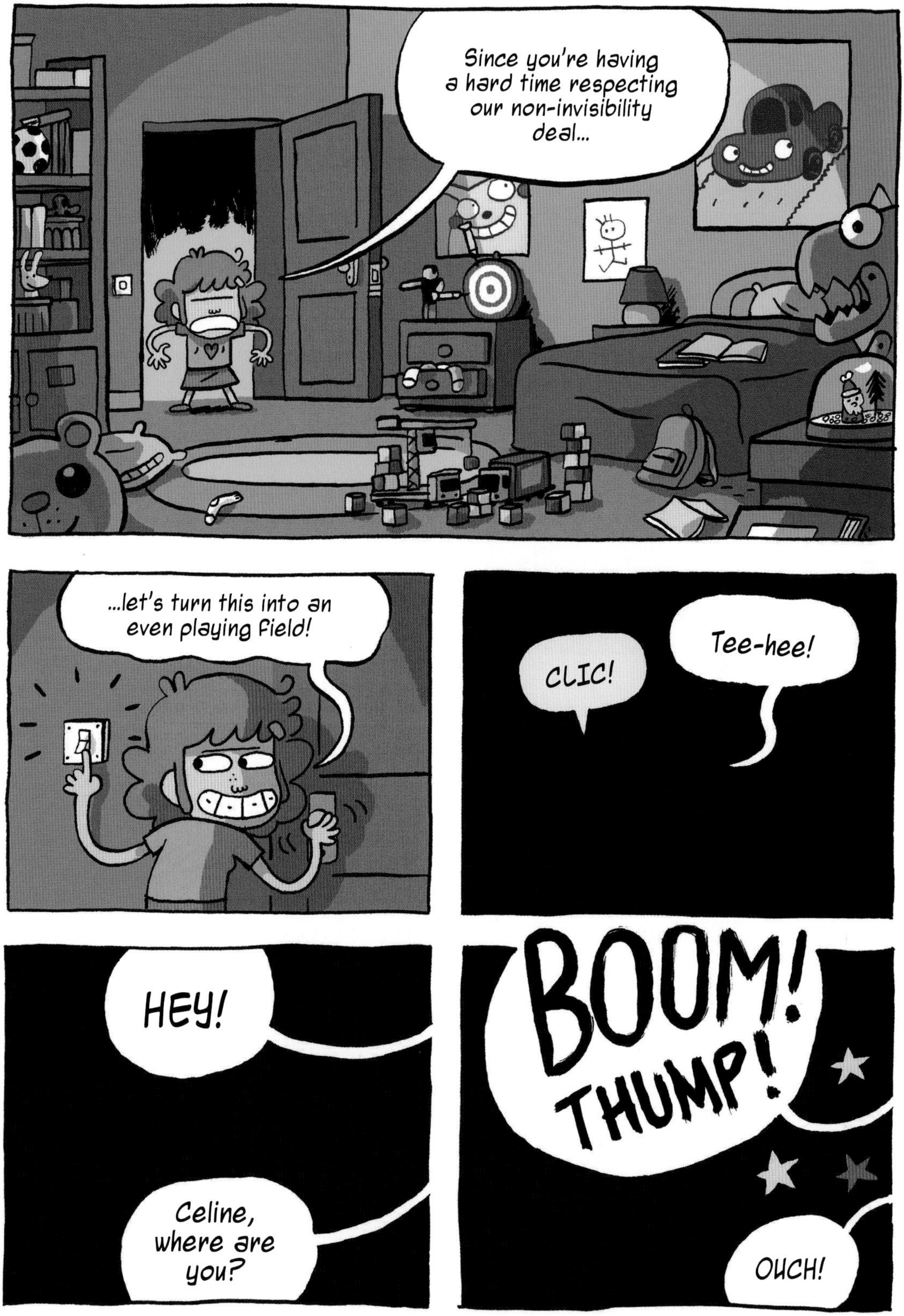
Since you're having a hard time respecting our non-invisibility deal...
...let's turn this into an even playing field!
CLIC!
Tee-hee!
HEY!
Celine, where are you?
BOOM!
THUMP!
OUCH!

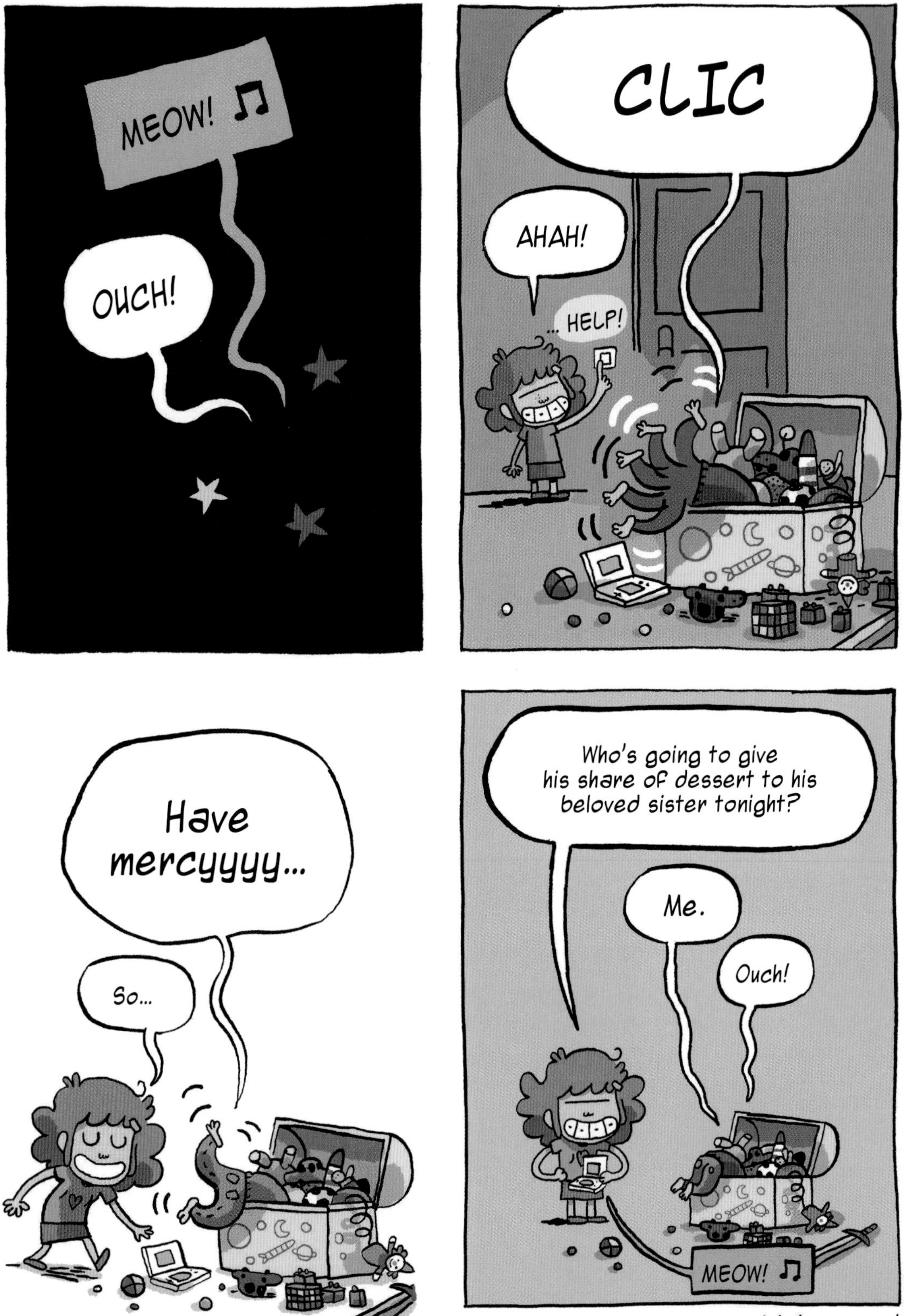
MEOW! ♫
OUCH!
CLIC
AHAH!
... HELP!
Have mercyyyy...
So...
Who's going to give his share of dessert to his beloved sister tonight?
Me.
Ouch!
MEOW! ♫

Michel-Yves + vincent

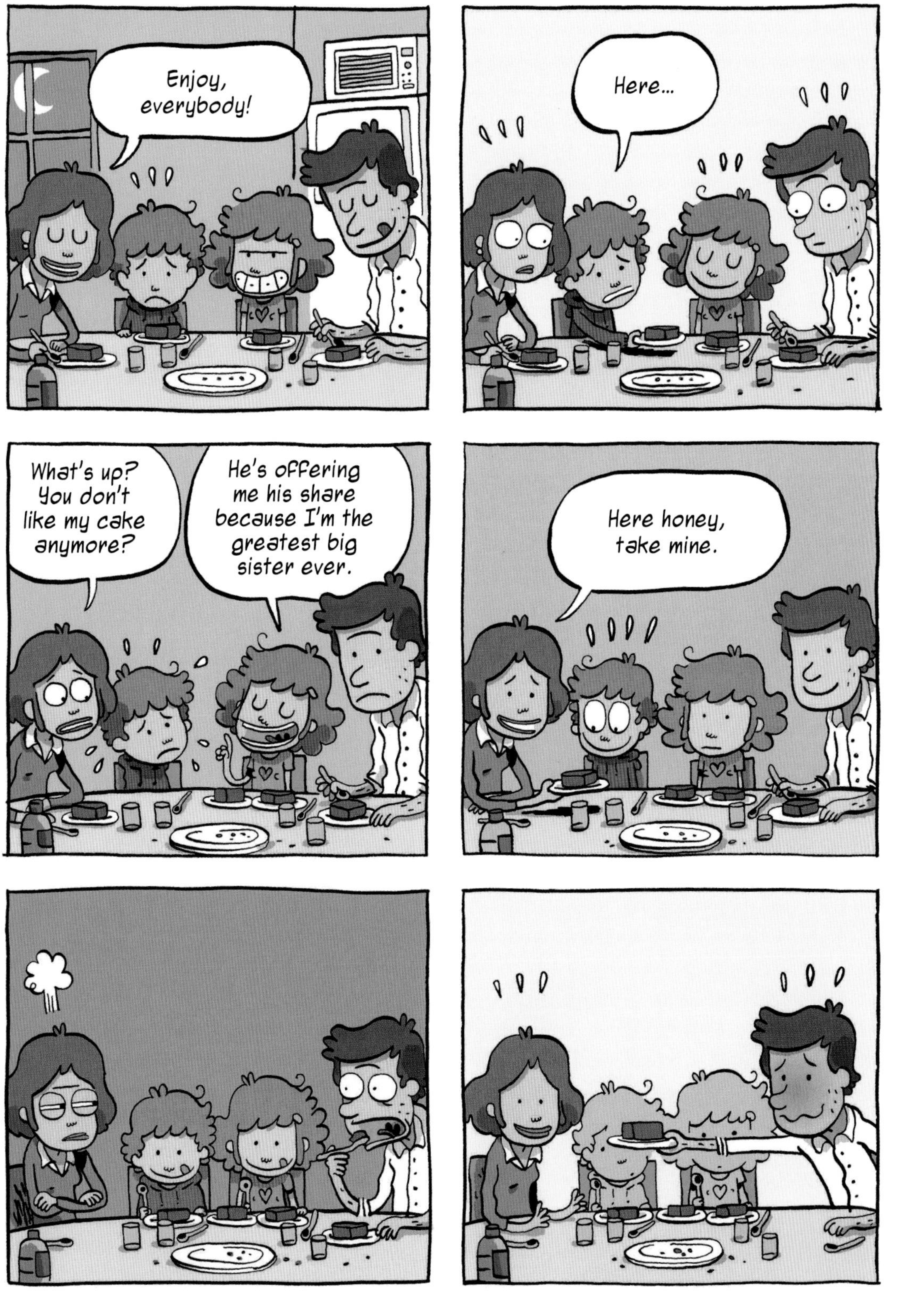
Enjoy, everybody!
Here...
What's up? You don't like my cake anymore?
He's offering me his share because I'm the greatest big sister ever.
Here honey, take mine.

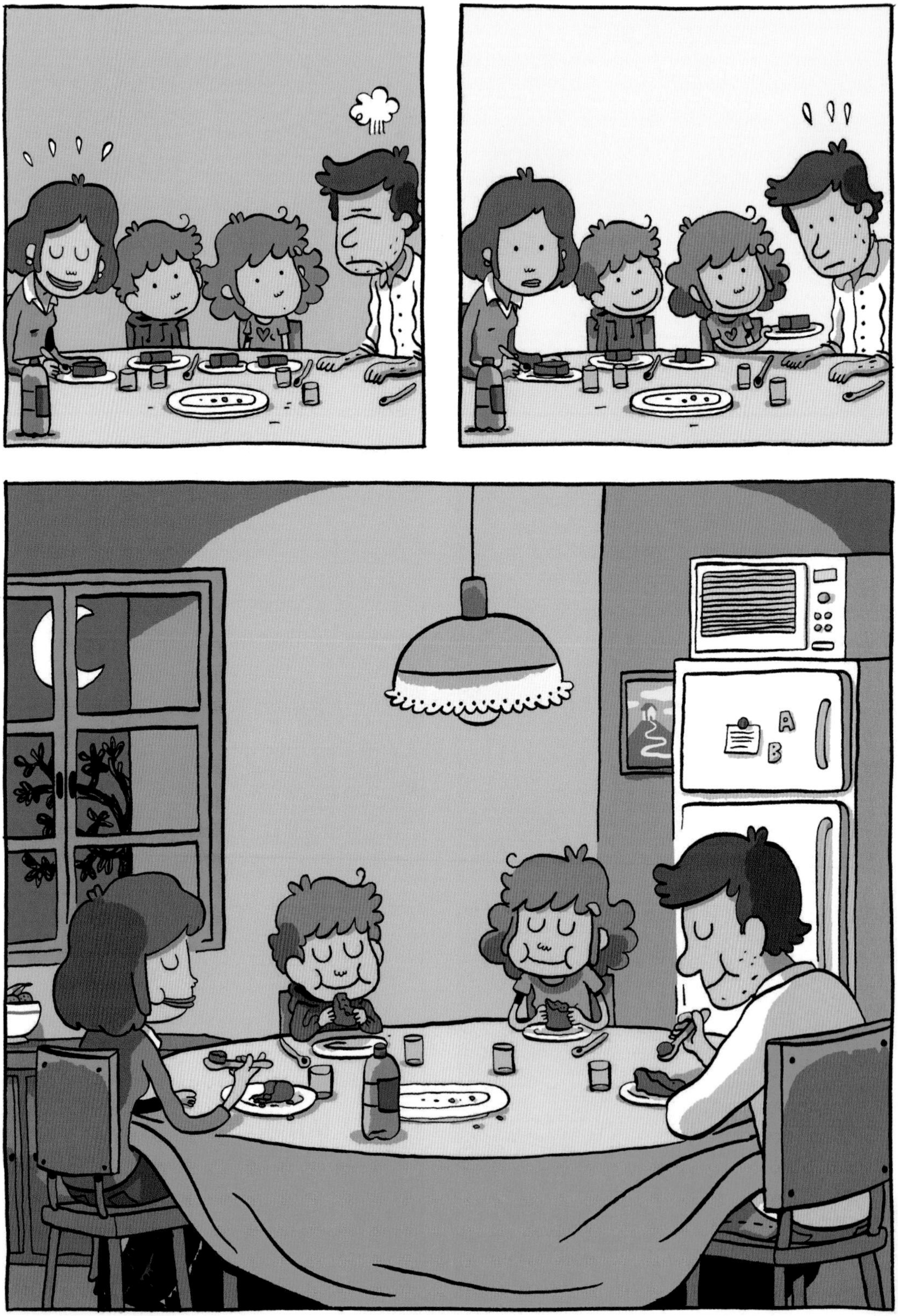

Michel-Yves+vincent

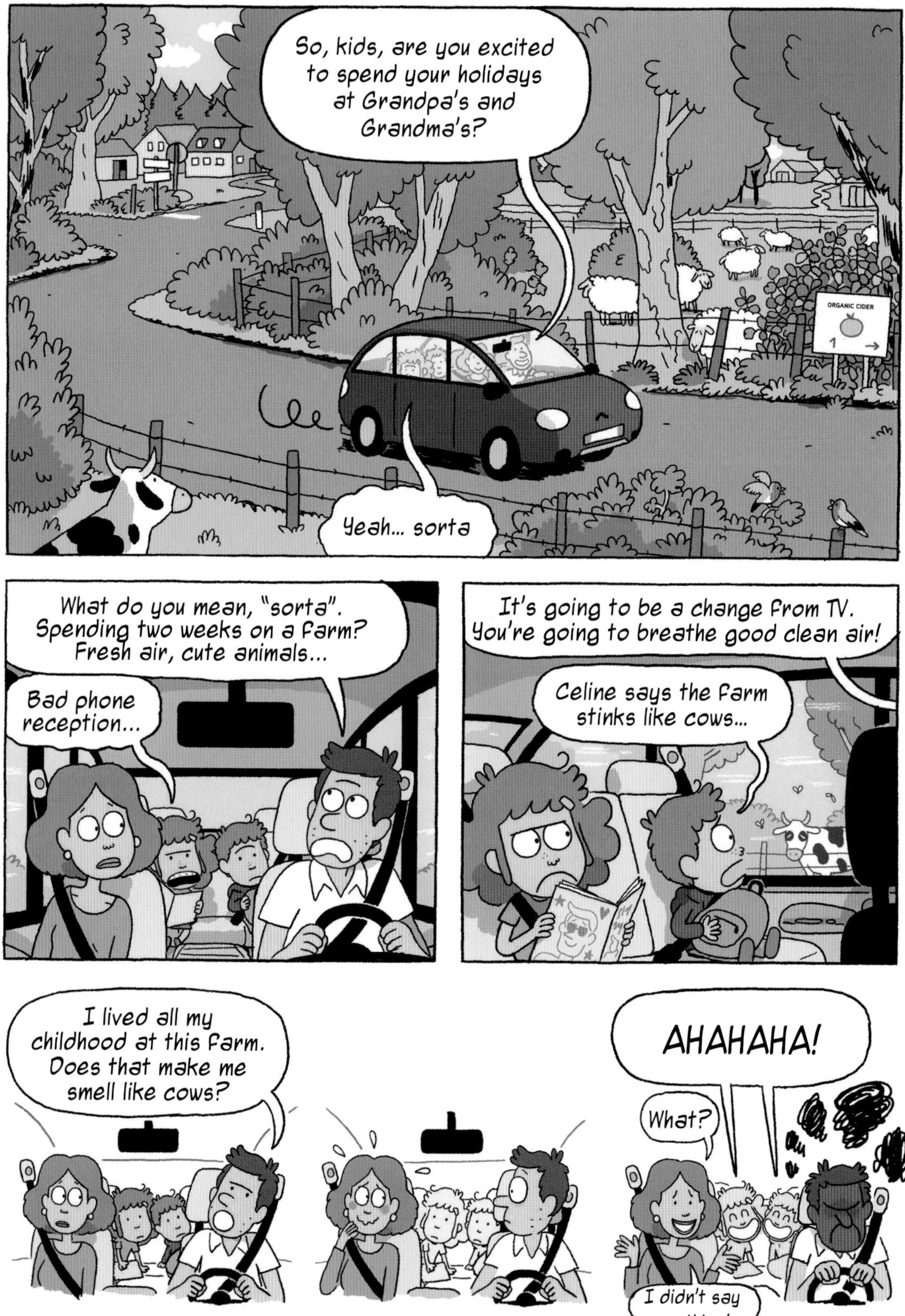
So, kids, are you excited to spend your holidays at Grandpa's and Grandma's?
ORGANIC CIDER
Yeah... sorta
What do you mean, "sorta". Spending two weeks on a farm? Fresh air, cute animals...
Bad phone reception...
It's going to be a change from TV. You're going to breathe good clean air!
Celine says the farm stinks like cows...
I lived all my childhood at this farm. Does that make me smell like cows?
AHAHAHA!
What?
I didn't say anything!

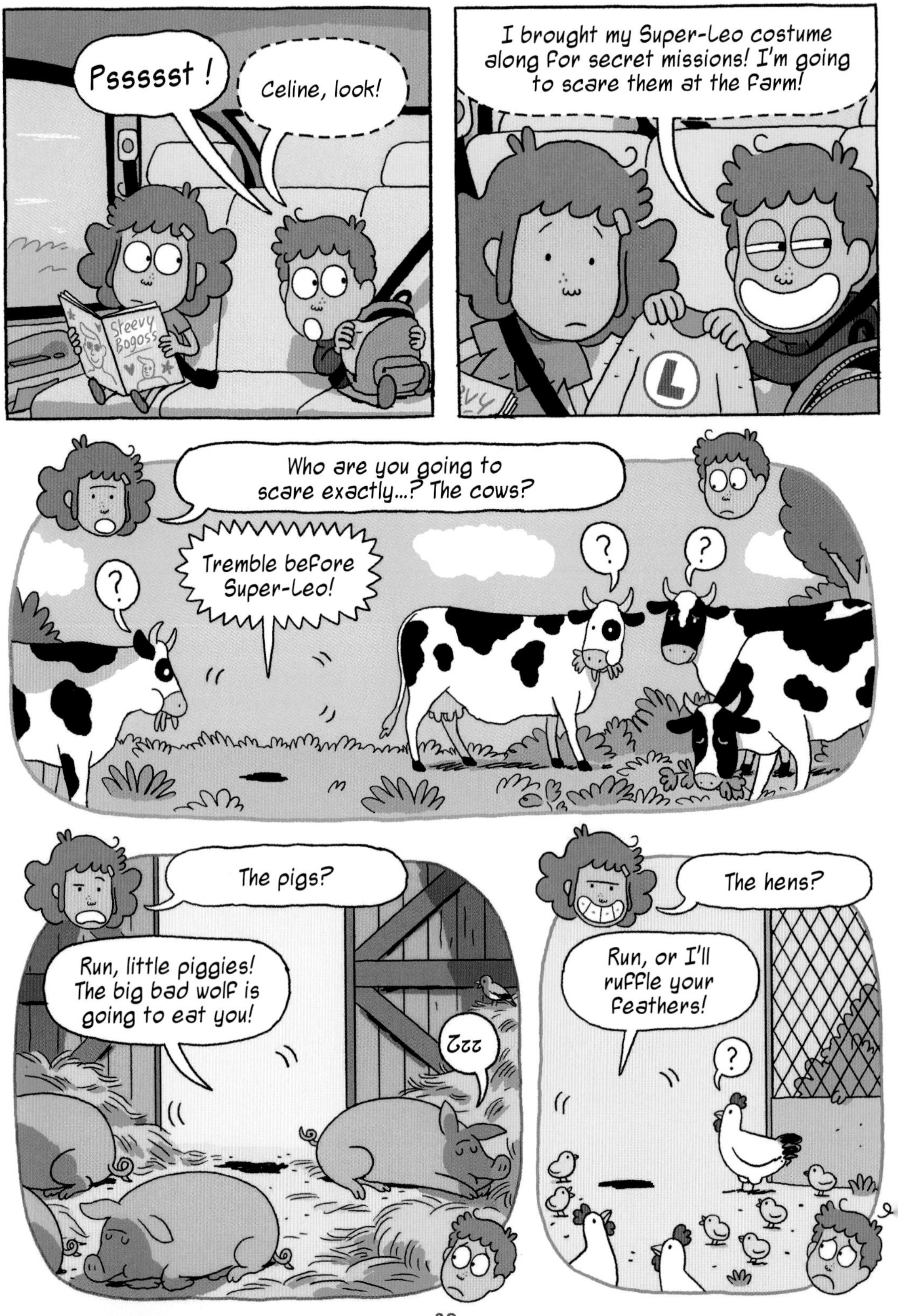
Psssssst !
Celine, look!
I brought my Super-Leo costume along for secret missions! I'm going to scare them at the farm!
Who are you going to scare exactly...? The cows?
Tremble before Super-Leo!
?
?
?
The pigs?
Run, little piggies! The big bad wolf is going to eat you!
zzz
The hens?
Run, or I'll ruffle your feathers!
?

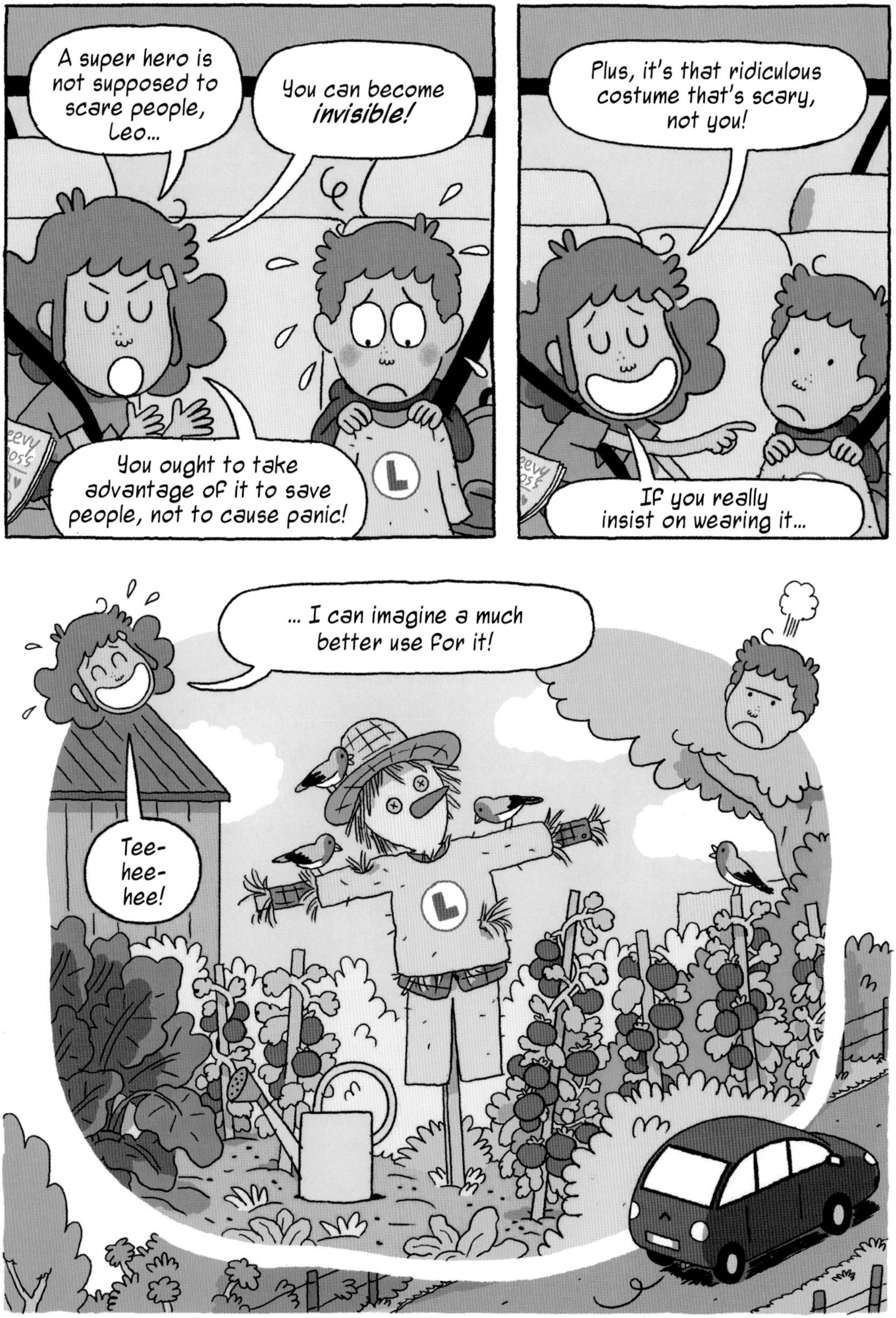
A super hero is not supposed to scare people, Leo...
You can become *invisible!*
You ought to take advantage of it to save people, not to cause panic!
Plus, it's that ridiculous costume that's scary, not you!
If you really insist on wearing it...
... I can imagine a much better use for it!
Tee-hee-hee!

Michel-Yves+vincent

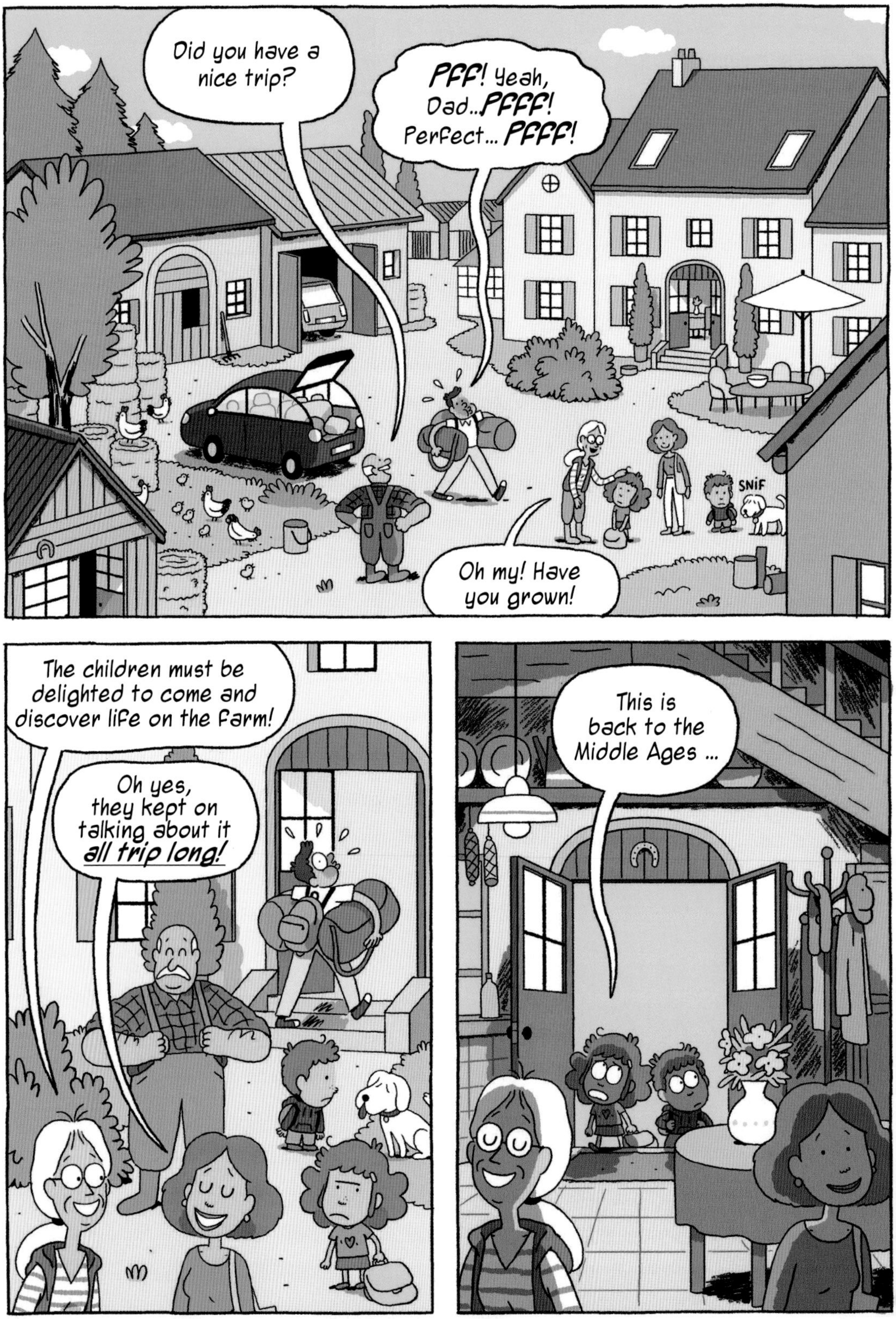
Did you have a nice trip?
PFF! Yeah, Dad...PFFF! Perfect... PFFF!
SNIF
Oh my! Have you grown!
The children must be delighted to come and discover life on the farm!
Oh yes, they kept on talking about it all trip long!
This is back to the Middle Ages ...

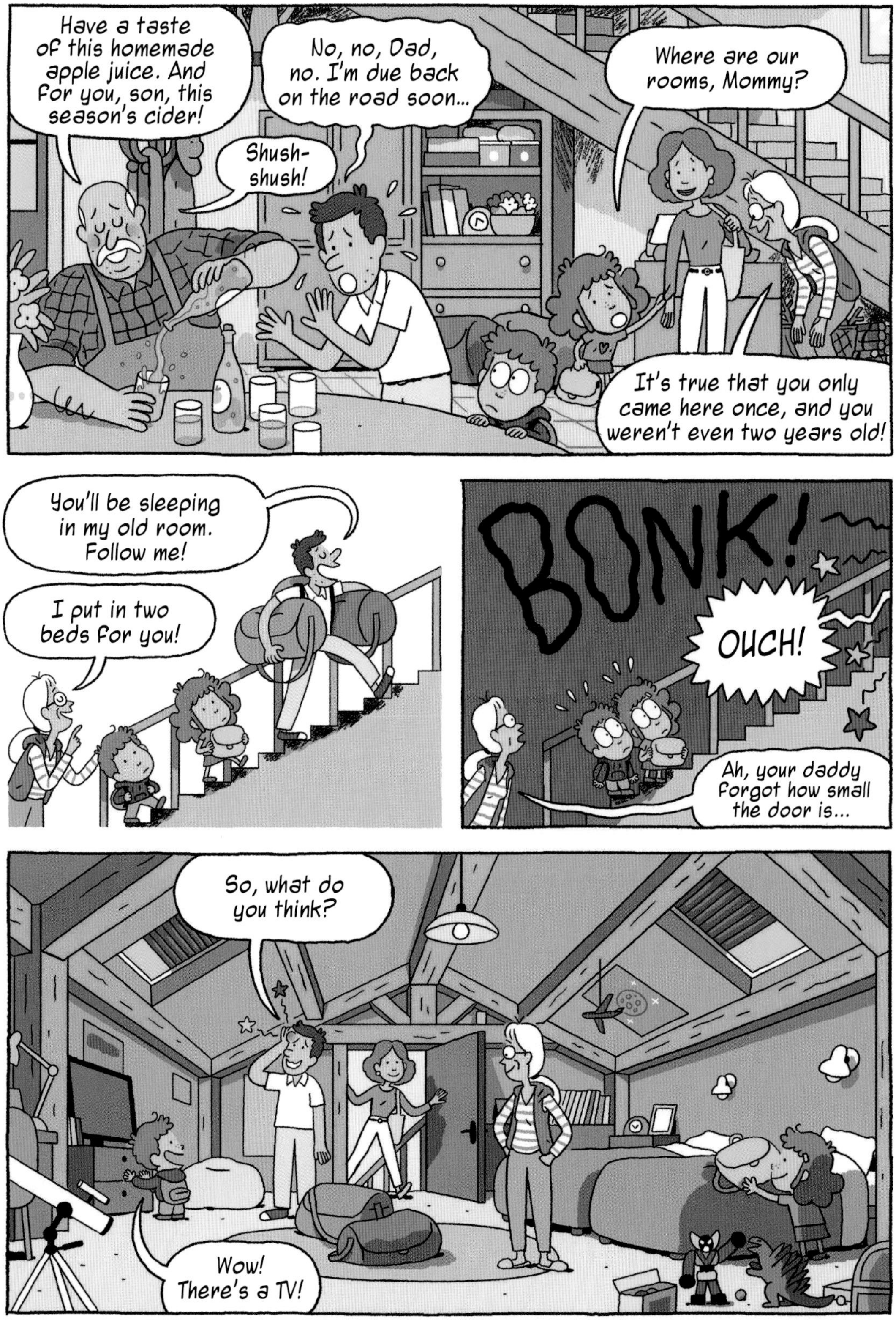
Have a taste of this homemade apple juice. And for you, son, this season's cider!
Shush-shush!
No, no, Dad, no. I'm due back on the road soon...
Where are our rooms, Mommy?
It's true that you only came here once, and you weren't even two years old!
You'll be sleeping in my old room. Follow me!
I put in two beds for you!
BONK!
OUCH!
Ah, your daddy forgot how small the door is...
So, what do you think?
Wow! There's a TV!

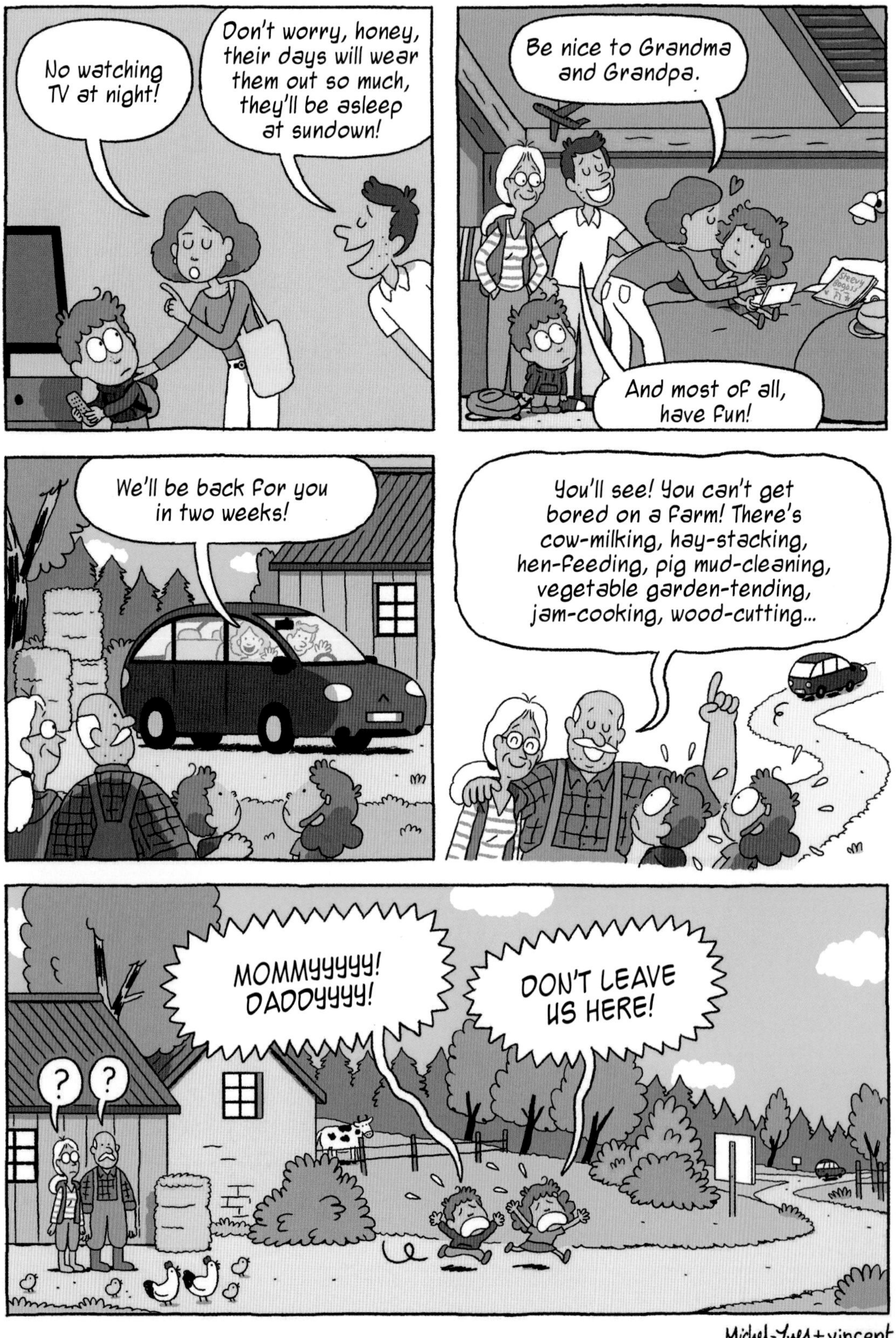
No watching TV at night!
Don't worry, honey, their days will wear them out so much, they'll be asleep at sundown!
Be nice to Grandma and Grandpa.
And most of all, have fun!
We'll be back for you in two weeks!
You'll see! You can't get bored on a farm! There's cow-milking, hay-stacking, hen-feeding, pig mud-cleaning, vegetable garden-tending, jam-cooking, wood-cutting...
?
?
MOMMYYYYY! DADDYYYY!
DON'T LEAVE US HERE!
Michel-Yves+vincent

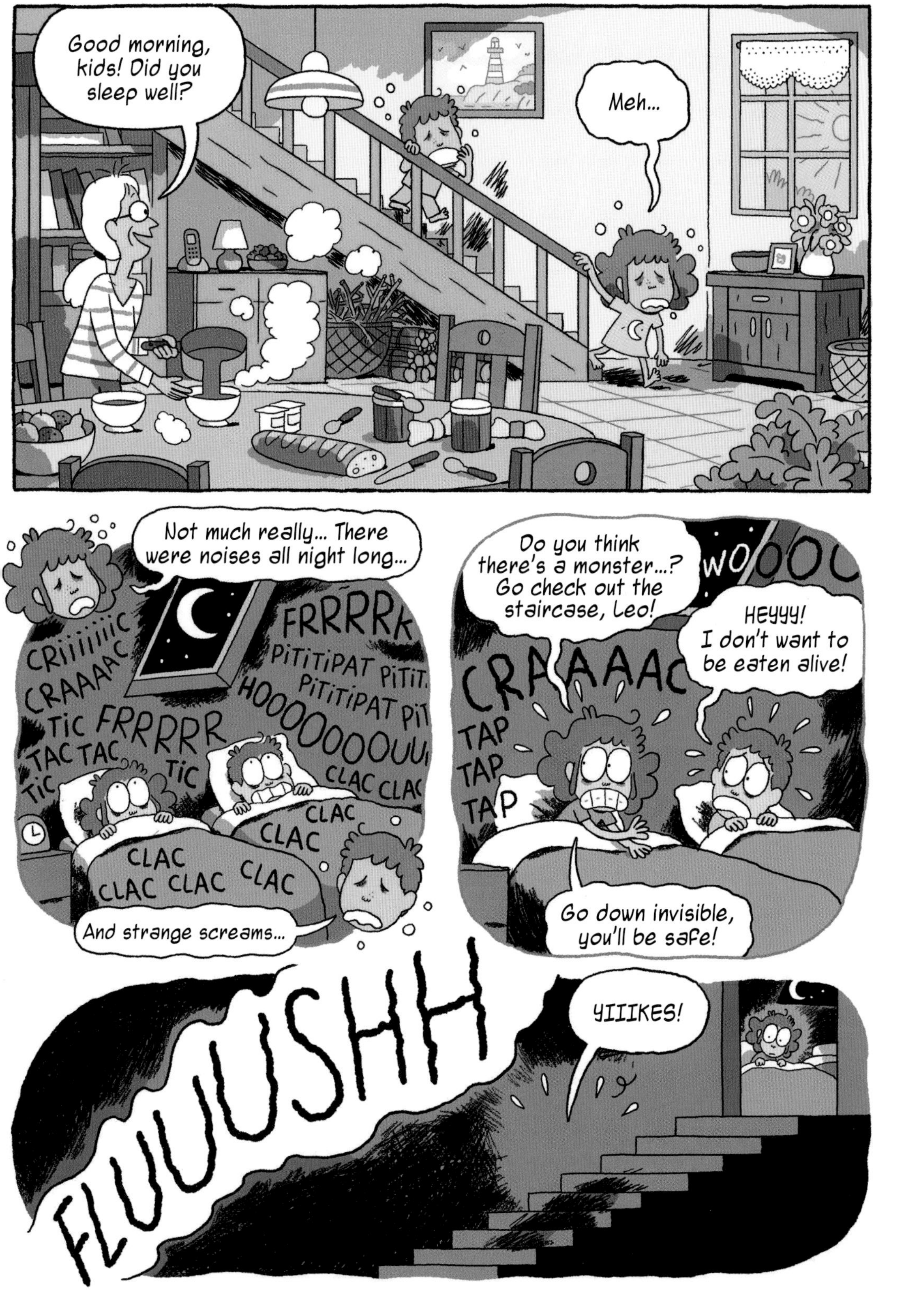
Good morning, kids! Did you sleep well?
Meh...
Not much really... There were noises all night long...
CRiiiiiiic
CRAAAAC
Tic
TAC TAC
Tic
FRRRRR
Tic
FRRRRK
PiTiTiPAT PiTiT
PiTiTiPAT PiT
HOOOOOOOOUU
CLAC CLAC
CLAC
CLAC
CLAC
CLAC CLAC CLAC
And strange screams...
Do you think there's a monster...? Go check out the staircase, Leo!
WOOOO
HEYYY! I don't want to be eaten alive!
CRAAAAC
TAP
TAP
TAP
Go down invisible, you'll be safe!
FLUUUSHH
YIIIKES!

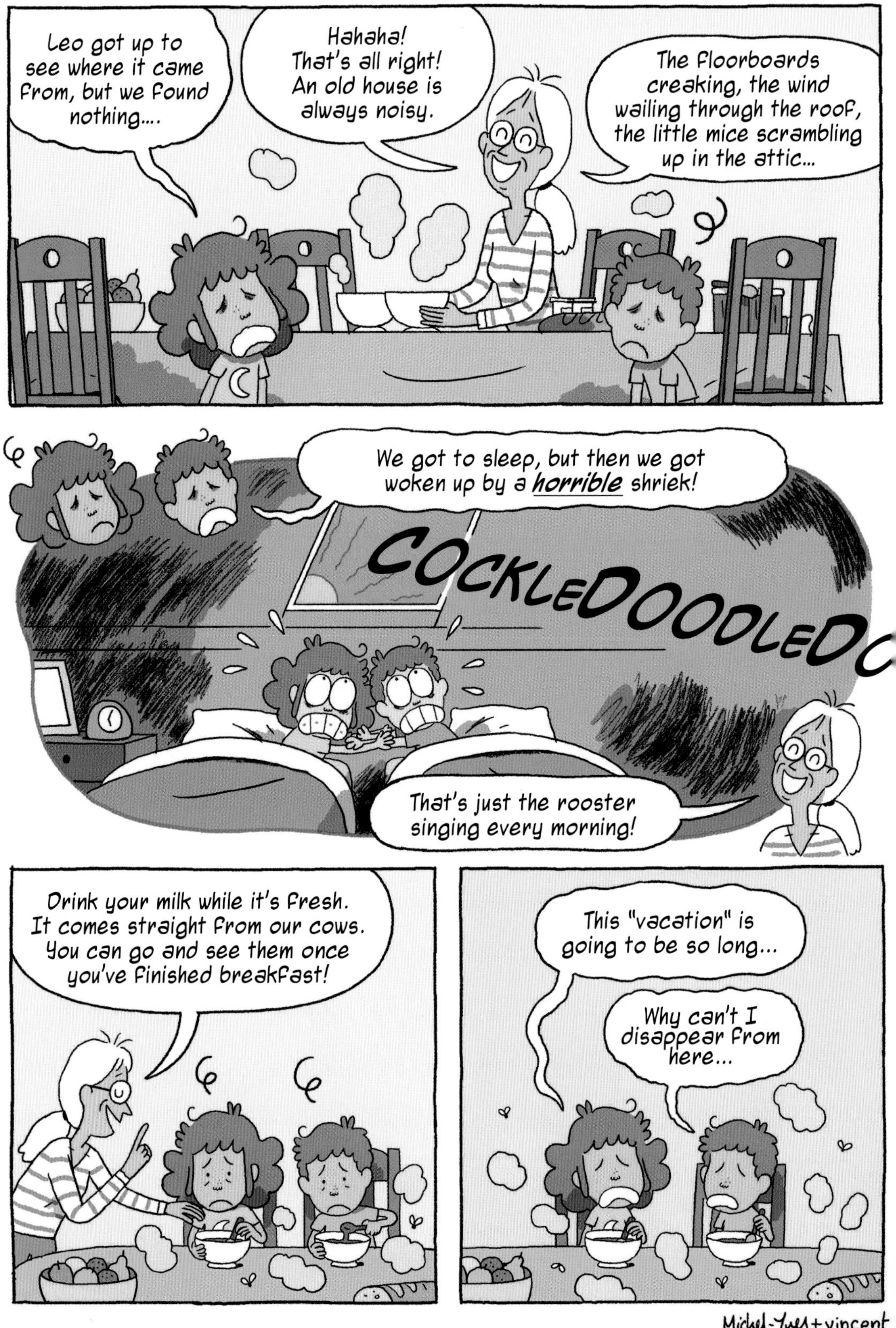
Leo got up to see where it came from, but we found nothing....
Hahaha! That's all right! An old house is always noisy.
The floorboards creaking, the wind wailing through the roof, the little mice scrambling up in the attic...
We got to sleep, but then we got woken up by a **horrible** shriek!
COCKLEDOOODLEDO
That's just the rooster singing every morning!
Drink your milk while it's fresh. It comes straight from our cows. You can go and see them once you've finished breakfast!
This "vacation" is going to be so long...
Why can't I disappear from here...

Michel-Yves+vincent

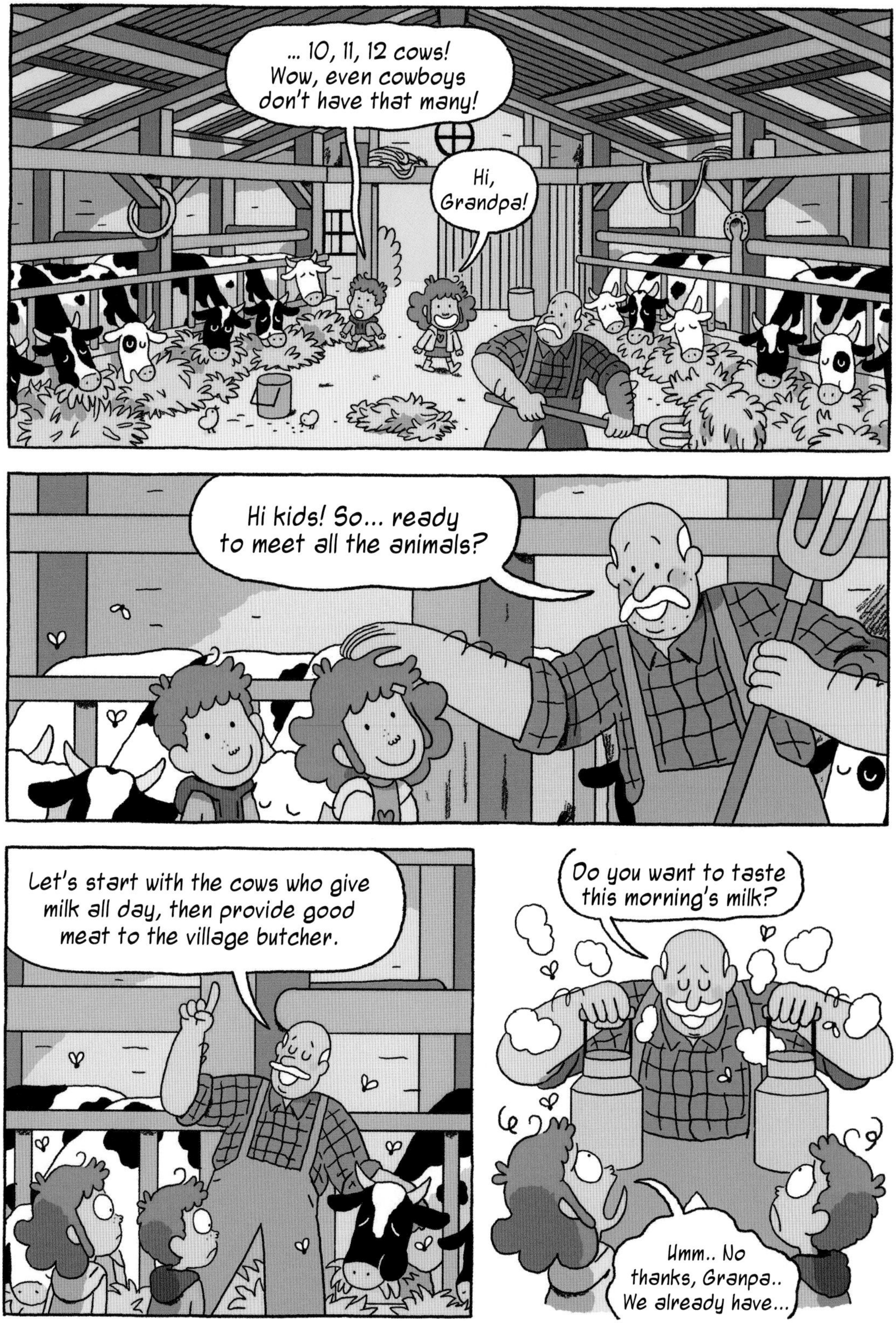
... 10, 11, 12 cows! Wow, even cowboys don't have that many!
Hi, Grandpa!
Hi kids! So... ready to meet all the animals?
Let's start with the cows who give milk all day, then provide good meat to the village butcher.
Do you want to taste this morning's milk?
Umm.. No thanks, Granpa.. We already have...

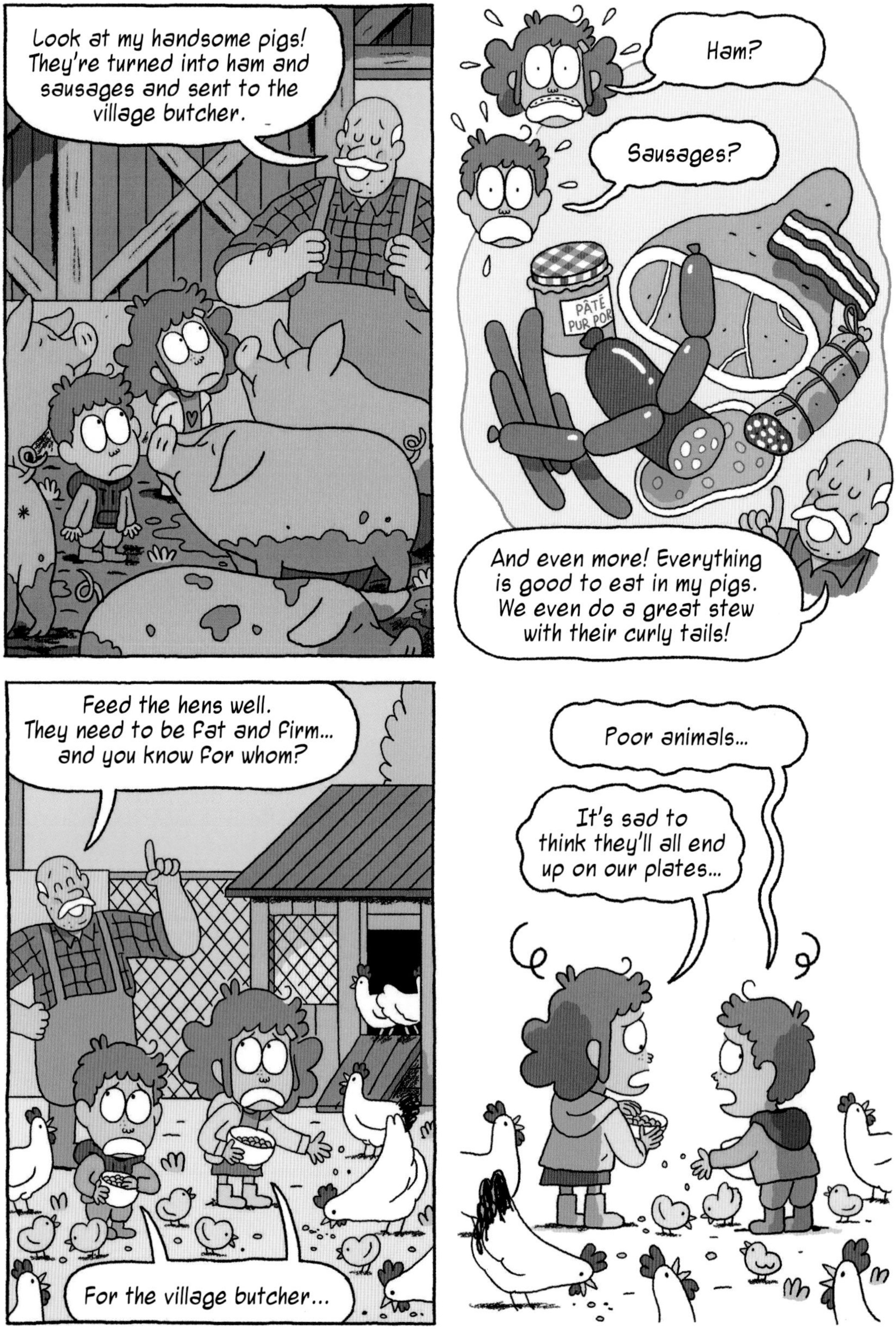
Look at my handsome pigs! They're turned into ham and sausages and sent to the village butcher.
Ham?
Sausages?
PÂTÉ PUR PORC
And even more! Everything is good to eat in my pigs. We even do a great stew with their curly tails!
Feed the hens well. They need to be fat and firm... and you know for whom?
For the village butcher...
Poor animals...
It's sad to think they'll all end up on our plates...

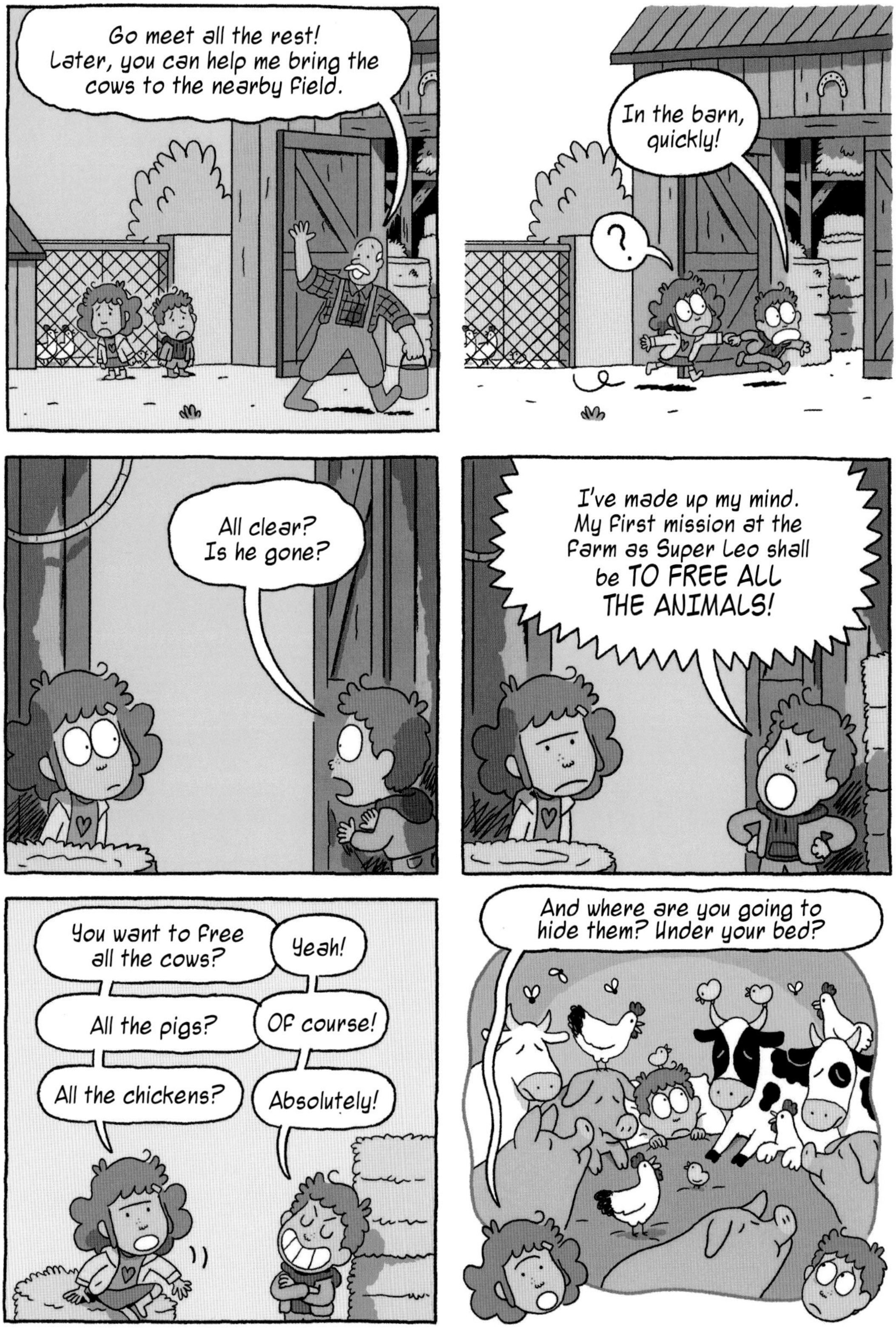
Go meet all the rest! Later, you can help me bring the cows to the nearby field.
In the barn, quickly!
?
All clear? Is he gone?
I've made up my mind. My first mission at the farm as Super Leo shall be TO FREE ALL THE ANIMALS!
You want to free all the cows?
Yeah!
All the pigs?
Of course!
All the chickens?
Absolutely!
And where are you going to hide them? Under your bed?

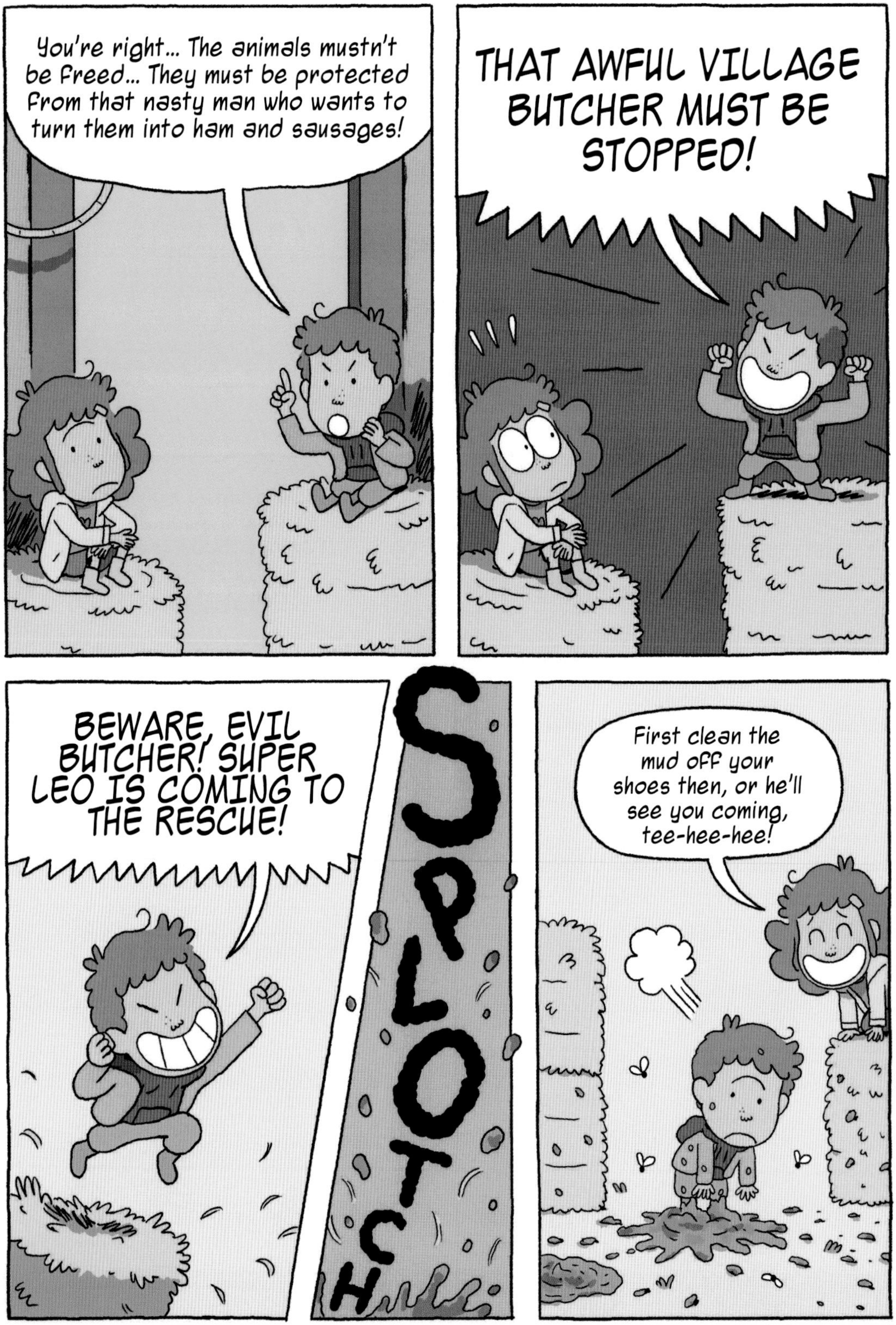
You're right... The animals mustn't be freed... They must be protected from that nasty man who wants to turn them into ham and sausages!
THAT AWFUL VILLAGE BUTCHER MUST BE STOPPED!
BEWARE, EVIL BUTCHER! SUPER LEO IS COMING TO THE RESCUE!
SPLOTCH
First clean the mud off your shoes then, or he'll see you coming, tee-hee-hee!

Michel-Yves+vincent

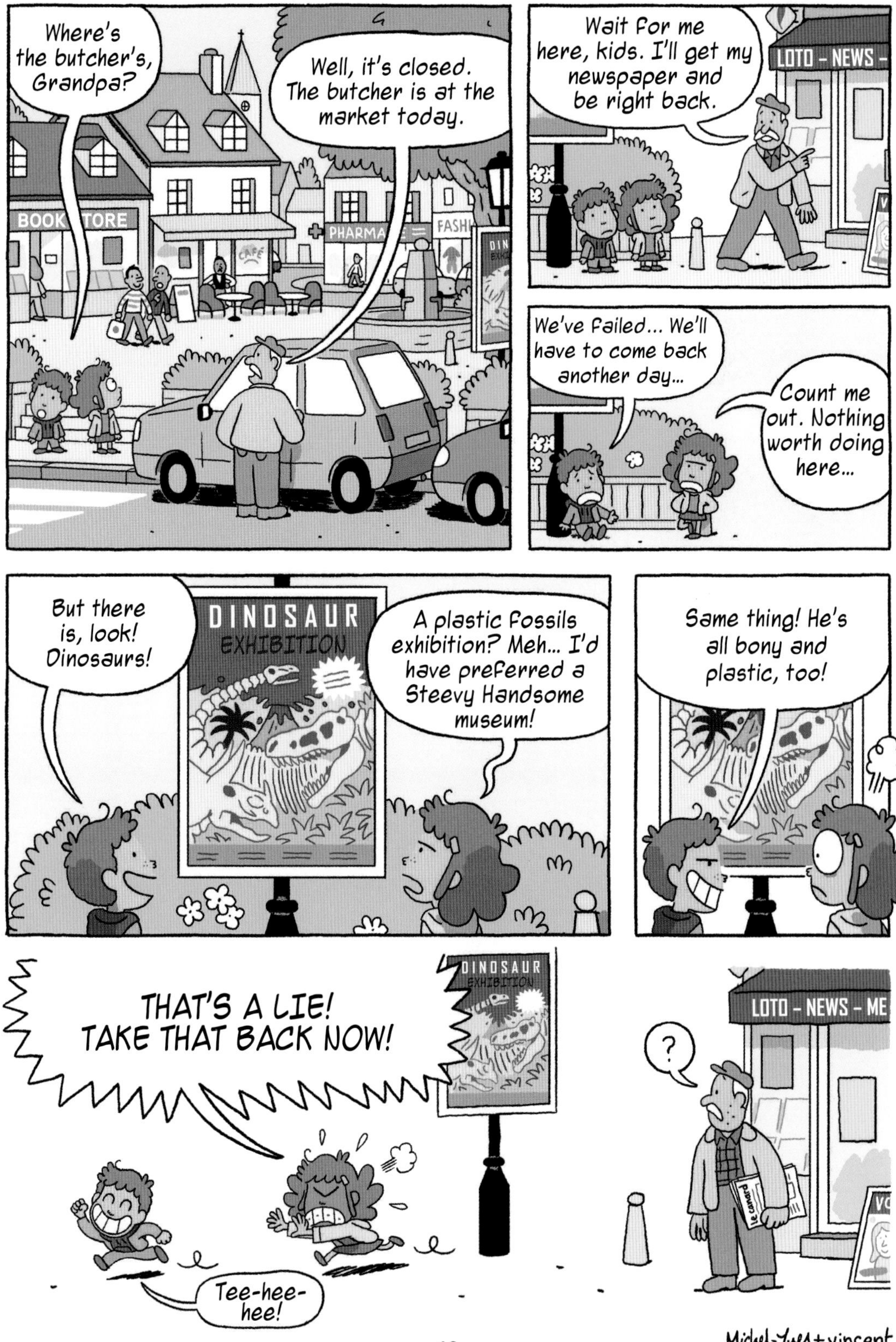
Where's the butcher's, Grandpa?
Well, it's closed. The butcher is at the market today.
BOOKSTORE
PHARMA
FASH
CAFÉ
Wait for me here, kids. I'll get my newspaper and be right back.
LOTO – NEWS –
We've failed... We'll have to come back another day...
Count me out. Nothing worth doing here...
But there is, look! Dinosaurs!
DINOSAUR EXHIBITION
A plastic fossils exhibition? Meh... I'd have preferred a Steevy Handsome museum!
Same thing! He's all bony and plastic, too!
THAT'S A LIE! TAKE THAT BACK NOW!
DINOSAUR EXHIBITION
LOTO – NEWS – ME
?
le canard
Tee-hee-hee!
Michel-Yves + vincent

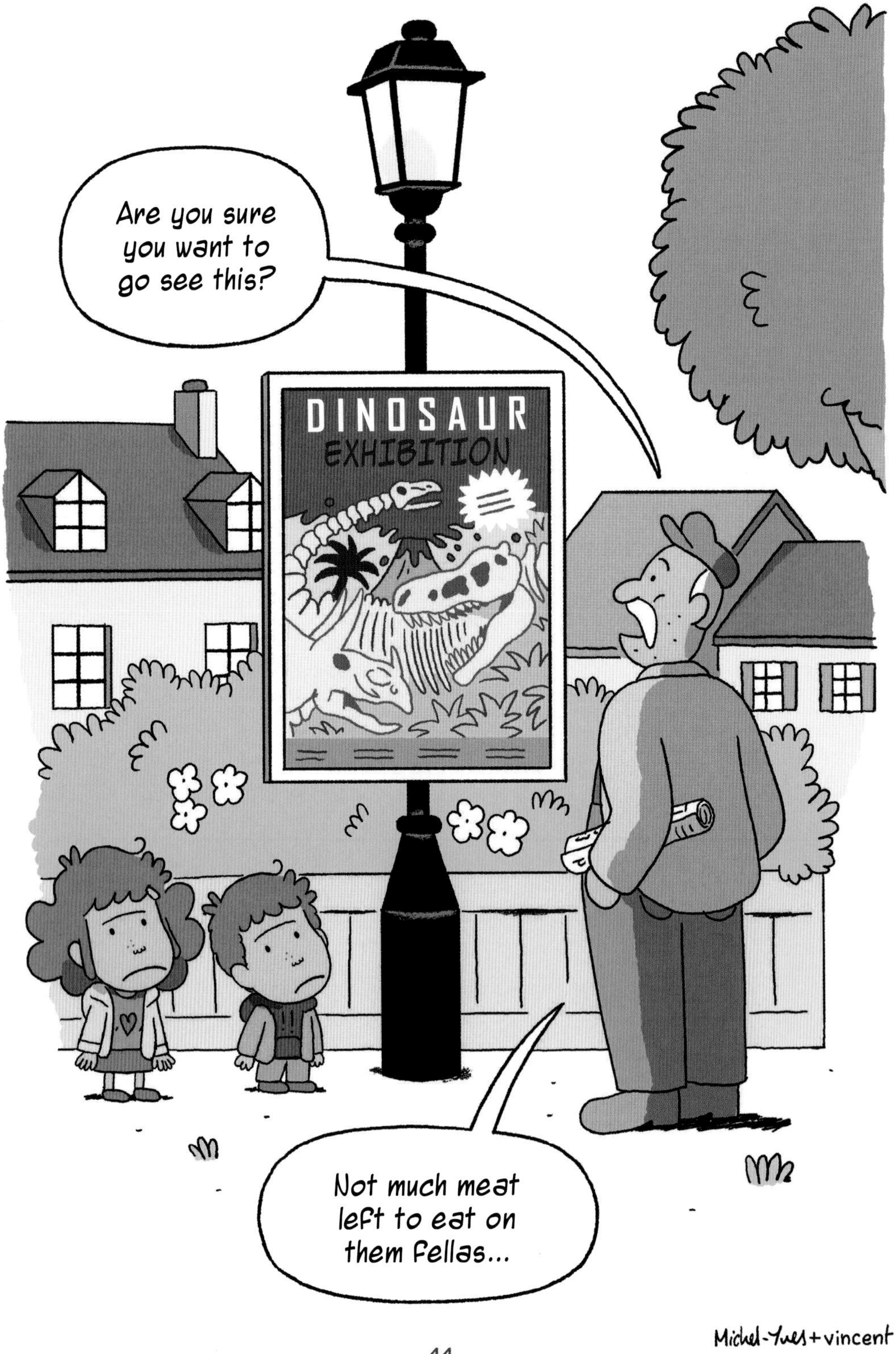
Are you sure you want to go see this?
DINOSAUR EXHIBITION
Not much meat left to eat on them fellas...
Michel-Yves + vincent

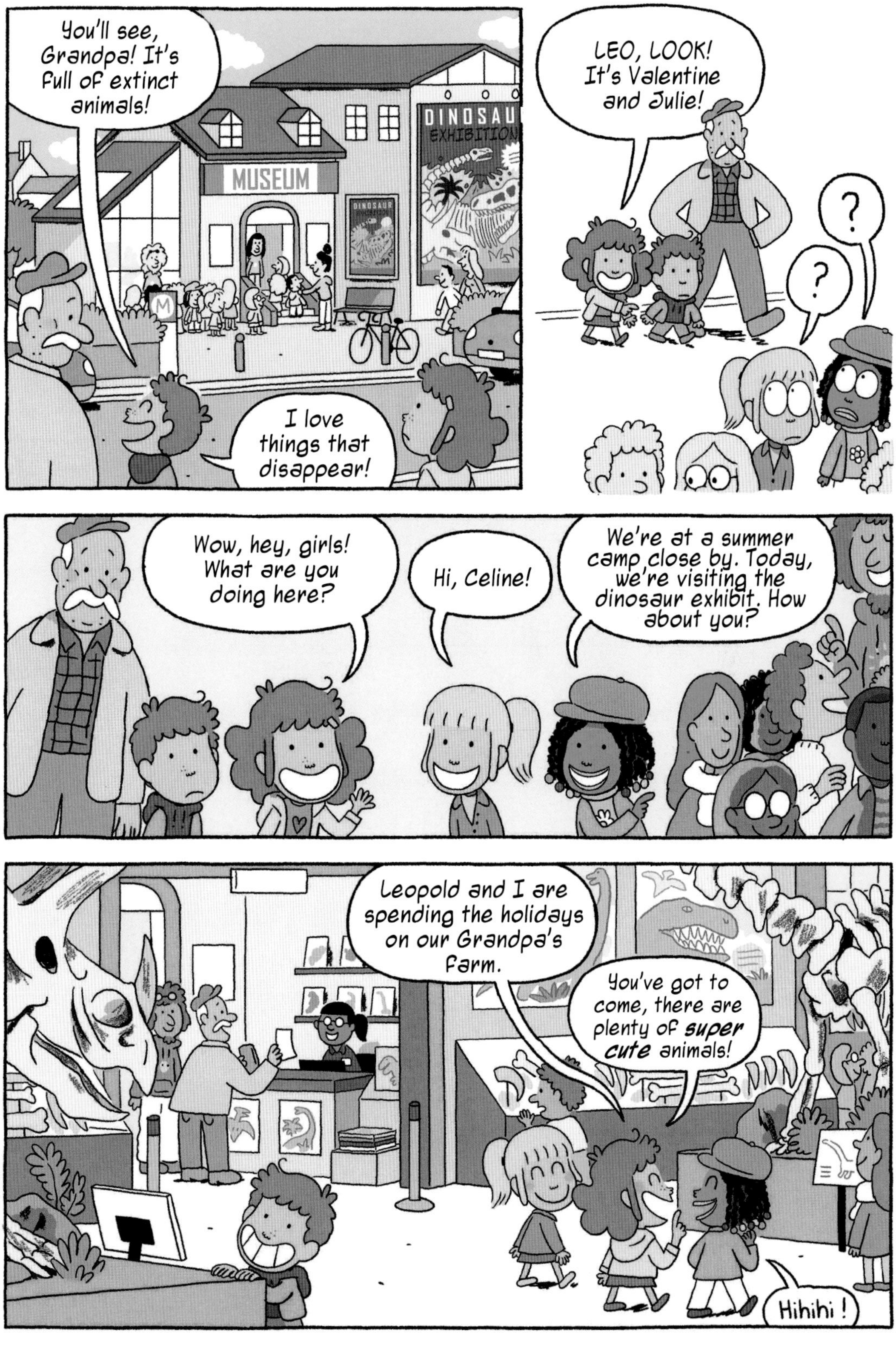

You'll see, Grandpa! It's full of extinct animals!
MUSEUM
DINOSAUR EXHIBITION
I love things that disappear!
LEO, LOOK! It's Valentine and Julie!
?
?
Wow, hey, girls! What are you doing here?
Hi, Celine!
We're at a summer camp close by. Today, we're visiting the dinosaur exhibit. How about you?
Leopold and I are spending the holidays on our Grandpa's farm.
You've got to come, there are plenty of **super cute** animals!
Hihihi!

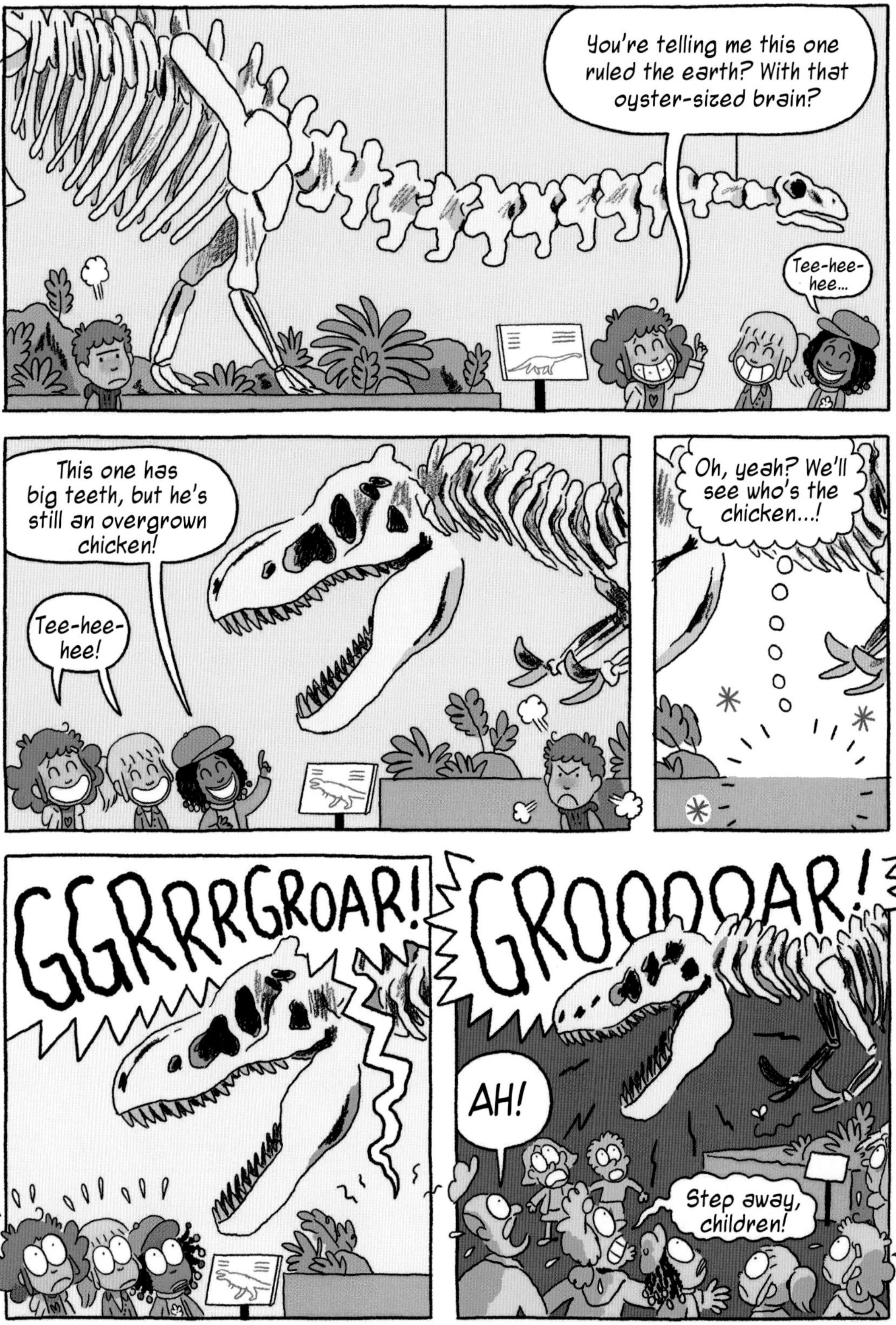
You're telling me this one ruled the earth? With that oyster-sized brain?
Tee-hee-hee...
This one has big teeth, but he's still an overgrown chicken!
Tee-hee-hee!
Oh, yeah? We'll see who's the chicken...!
GGRRRGROAR!
GROOOOOAR!
AH!
Step away, children!

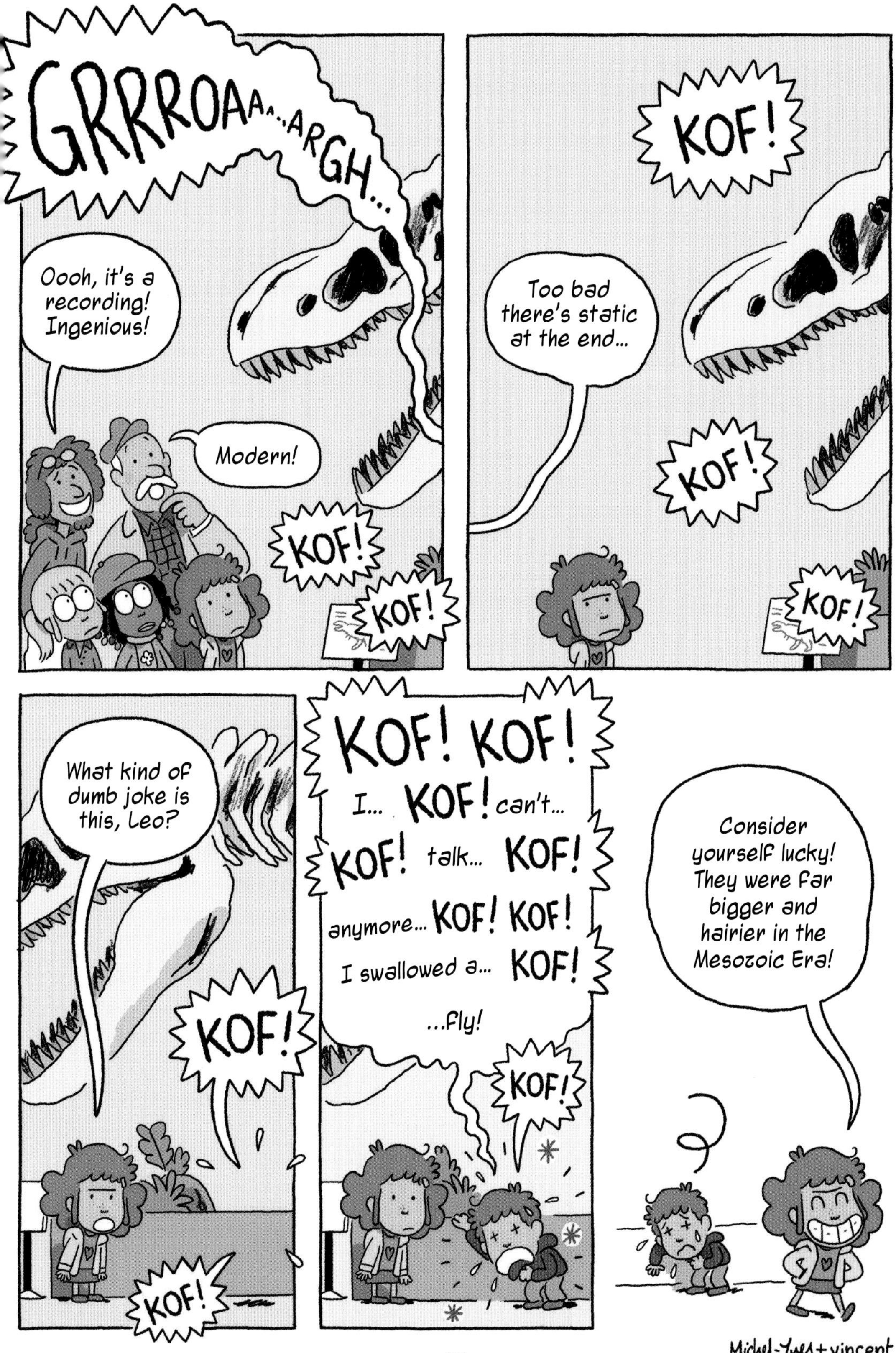
GRRROAA...ARGH...
Oooh, it's a recording! Ingenious!
Modern!
KOF!
KOF!
KOF!
Too bad there's static at the end...
KOF!
KOF!
What kind of dumb joke is this, Leo?
KOF!
KOF!
KOF! KOF! I... KOF! can't... KOF! talk... KOF! anymore... KOF! KOF! I swallowed a... KOF! ...fly!
KOF!
Consider yourself lucky! They were far bigger and hairier in the Mesozoic Era!
Michel-Yves + vincent

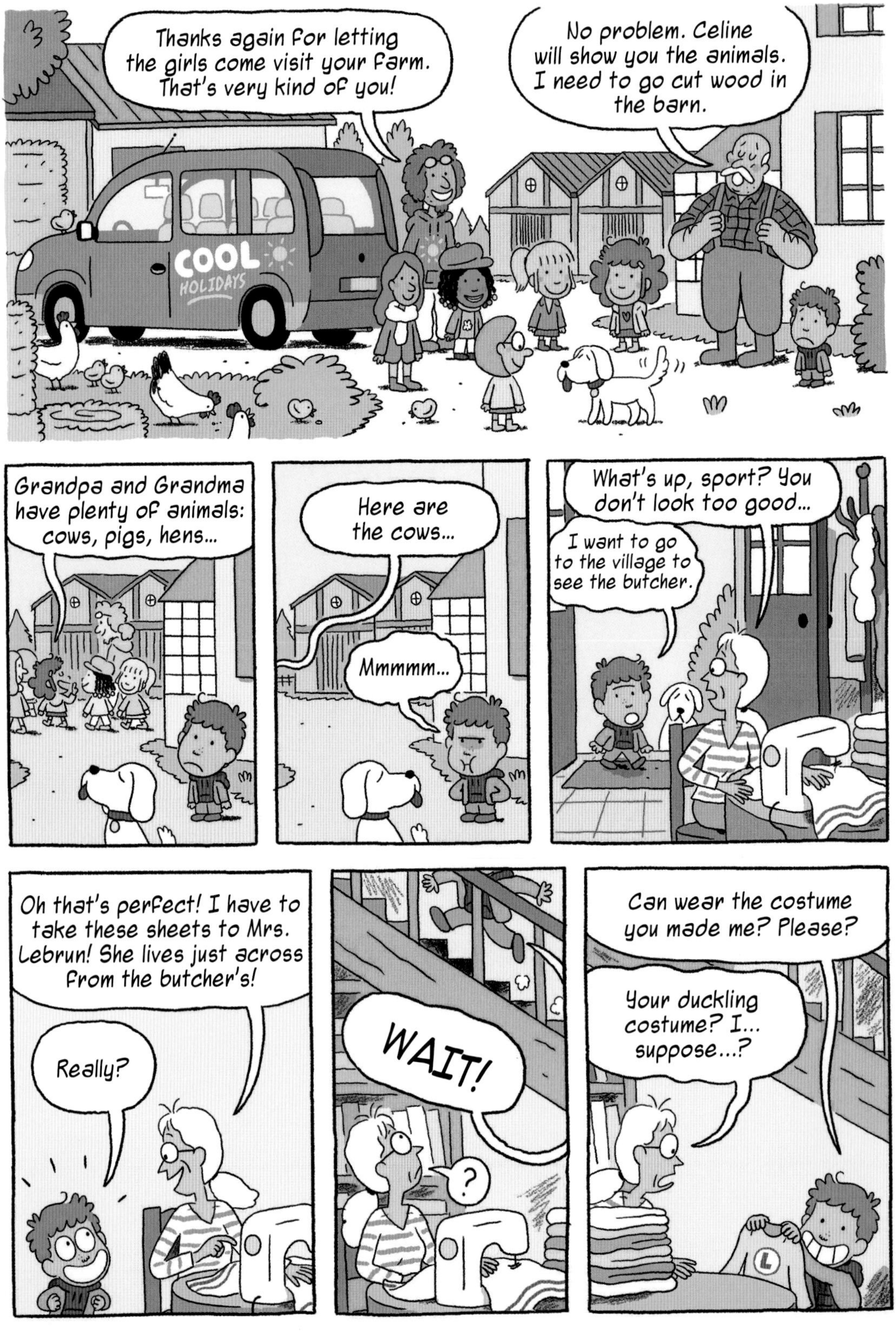
Thanks again for letting the girls come visit your farm. That's very kind of you!
No problem. Celine will show you the animals. I need to go cut wood in the barn.
COOL HOLIDAYS
Grandpa and Grandma have plenty of animals: cows, pigs, hens...
Here are the cows...
Mmmmm...
What's up, sport? You don't look too good...
I want to go to the village to see the butcher.
Oh that's perfect! I have to take these sheets to Mrs. Lebrun! She lives just across from the butcher's!
Really?
WAIT!
?
Can wear the costume you made me? Please?
Your duckling costume? I... suppose...?

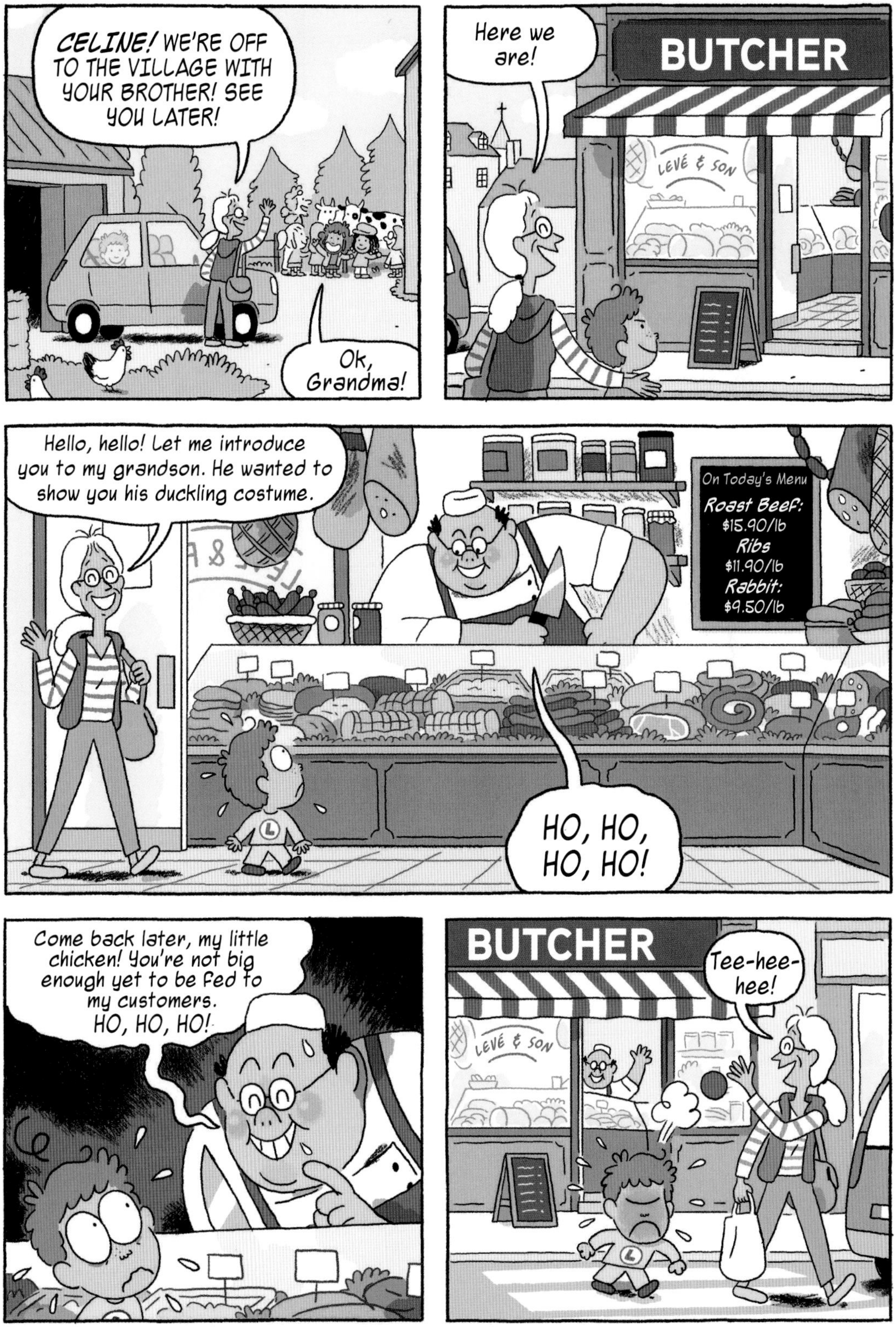
CELINE! WE'RE OFF TO THE VILLAGE WITH YOUR BROTHER! SEE YOU LATER!
Ok, Grandma!
Here we are!
BUTCHER
LEVÉ & SON
Hello, hello! Let me introduce you to my grandson. He wanted to show you his duckling costume.
On Today's Menu
Roast Beef: $15.90/lb
Ribs $11.90/lb
Rabbit: $9.50/lb
HO, HO, HO, HO!
Come back later, my little chicken! You're not big enough yet to be fed to my customers. HO, HO, HO!
BUTCHER
LEVÉ & SON
Tee-hee-hee!

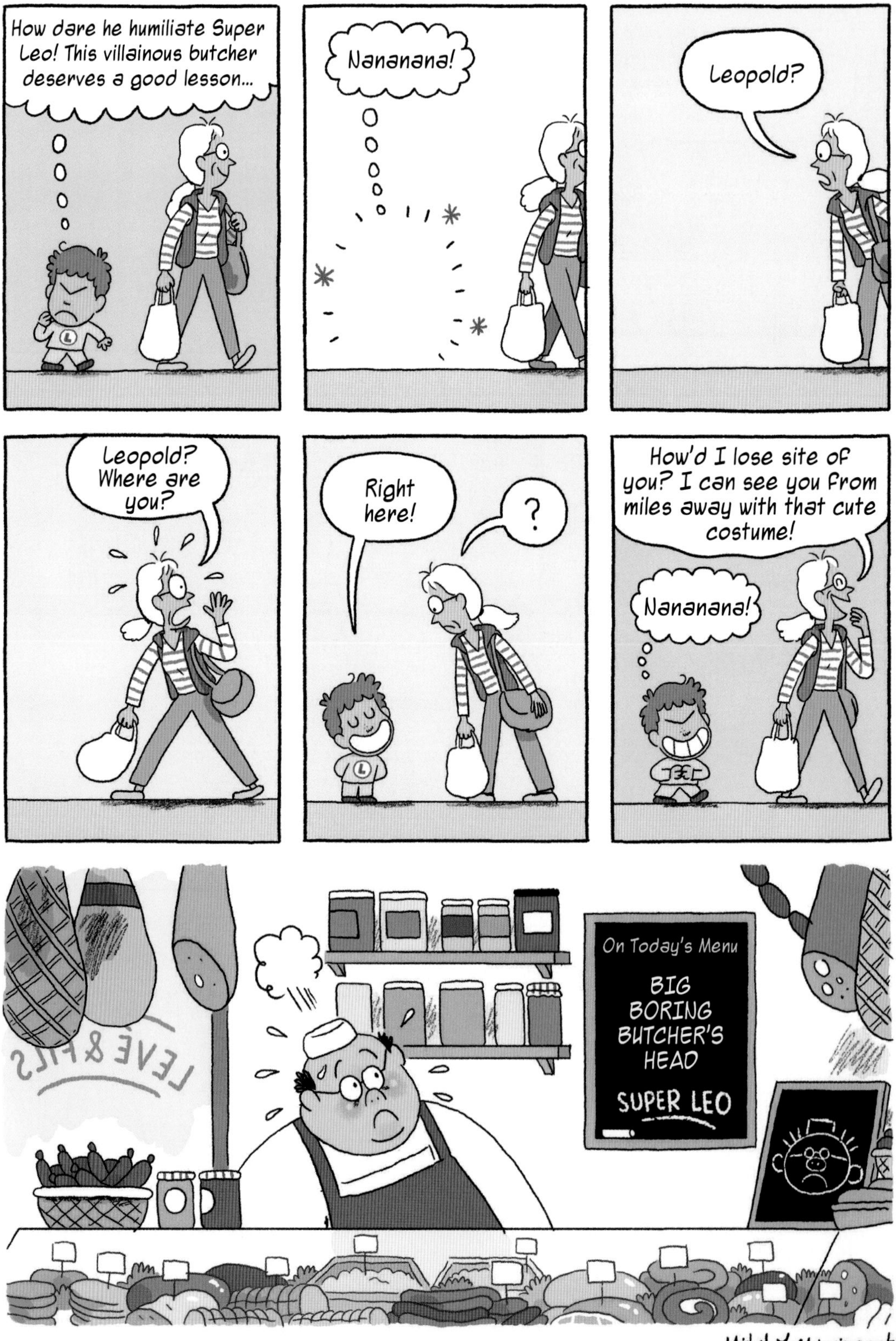
How dare he humiliate Super Leo! This villainous butcher deserves a good lesson...
Nananana!
Leopold?
Leopold? Where are you?
Right here!
?
How'd I lose site of you? I can see you from miles away with that cute costume!
Nananana!
On Today's Menu
BIG BORING BUTCHER'S HEAD
SUPER LEO
Michel-Yves+vincent

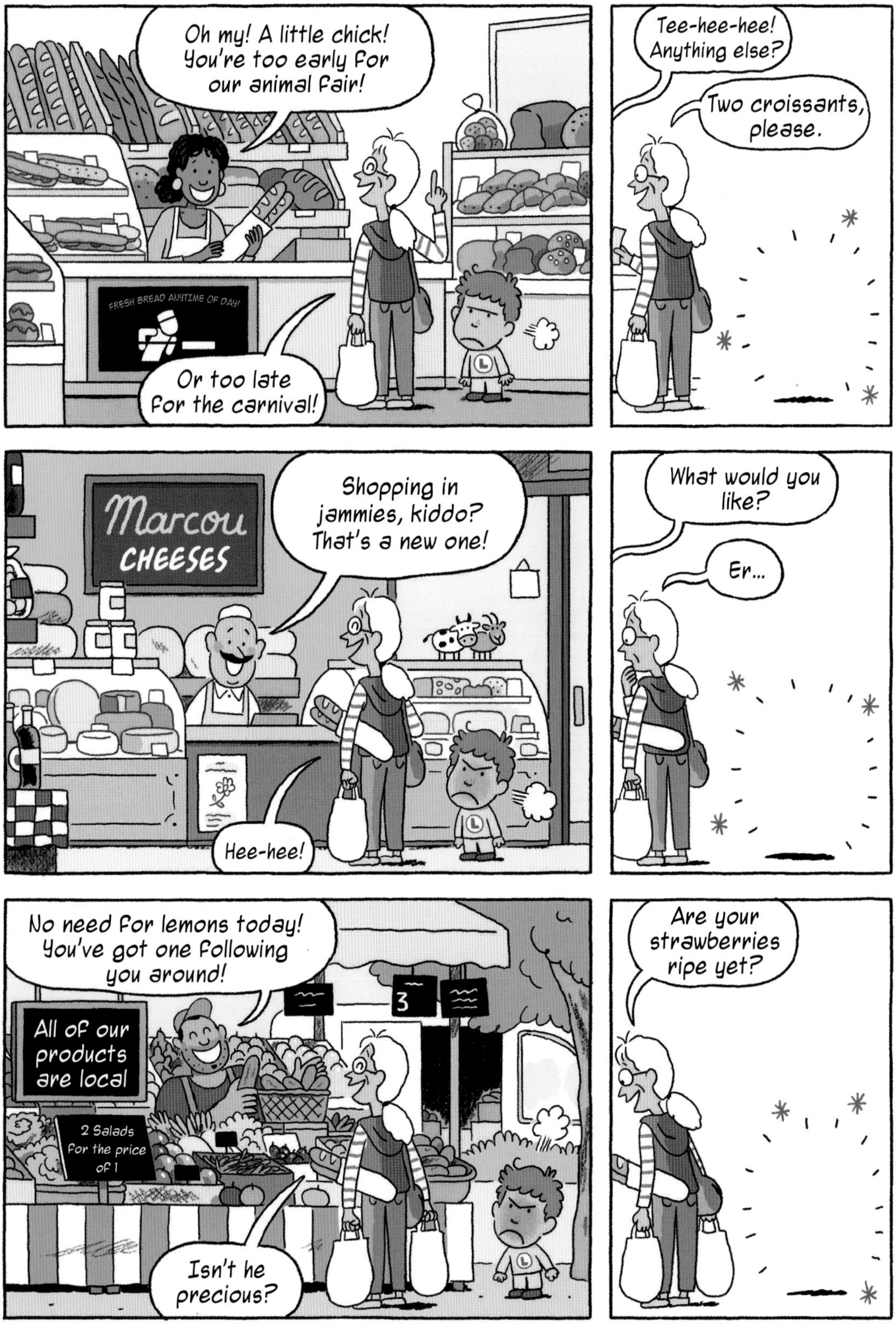

Oh my! A little chick! You're too early for our animal fair!
FRESH BREAD ANYTIME OF DAY!
Or too late for the carnival!
Tee-hee-hee! Anything else?
Two croissants, please.
Marcou CHEESES
Shopping in jammies, kiddo? That's a new one!
Hee-hee!
What would you like?
Er...
No need for lemons today! You've got one following you around!
All of our products are local
2 Salads for the price of 1
3
Isn't he precious?
Are your strawberries ripe yet?

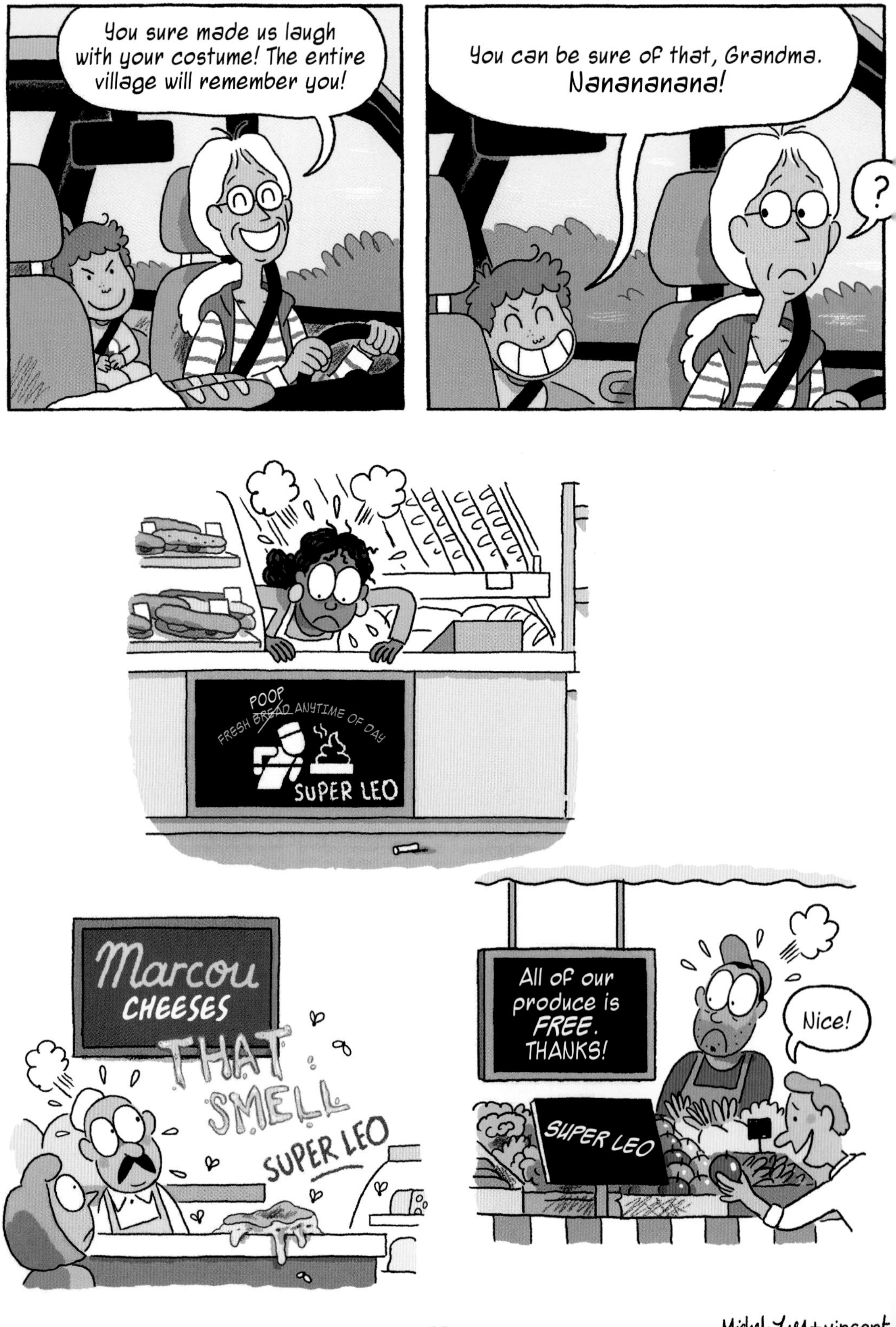
You sure made us laugh with your costume! The entire village will remember you!
You can be sure of that, Grandma. Nanananana!
?
POOP
FRESH BREAD ANYTIME OF DAY
SUPER LEO
Marcou CHEESES
THAT SMELL
SUPER LEO
All of our produce is FREE. THANKS!
SUPER LEO
Nice!
Michel-Yves + vincent

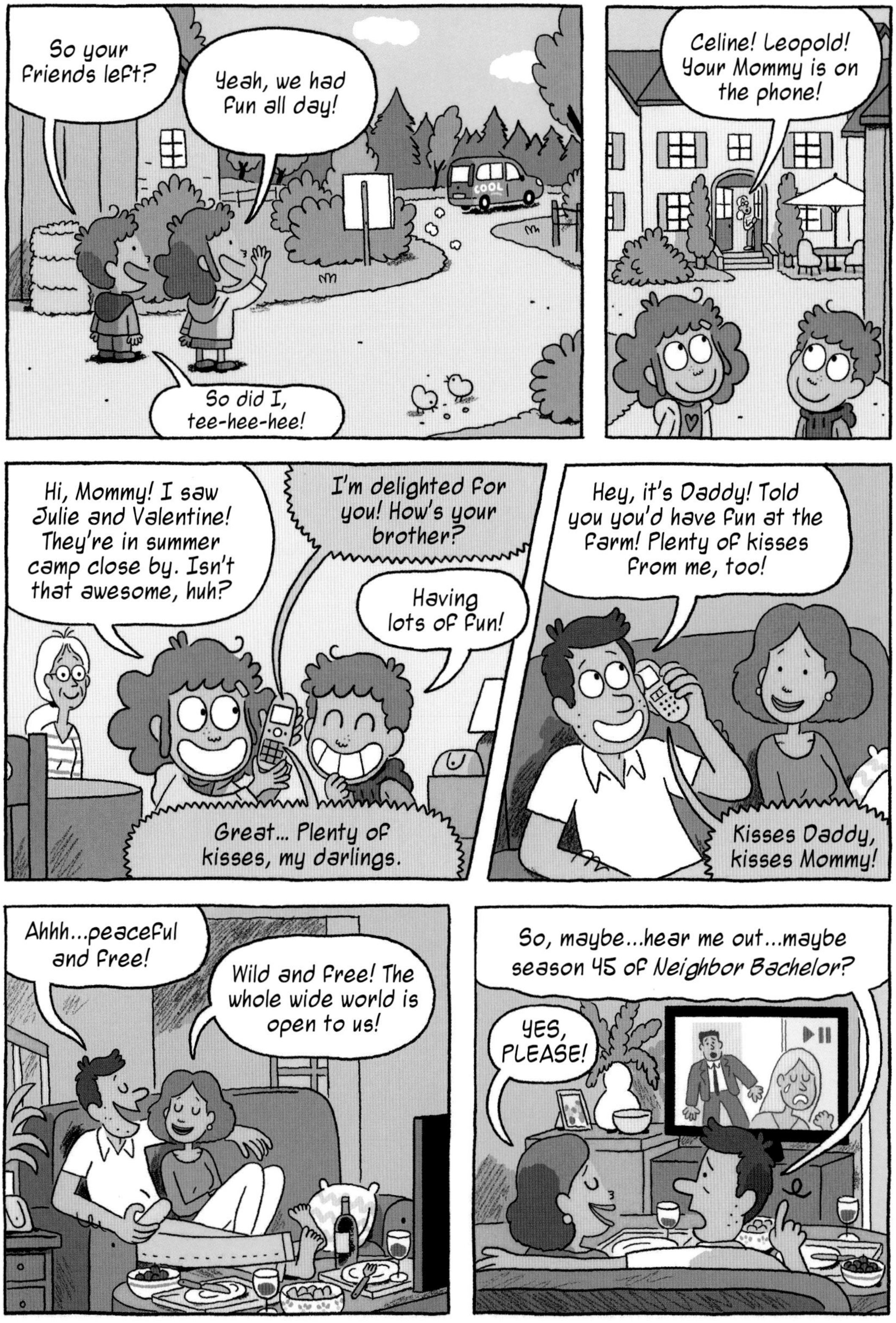
So your friends left?
Yeah, we had fun all day!
COOL
So did I, tee-hee-hee!
Celine! Leopold! Your Mommy is on the phone!
Hi, Mommy! I saw Julie and Valentine! They're in summer camp close by. Isn't that awesome, huh?
I'm delighted for you! How's your brother?
Having lots of fun!
Great... Plenty of kisses, my darlings.
Hey, it's Daddy! Told you you'd have fun at the farm! Plenty of kisses from me, too!
Kisses Daddy, kisses Mommy!
Ahhh...peaceful and free!
Wild and free! The whole wide world is open to us!
So, maybe...hear me out...maybe season 45 of *Neighbor Bachelor*?
YES, PLEASE!

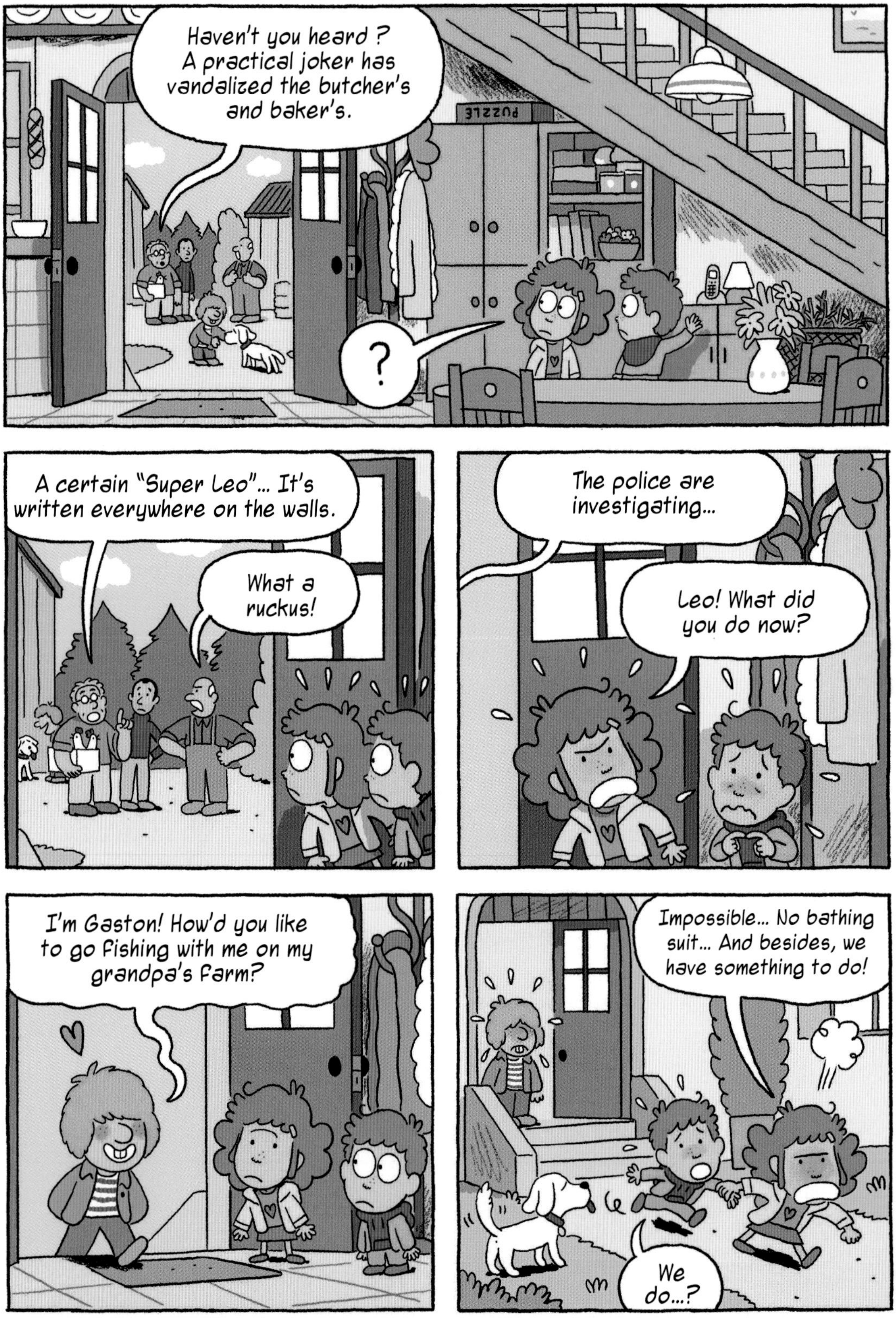
Haven't you heard ? A practical joker has vandalized the butcher's and baker's.
PUZZLE
?
A certain "Super Leo"... It's written everywhere on the walls.
What a ruckus!
The police are investigating...
Leo! What did you do now?
I'm Gaston! How'd you like to go fishing with me on my grandpa's farm?
Impossible... No bathing suit... And besides, we have something to do!
We do...?

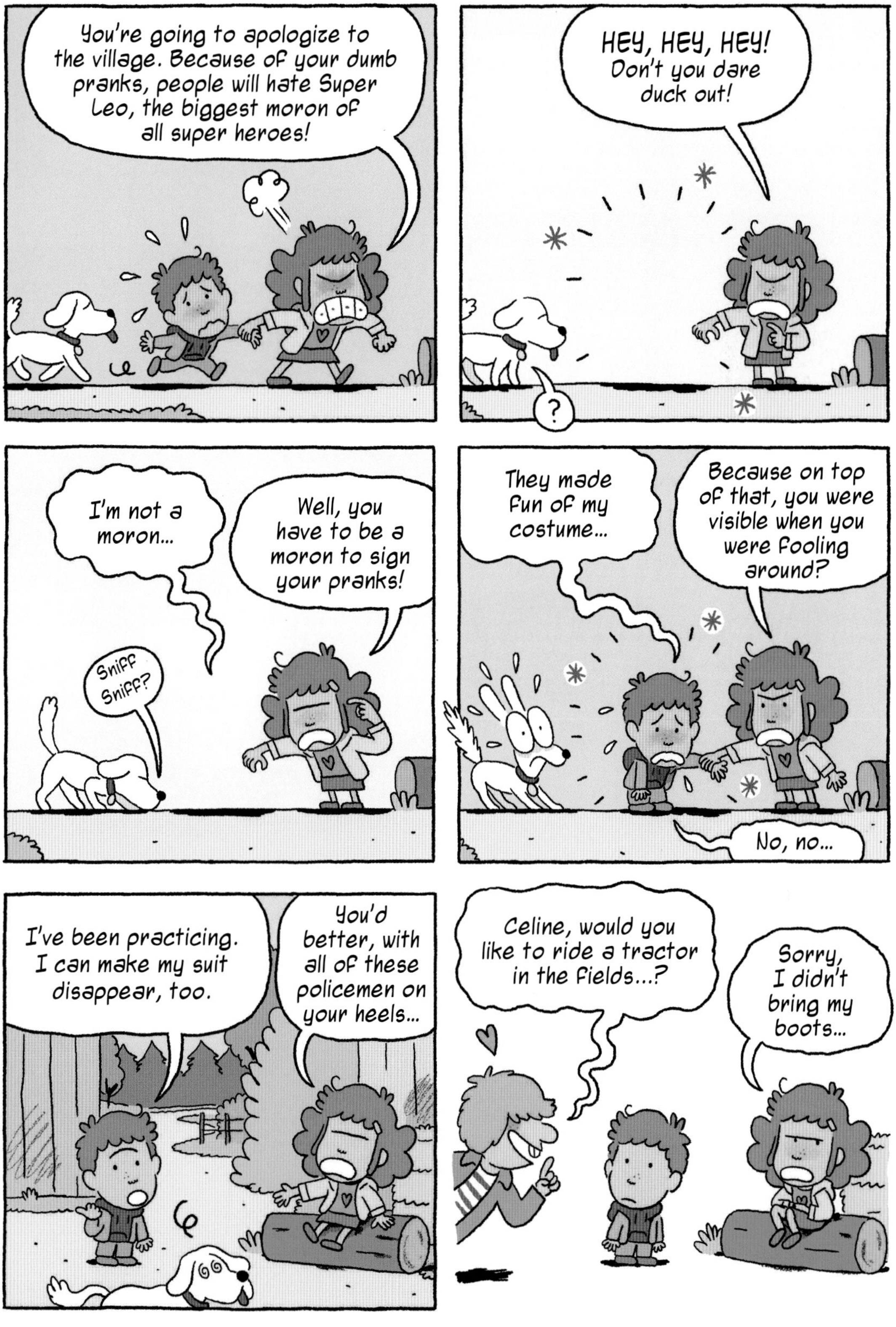
You're going to apologize to the village. Because of your dumb pranks, people will hate Super Leo, the biggest moron of all super heroes!
HEY, HEY, HEY! Don't you dare duck out!
?
I'm not a moron...
Well, you have to be a moron to sign your pranks!
Sniff Sniff?
They made fun of my costume...
Because on top of that, you were visible when you were fooling around?
No, no...
I've been practicing. I can make my suit disappear, too.
You'd better, with all of these policemen on your heels...
Celine, would you like to ride a tractor in the fields...?
Sorry, I didn't bring my boots...

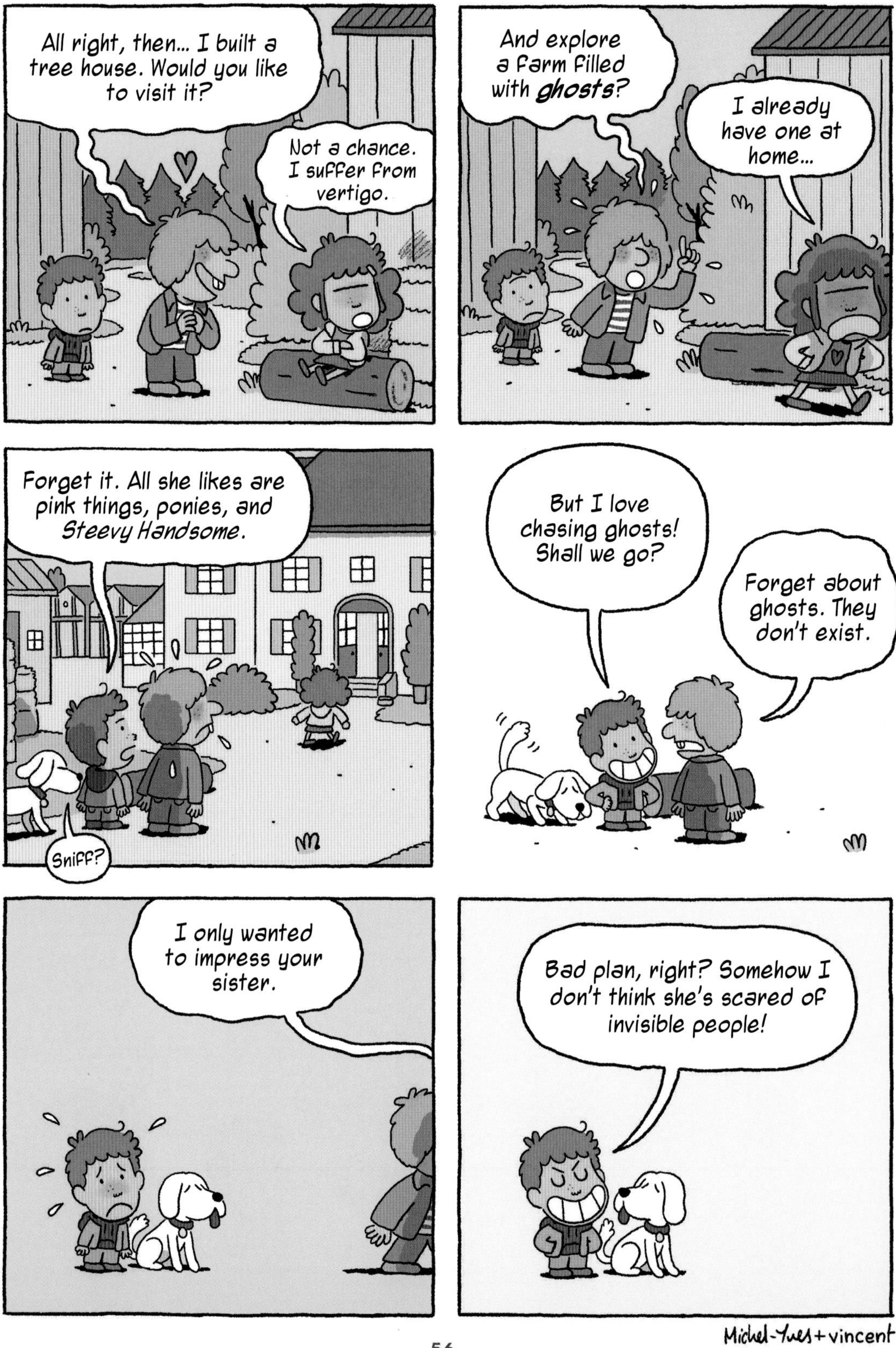
All right, then... I built a tree house. Would you like to visit it?
Not a chance. I suffer from vertigo.
And explore a farm filled with ghosts?
I already have one at home...
Forget it. All she likes are pink things, ponies, and Steevy Handsome.
Sniff?
But I love chasing ghosts! Shall we go?
Forget about ghosts. They don't exist.
I only wanted to impress your sister.
Bad plan, right? Somehow I don't think she's scared of invisible people!
Michel-Yves+vincent

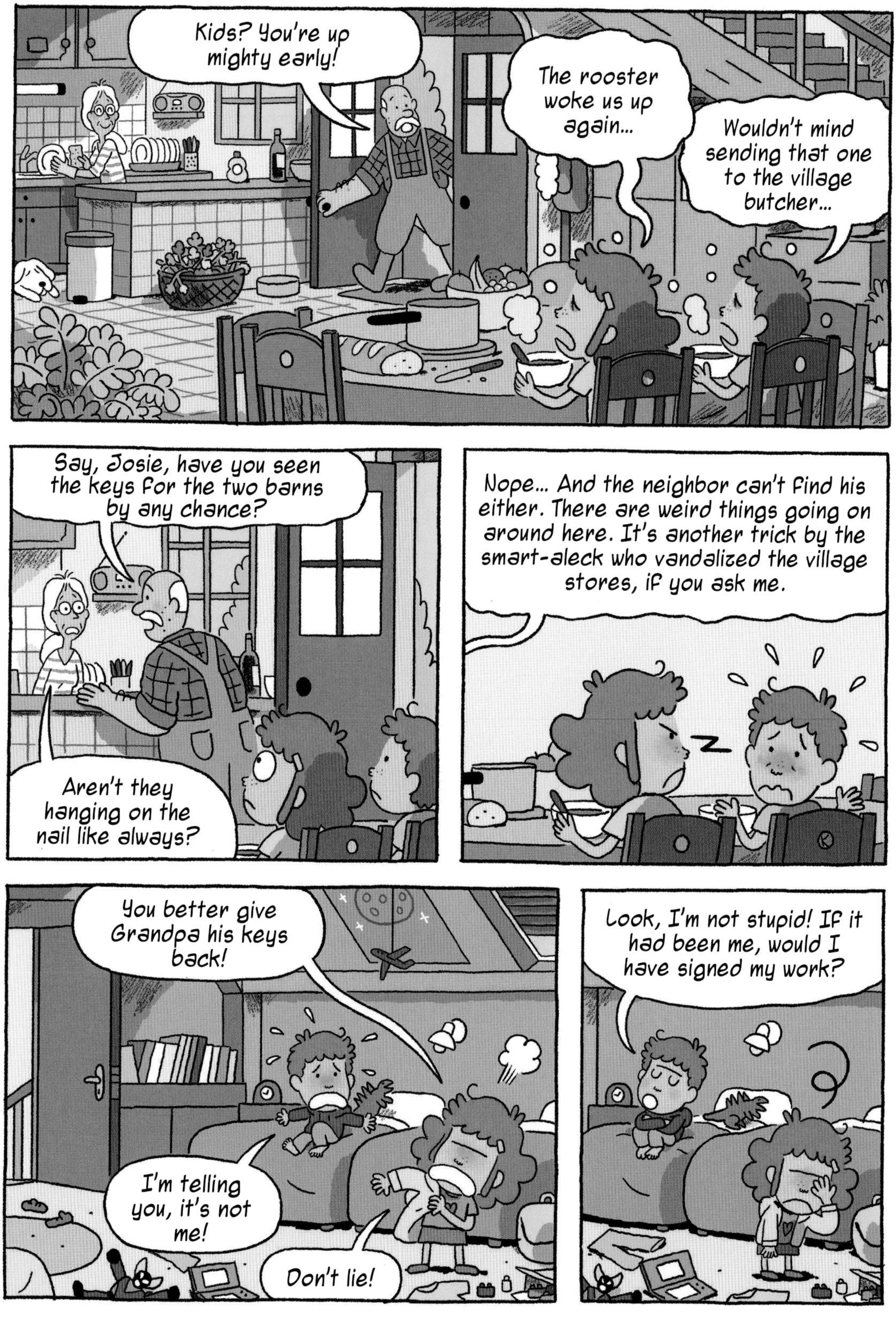
Kids? You're up mighty early!
The rooster woke us up again...
Wouldn't mind sending that one to the village butcher...
Say, Josie, have you seen the keys for the two barns by any chance?
Aren't they hanging on the nail like always?
Nope... And the neighbor can't find his either. There are weird things going on around here. It's another trick by the smart-aleck who vandalized the village stores, if you ask me.
You better give Grandpa his keys back!
I'm telling you, it's not me!
Don't lie!
Look, I'm not stupid! If it had been me, would I have signed my work?

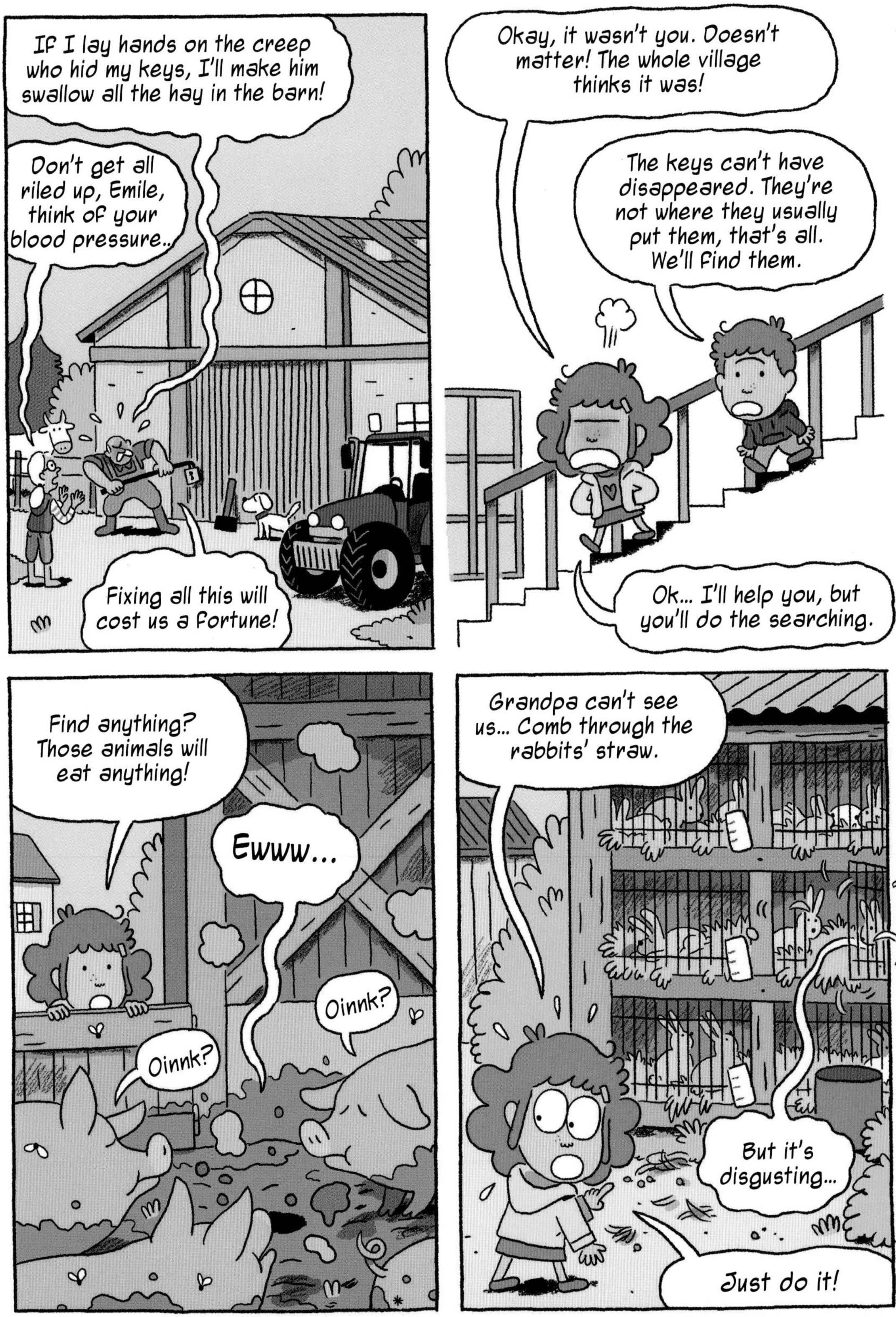
If I lay hands on the creep who hid my keys, I'll make him swallow all the hay in the barn!
Don't get all riled up, Emile, think of your blood pressure...
Fixing all this will cost us a fortune!
Okay, it wasn't you. Doesn't matter! The whole village thinks it was!
The keys can't have disappeared. They're not where they usually put them, that's all. We'll find them.
Ok... I'll help you, but you'll do the searching.
Find anything? Those animals will eat anything!
Ewww...
Oinnk?
Oinnk?
Grandpa can't see us... Comb through the rabbits' straw.
But it's disgusting...
Just do it!

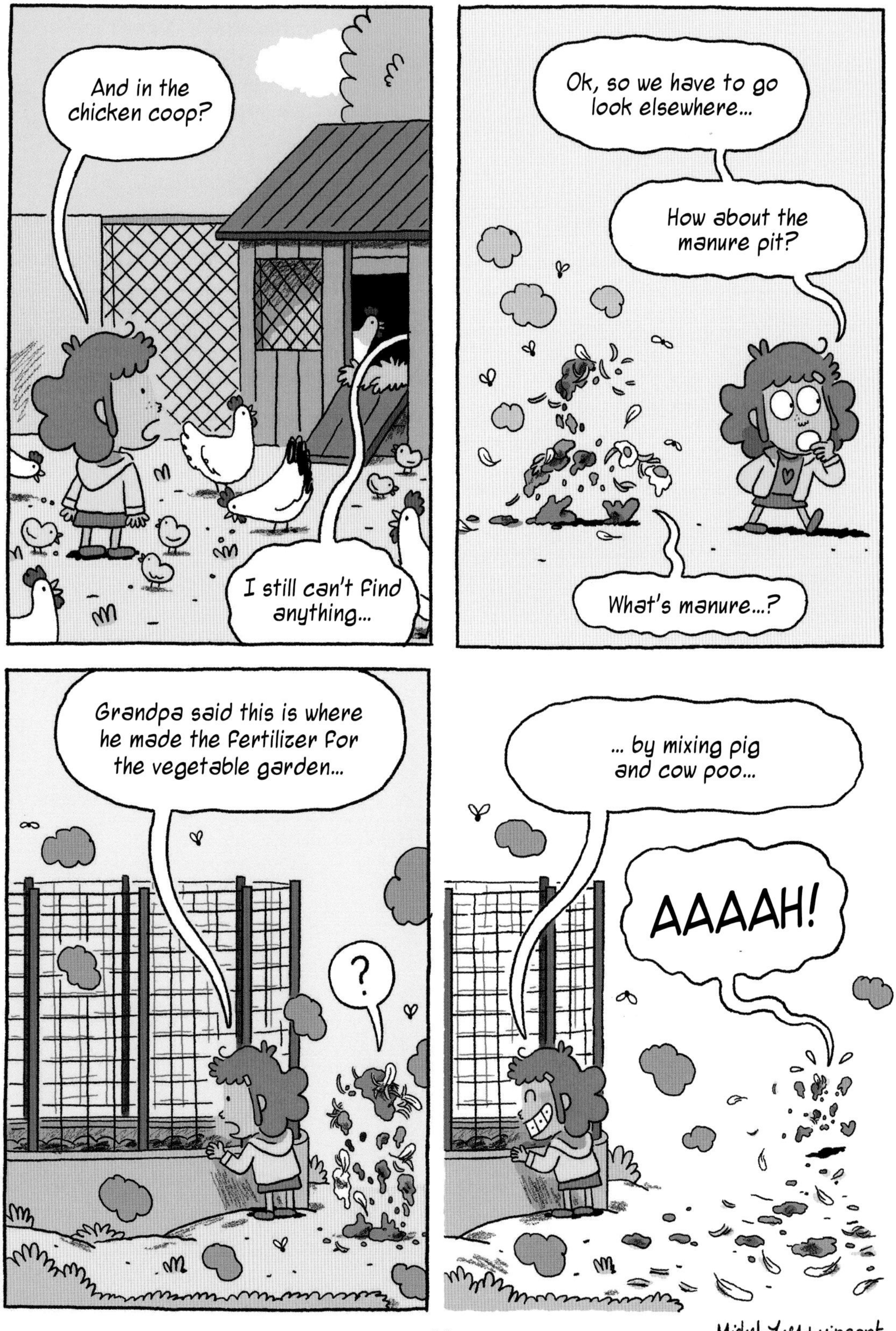

And in the chicken coop?
I still can't find anything...
Ok, so we have to go look elsewhere...
How about the manure pit?
What's manure...?
Grandpa said this is where he made the fertilizer for the vegetable garden...
?
... by mixing pig and cow poo...
AAAAH!
Michel-Yves + vincent

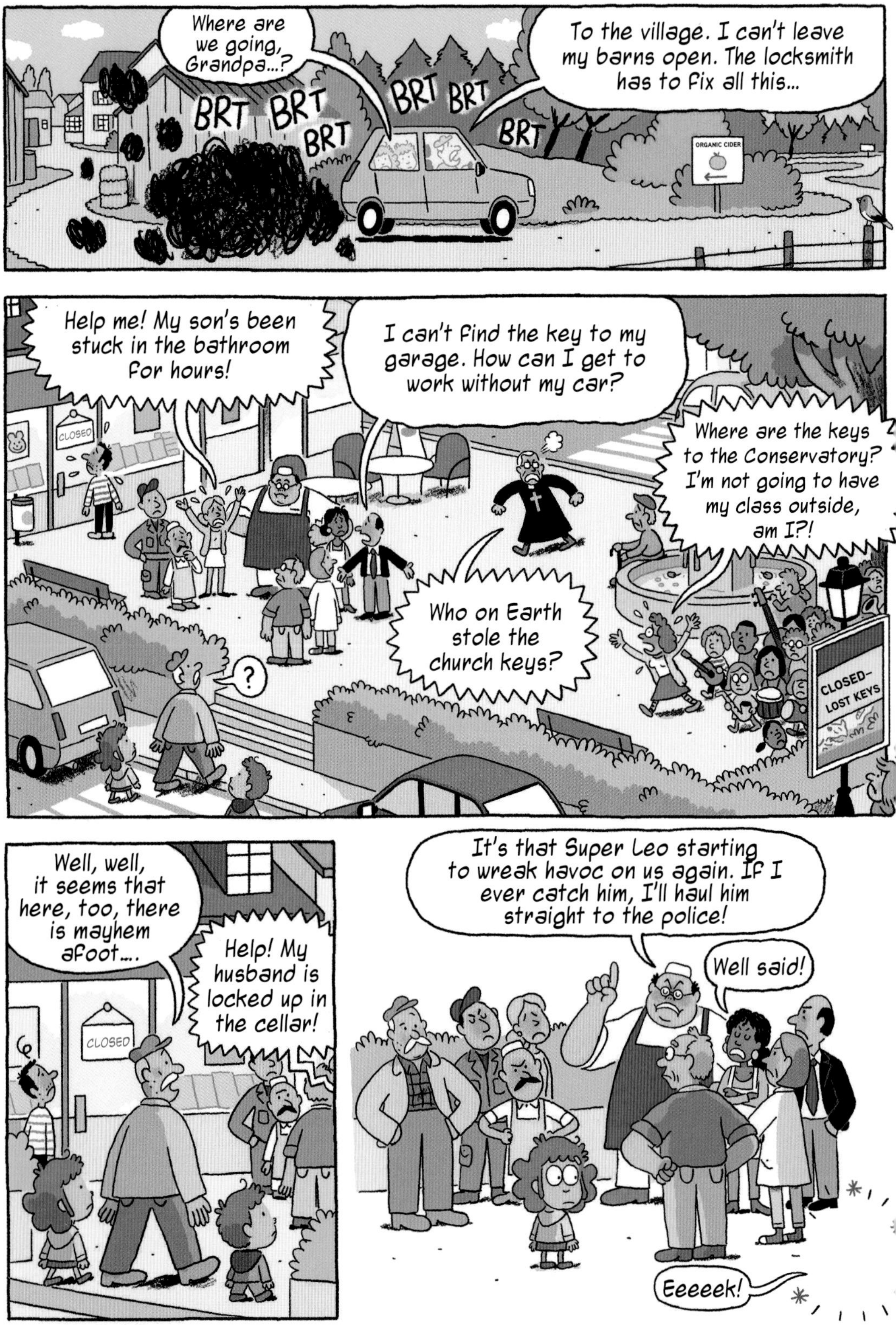
Where are we going, Grandpa...?
BRT BRT BRT BRT BRT BRT
To the village. I can't leave my barns open. The locksmith has to fix all this...
ORGANIC CIDER
Help me! My son's been stuck in the bathroom for hours!
I can't find the key to my garage. How can I get to work without my car?
CLOSED
Where are the keys to the Conservatory? I'm not going to have my class outside, am I?!
Who on Earth stole the church keys?
?
CLOSED–
LOST KEYS
Well, well, it seems that here, too, there is mayhem afoot....
Help! My husband is locked up in the cellar!
CLOSED
It's that Super Leo starting to wreak havoc on us again. If I ever catch him, I'll haul him straight to the police!
Well said!
Eeeeek!

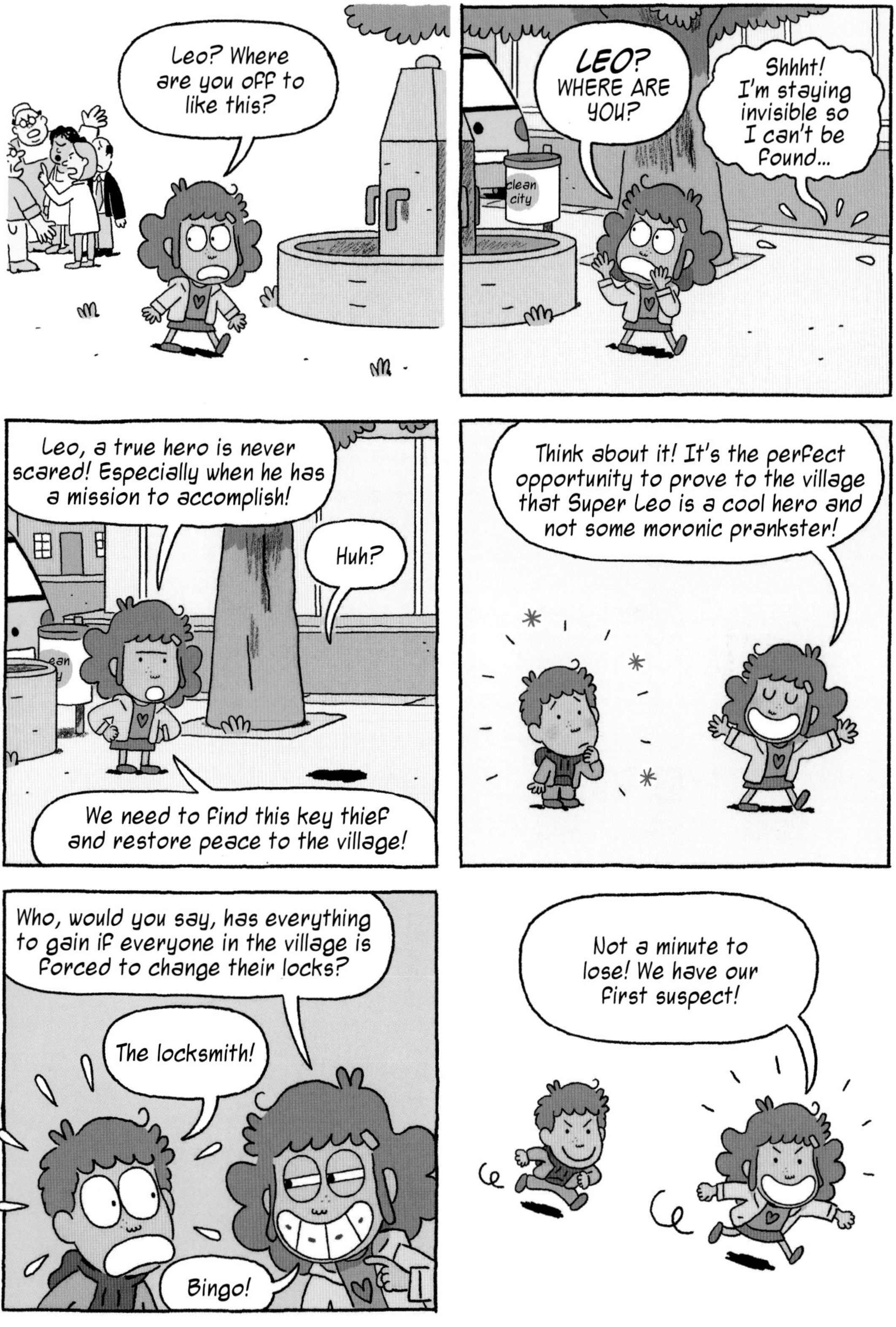
Leo? Where are you off to like this?
LEO? WHERE ARE YOU?
Shhht! I'm staying invisible so I can't be found...
clean city
Leo, a true hero is never scared! Especially when he has a mission to accomplish!
Huh?
We need to find this key thief and restore peace to the village!
Think about it! It's the perfect opportunity to prove to the village that Super Leo is a cool hero and not some moronic prankster!
Who, would you say, has everything to gain if everyone in the village is forced to change their locks?
The locksmith!
Bingo!
Not a minute to lose! We have our first suspect!

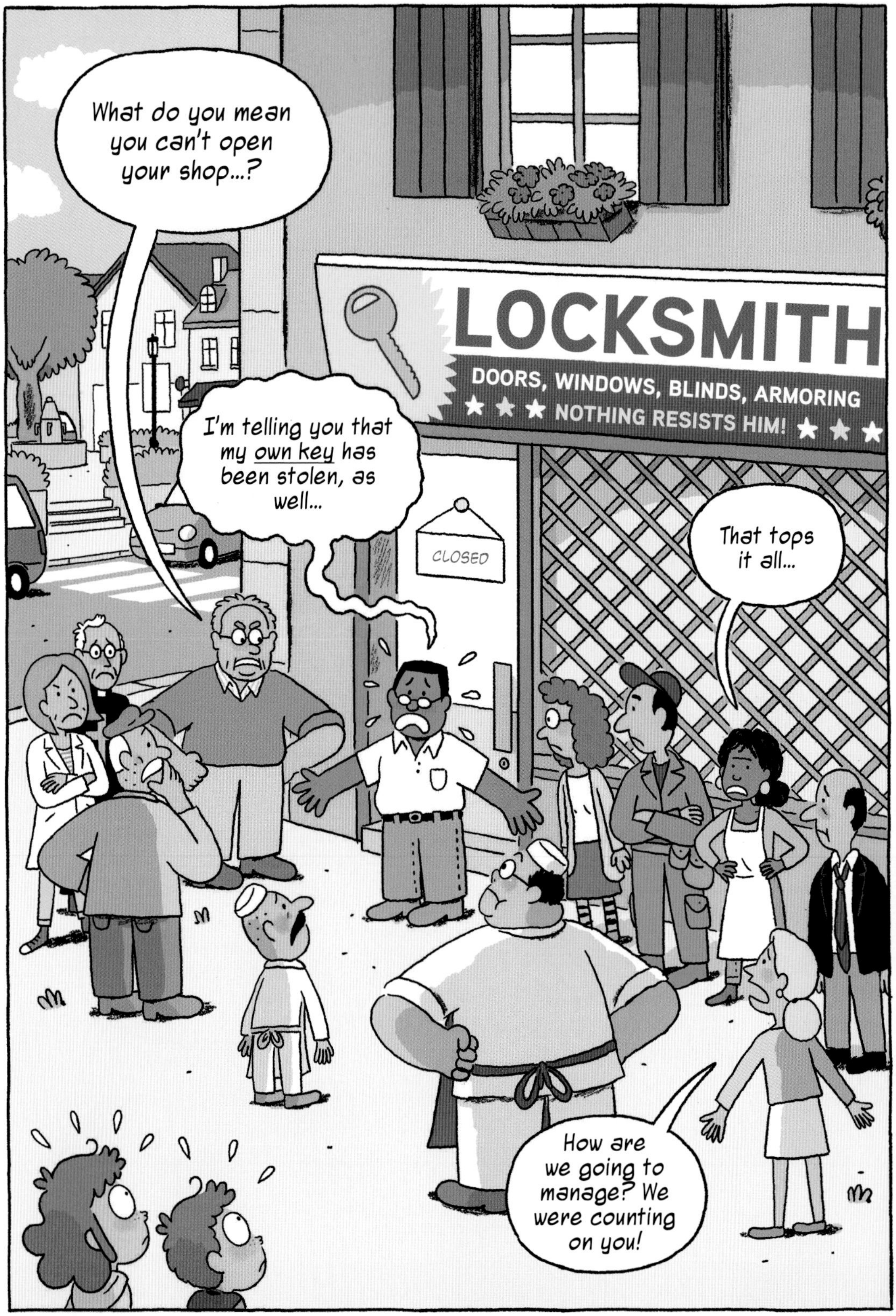
What do you mean you can't open your shop...?
I'm telling you that my own key has been stolen, as well...
LOCKSMITH
DOORS, WINDOWS, BLINDS, ARMORING
NOTHING RESISTS HIM!
CLOSED
That tops it all...
How are we going to manage? We were counting on you!

Michel-Yves+vincent

Your mission, should you accept it, Super Leo, is to discover who among the villagers is the key thief.

Why are you talking to me like that?

- LOCKSMITH
- PHARMACIST
- MECHANIC
- BUTCHER
- BAKER
- MUSIC TEACHER

That's always how they speak in spy movies... Don't interrupt me, please.

Here is our list of suspects. You are going to use your powers of invisibility to watch each of them without getting noticed.

- LOCKSMITH
- PHARMACIST
- MECHANIC
- BUTCHER
- BAKER
- MUSIC TEACHER

Cool!

For that, you'll need...

HEY! Where are you hiding?

Here! tee-hee-hee!

Pay attention Leopold! This could get tricky!

- LOCKSMITH
- PHARMACIST
- MECHANIC
- BUTCHER
- BAKER
- MUSIC TEACHER

One of them isn't telling the truth... But which one is it?

63

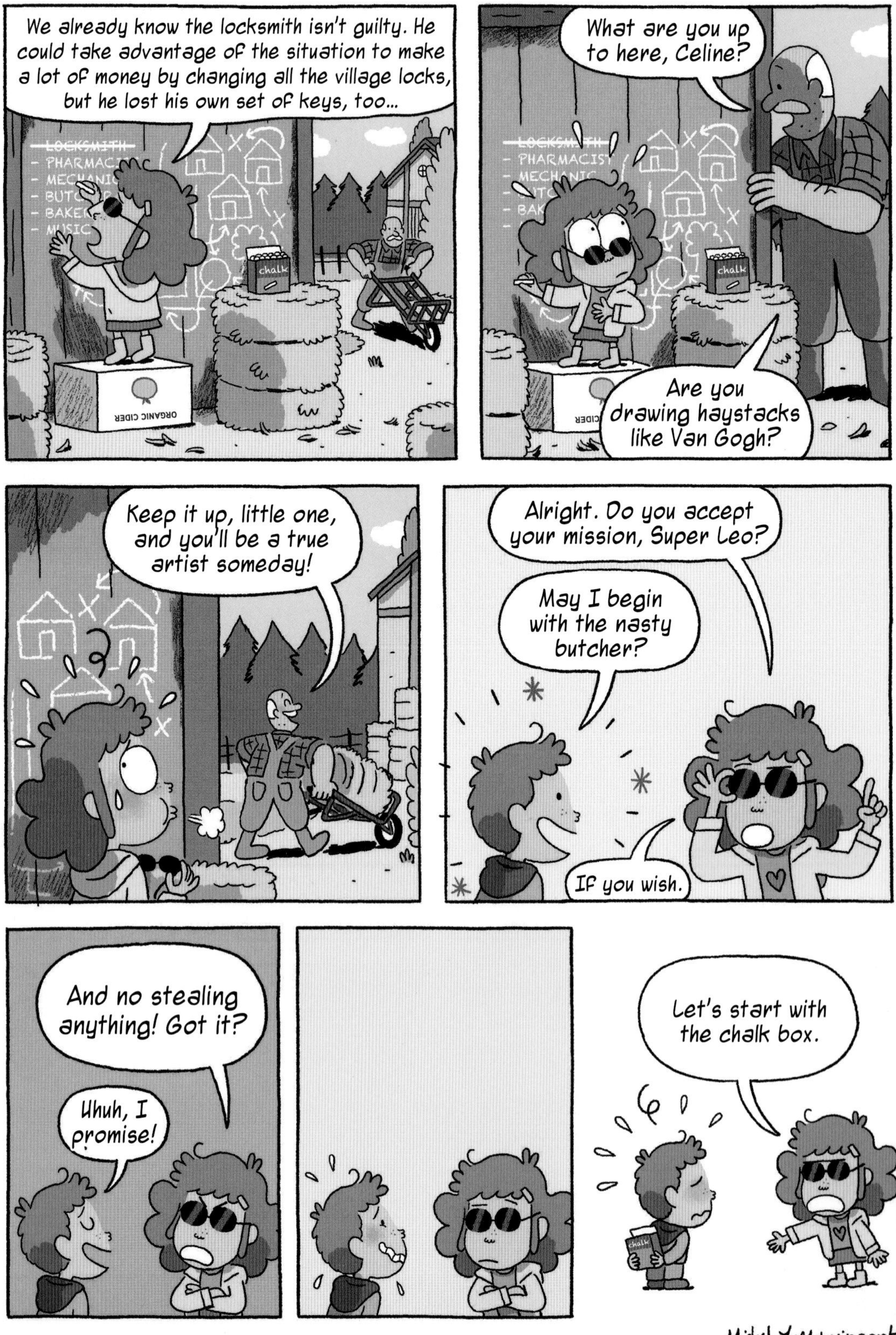
We already know the locksmith isn't guilty. He could take advantage of the situation to make a lot of money by changing all the village locks, but he lost his own set of keys, too...
LOCKSMITH
MECHANIC
chalk
ORGANIC CIDER
What are you up to here, Celine?
Are you drawing haystacks like Van Gogh?
Keep it up, little one, and you'll be a true artist someday!
Alright. Do you accept your mission, Super Leo?
May I begin with the nasty butcher?
If you wish.
And no stealing anything! Got it?
Uhuh, I promise!
Let's start with the chalk box.
chalk

Michel-Yves+vincent

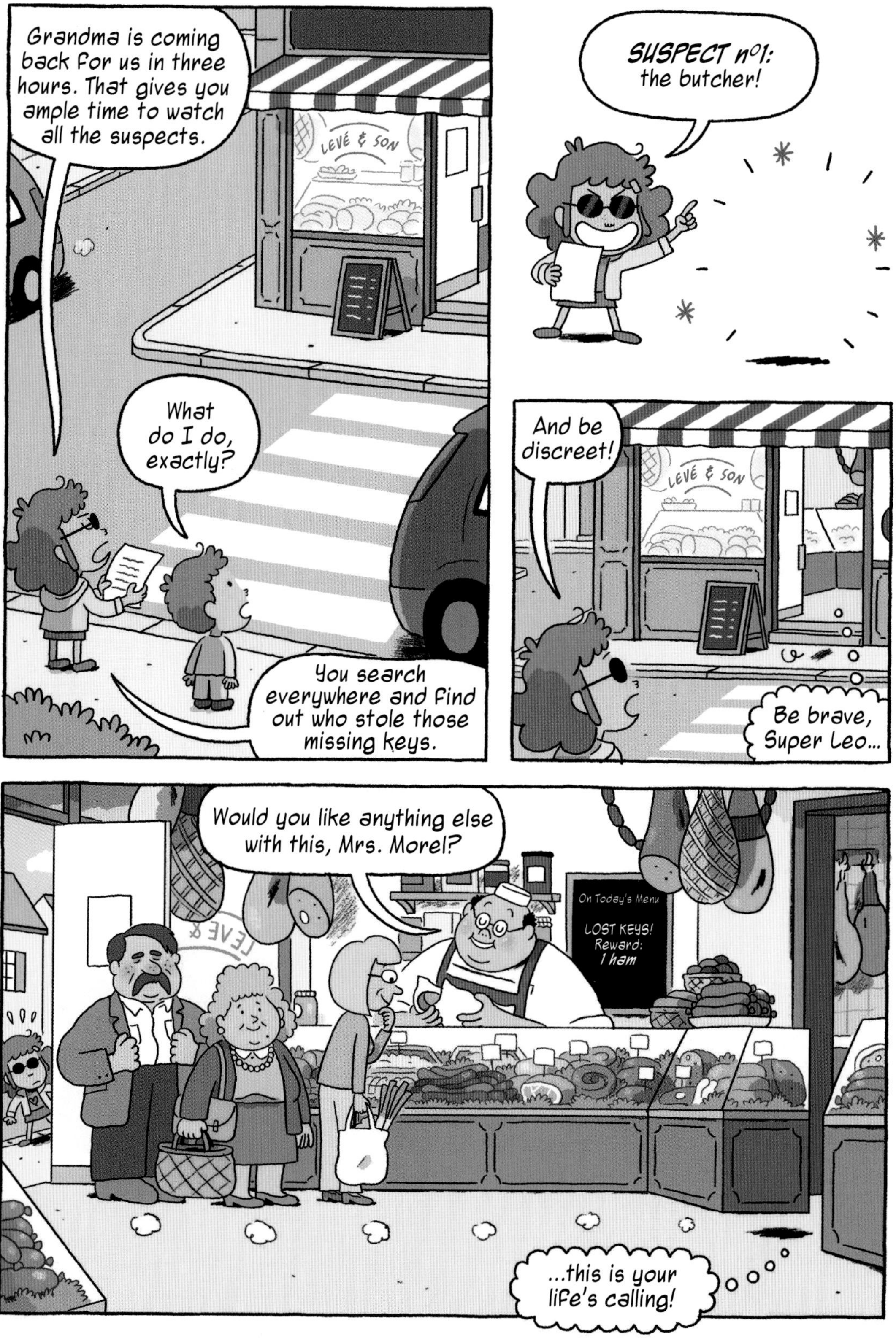
Grandma is coming back for us in three hours. That gives you ample time to watch all the suspects.
LEVÉ & SON
What do I do, exactly?
You search everywhere and find out who stole those missing keys.
SUSPECT nº1: the butcher!
And be discreet!
LEVÉ & SON
Be brave, Super Leo...
Would you like anything else with this, Mrs. Morel?
On Today's Menu
LOST KEYS!
Reward:
1 ham
...this is your life's calling!

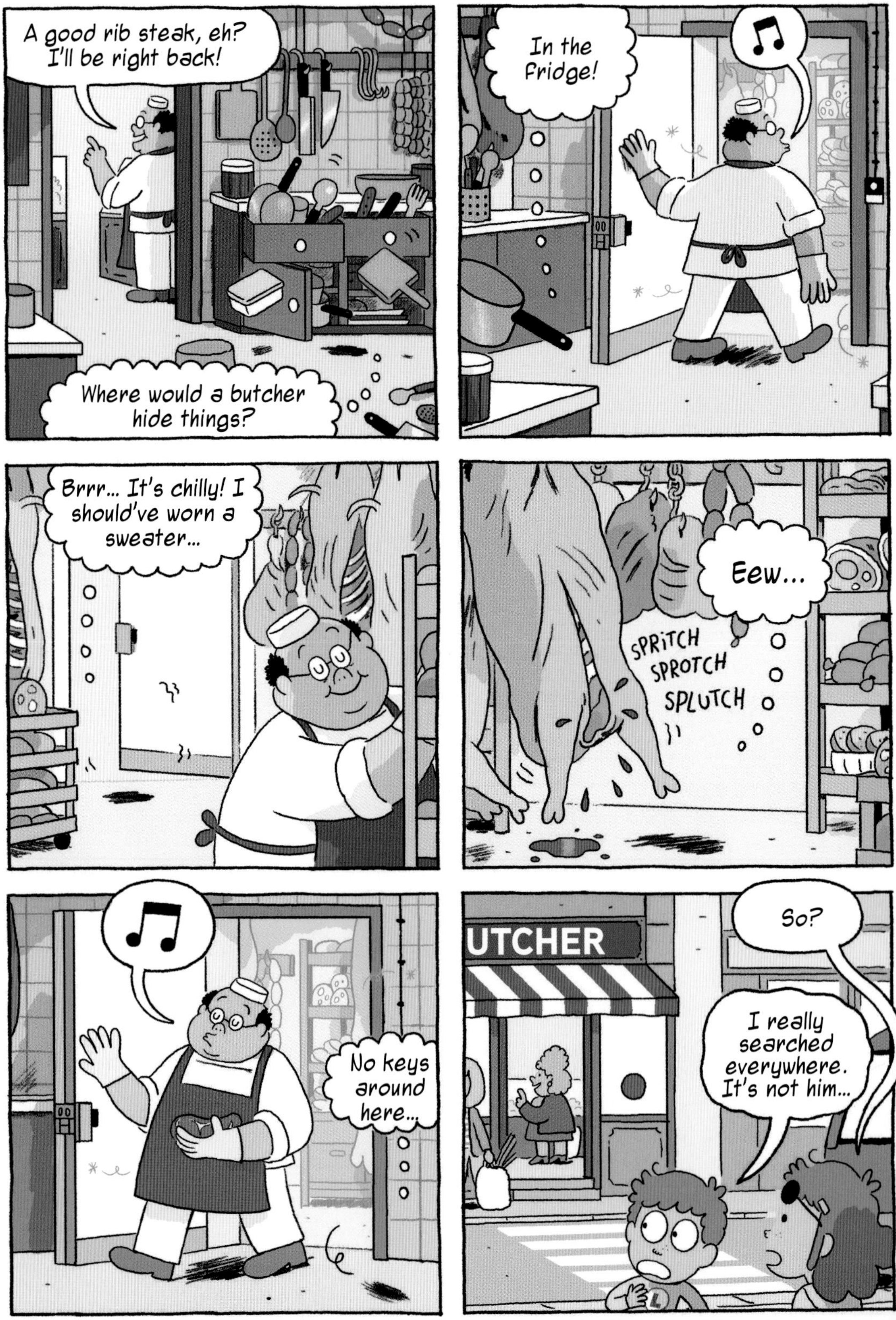

A good rib steak, eh? I'll be right back!
Where would a butcher hide things?
In the fridge!
♫
Brrr... It's chilly! I should've worn a sweater...
Eew...
SPRITCH
SPROTCH
SPLUTCH
♫
No keys around here...
UTCHER
So?
I really searched everywhere. It's not him...

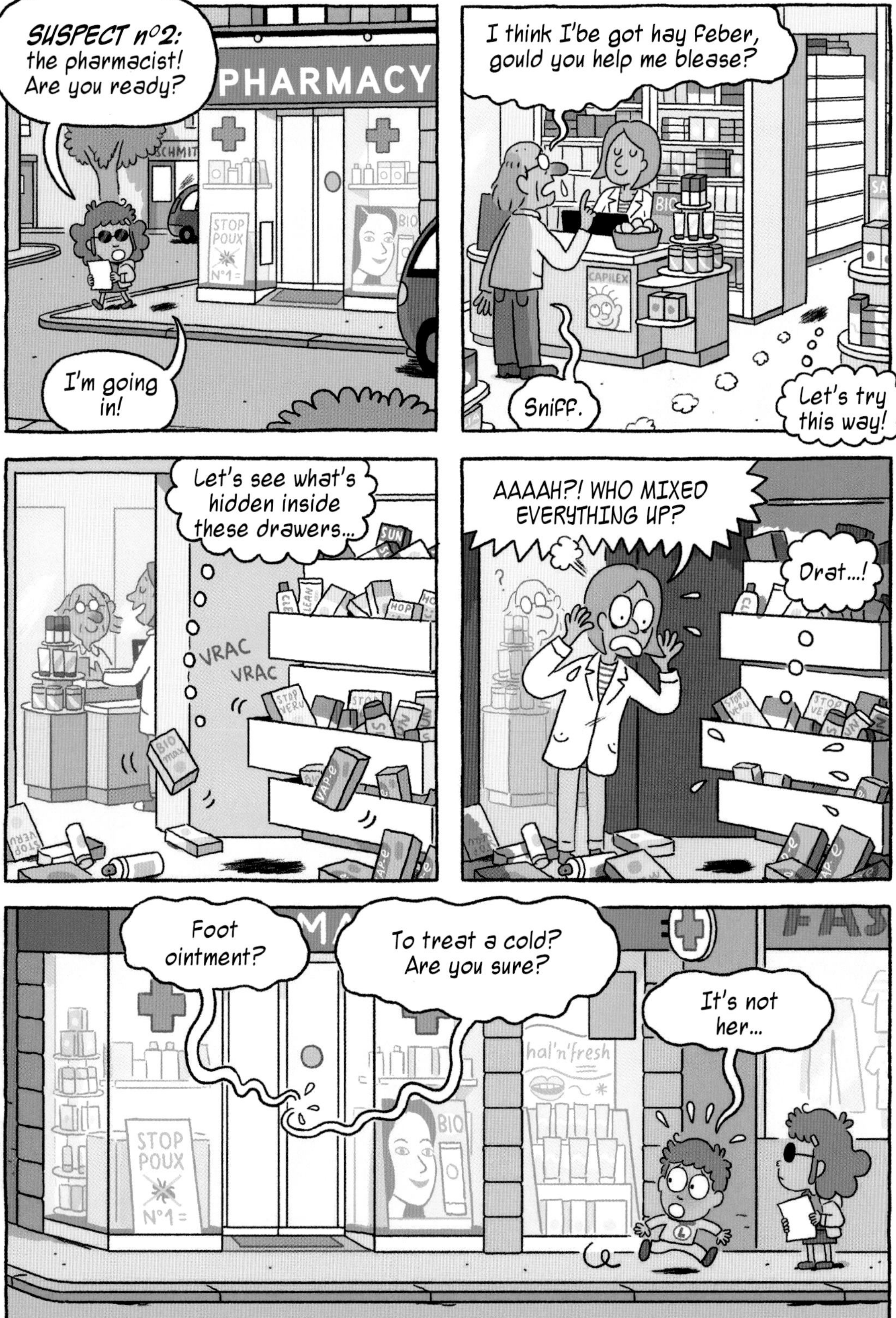
SUSPECT n°2: the pharmacist! Are you ready?
PHARMACY
STOP POUX N°1 =
BIO
I'm going in!
I think I'be got hay feber, gould you help me blease?
CAPILEX
Sniff.
Let's try this way!
Let's see what's hidden inside these drawers...
VRAC
VRAC
AAAAH?! WHO MIXED EVERYTHING UP?
Drat...!
Foot ointment?
To treat a cold? Are you sure?
It's not her...
hal'n'fresh
STOP POUX N°1 =

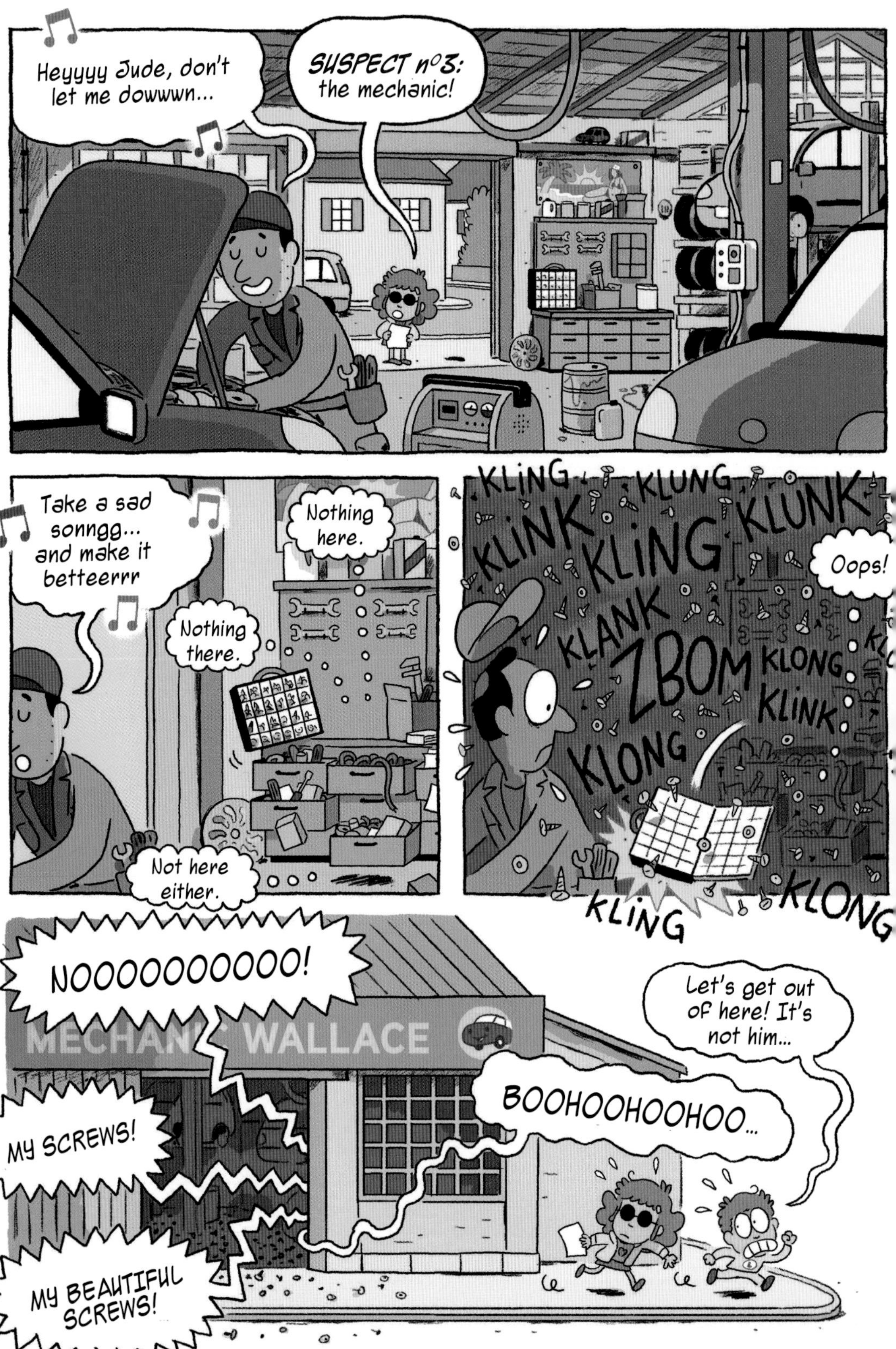

Heyyyy Jude, don't let me dowwwn...
SUSPECT n°3: the mechanic!
Take a sad sonngg... and make it betteerrr
Nothing here.
Nothing there.
Not here either.
KLING KLUNG KLINK KLING KLUNK
Oops!
KLANK ZBOM KLONG KLINK KLONG
KLING KLONG
NOOOOOOOOOO!
MECHANIC WALLACE
Let's get out of here! It's not him...
BOOHOOHOOHOO...
MY SCREWS!
MY BEAUTIFUL SCREWS!

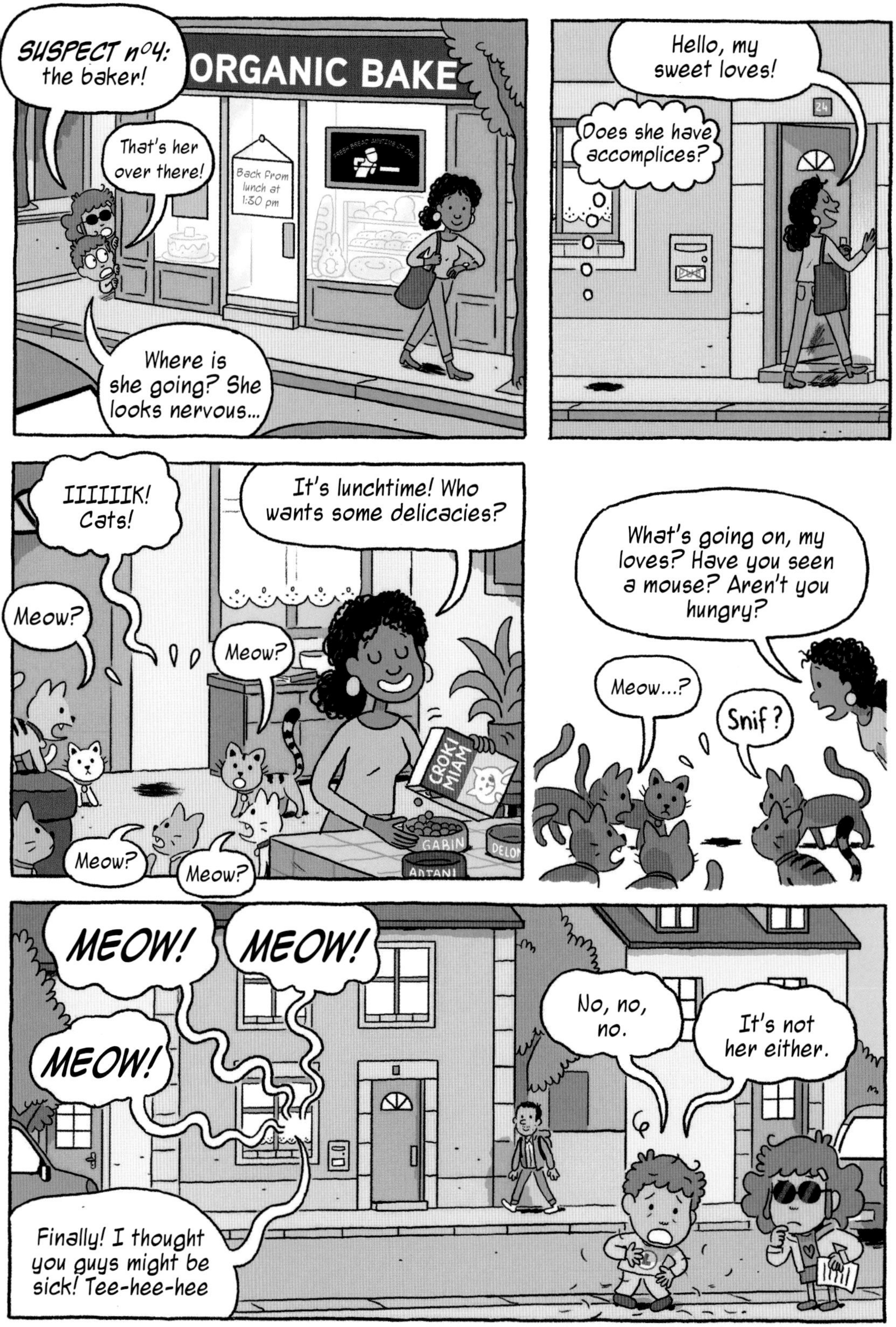
SUSPECT nº4: the baker!
ORGANIC BAKE
That's her over there!
Back from lunch at 1:30 pm
Where is she going? She looks nervous...
Hello, my sweet loves!
Does she have accomplices?
IIIIIIK! Cats!
It's lunchtime! Who wants some delicacies?
Meow?
Meow?
CROKI MIAM
GABIN
DELON
Meow?
Meow?
What's going on, my loves? Have you seen a mouse? Aren't you hungry?
Meow...?
Snif?
MEOW!
MEOW!
MEOW!
No, no, no.
It's not her either.
Finally! I thought you guys might be sick! Tee-hee-hee

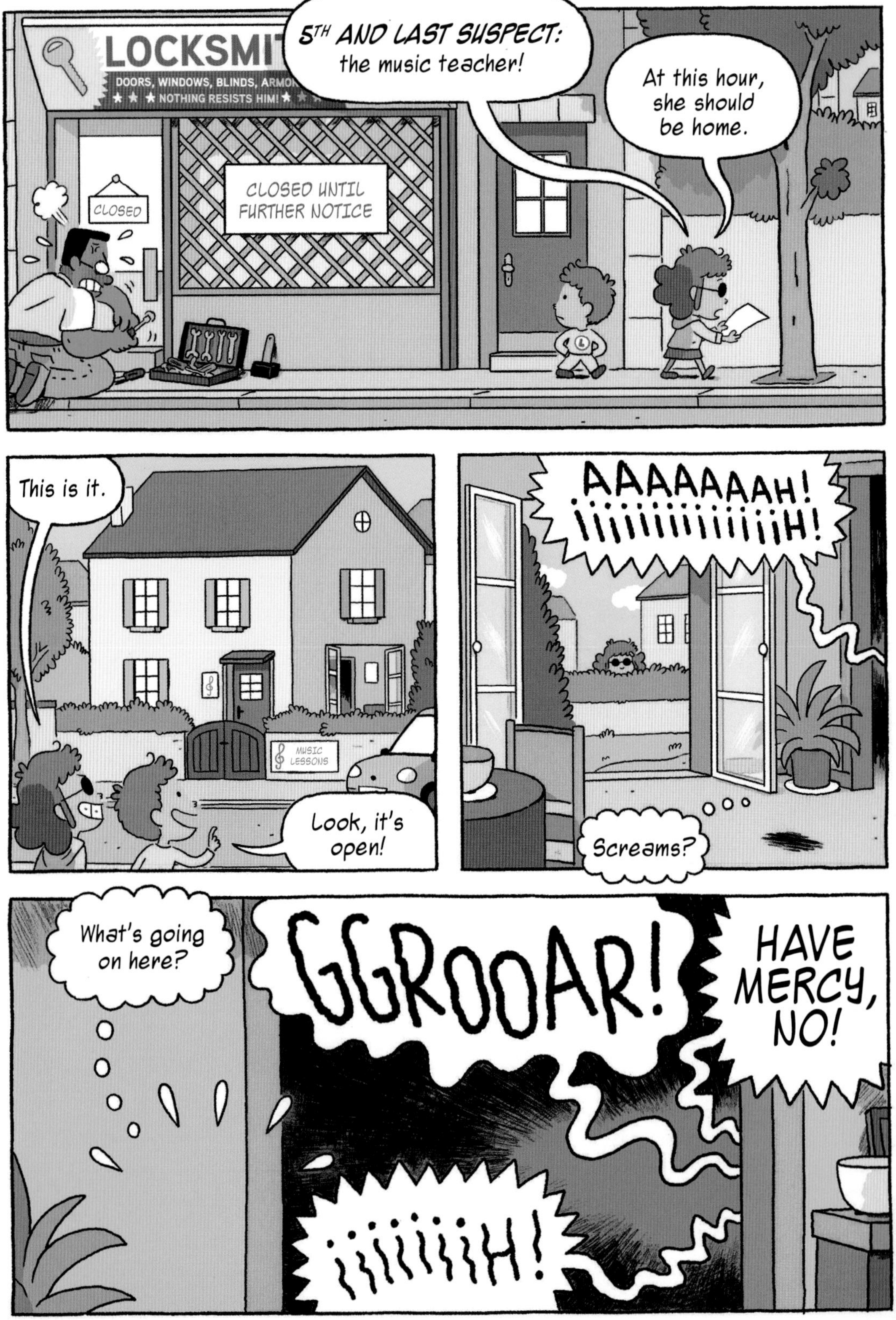

LOCKSMIT
DOORS, WINDOWS, BLINDS, ARMOR
★ ★ ★ NOTHING RESISTS HIM! ★
CLOSED
CLOSED UNTIL FURTHER NOTICE
5TH AND LAST SUSPECT: the music teacher!
At this hour, she should be home.
This is it.
MUSIC LESSONS
Look, it's open!
AAAAAAAH! iiiiiiiiiiiiiH!
Screams?
What's going on here?
GGROOAR!
HAVE MERCY, NO!
iiiiiiiiH!

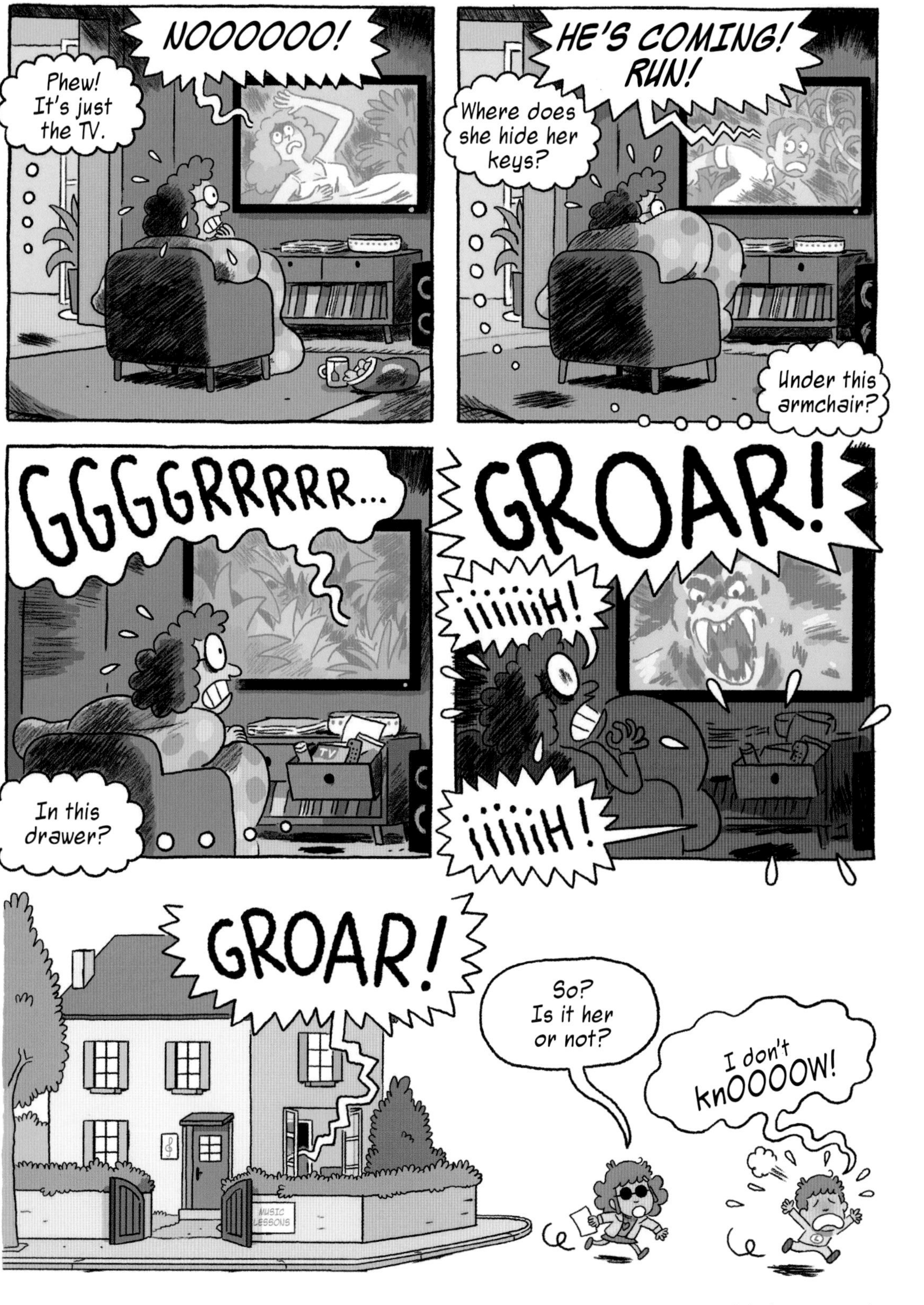
NOOOOOO!
Phew! It's just the TV.
HE'S COMING! RUN!
Where does she hide her keys?
Under this armchair?
GGGGRRRRR...
In this drawer?
GROAR!
iiiiiiH!
iiiiiH!
GROAR!
MUSIC LESSONS
So? Is it her or not?
I don't knOOOOW!
Michel-Yves + vincent

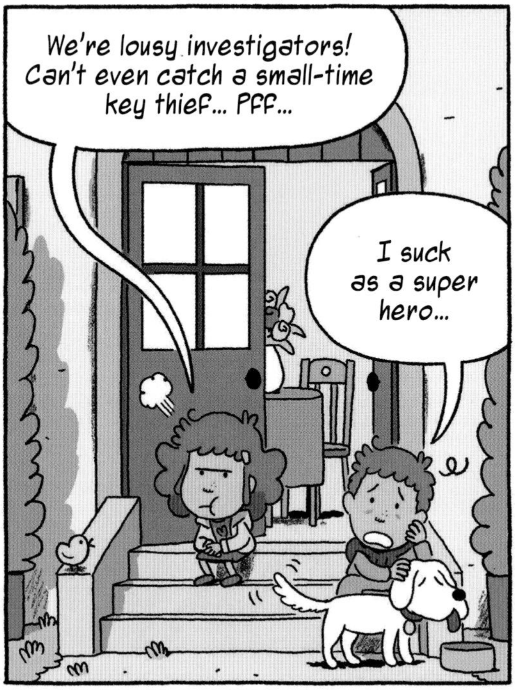
We're lousy investigators! Can't even catch a small-time key thief... PFF...
I suck as a super hero...

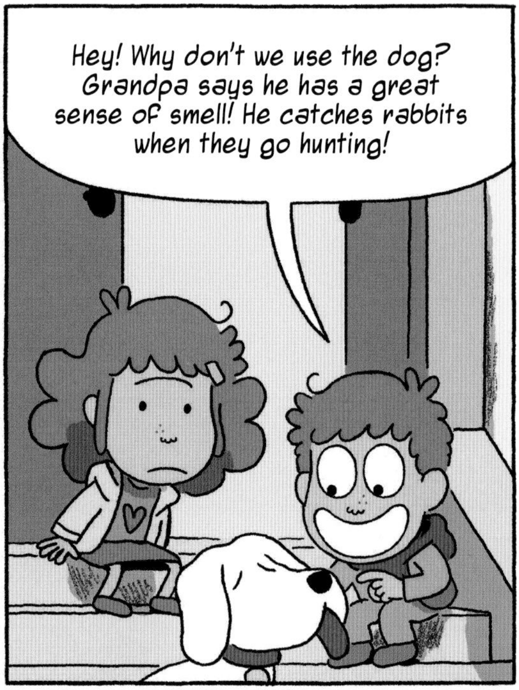
Hey! Why don't we use the dog? Grandpa says he has a great sense of smell! He catches rabbits when they go hunting!

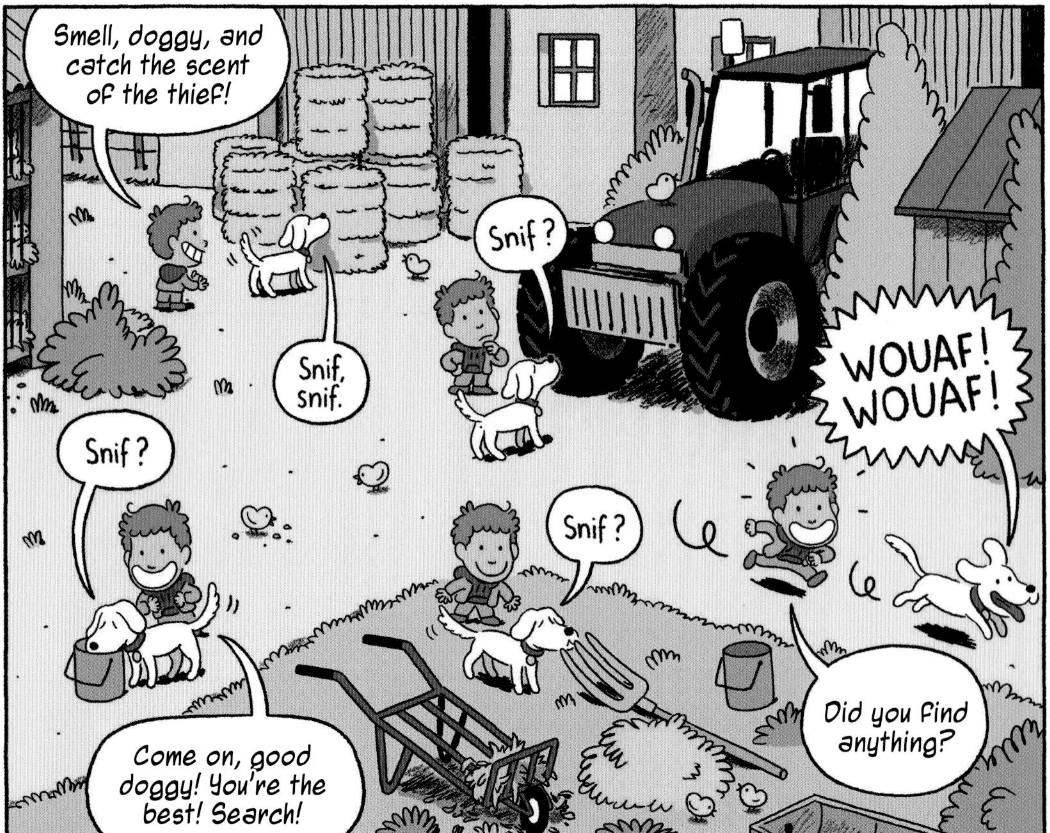
Smell, doggy, and catch the scent of the thief!
Snif, snif.
Snif ?
Snif ?
Snif ?
WOUAF! WOUAF!
Did you find anything?
Come on, good doggy! You're the best! Search!

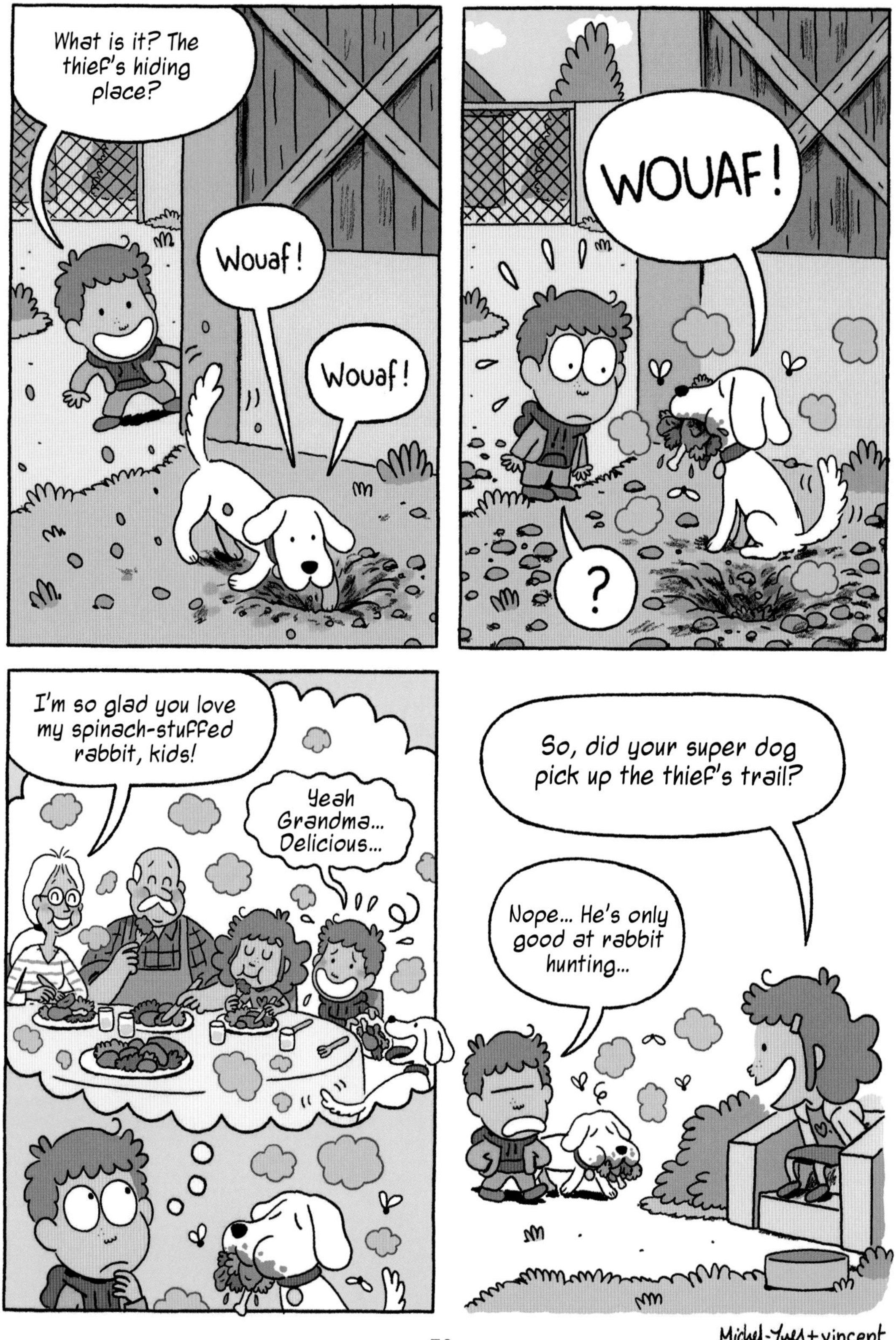
What is it? The thief's hiding place?
Wouaf!
Wouaf!
WOUAF!
?
I'm so glad you love my spinach-stuffed rabbit, kids!
Yeah Grandma... Delicious...
So, did your super dog pick up the thief's trail?
Nope... He's only good at rabbit hunting...
Michel-Yves+vincent

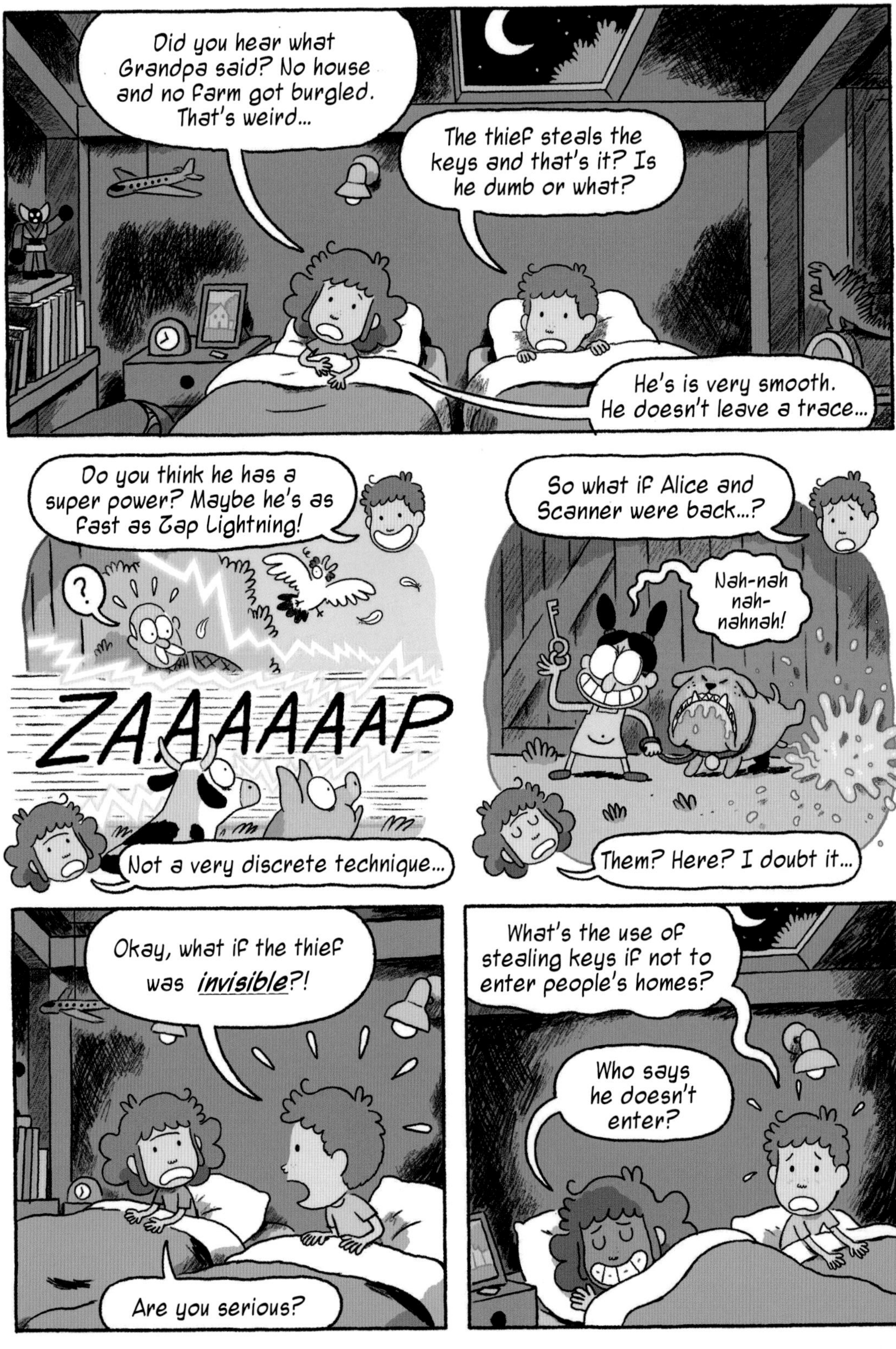
Did you hear what Grandpa said? No house and no farm got burgled. That's weird...
The thief steals the keys and that's it? Is he dumb or what?
He's is very smooth. He doesn't leave a trace...
Do you think he has a super power? Maybe he's as fast as Zap Lightning!
?
ZAAAAAAP
Not a very discrete technique...
So what if Alice and Scanner were back...?
Nah-nah nah-nahnah!
Them? Here? I doubt it...
Okay, what if the thief was invisible?!
Are you serious?
What's the use of stealing keys if not to enter people's homes?
Who says he doesn't enter?

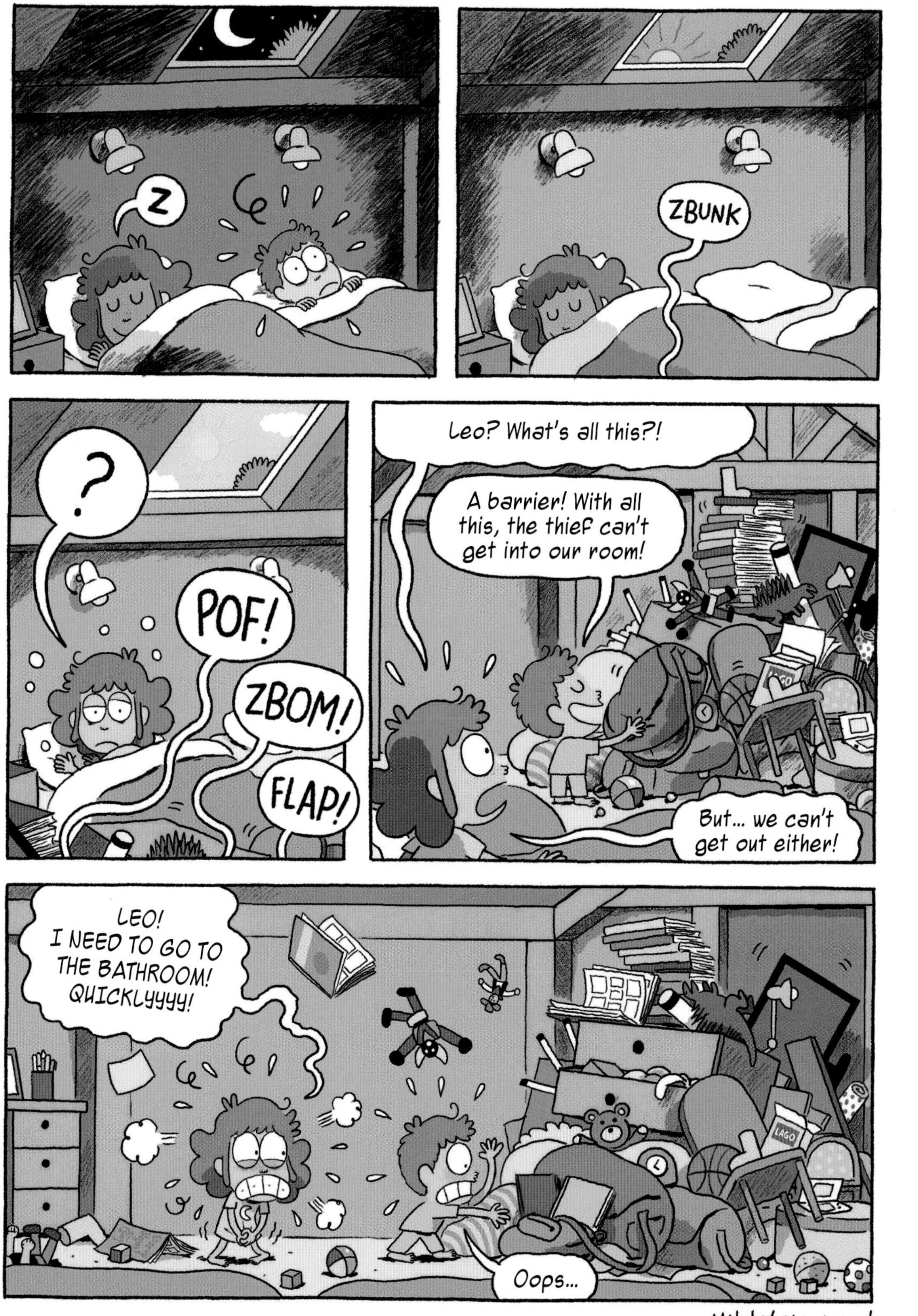
Z
ZBUNK
?
POF!
ZBOM!
FLAP!
Leo? What's all this?!
A barrier! With all this, the thief can't get into our room!
But... we can't get out either!
LAGO
LEO! I NEED TO GO TO THE BATHROOM! QUICKLYYYY!
LAGO
Oops...

Michel-Yves + vincent

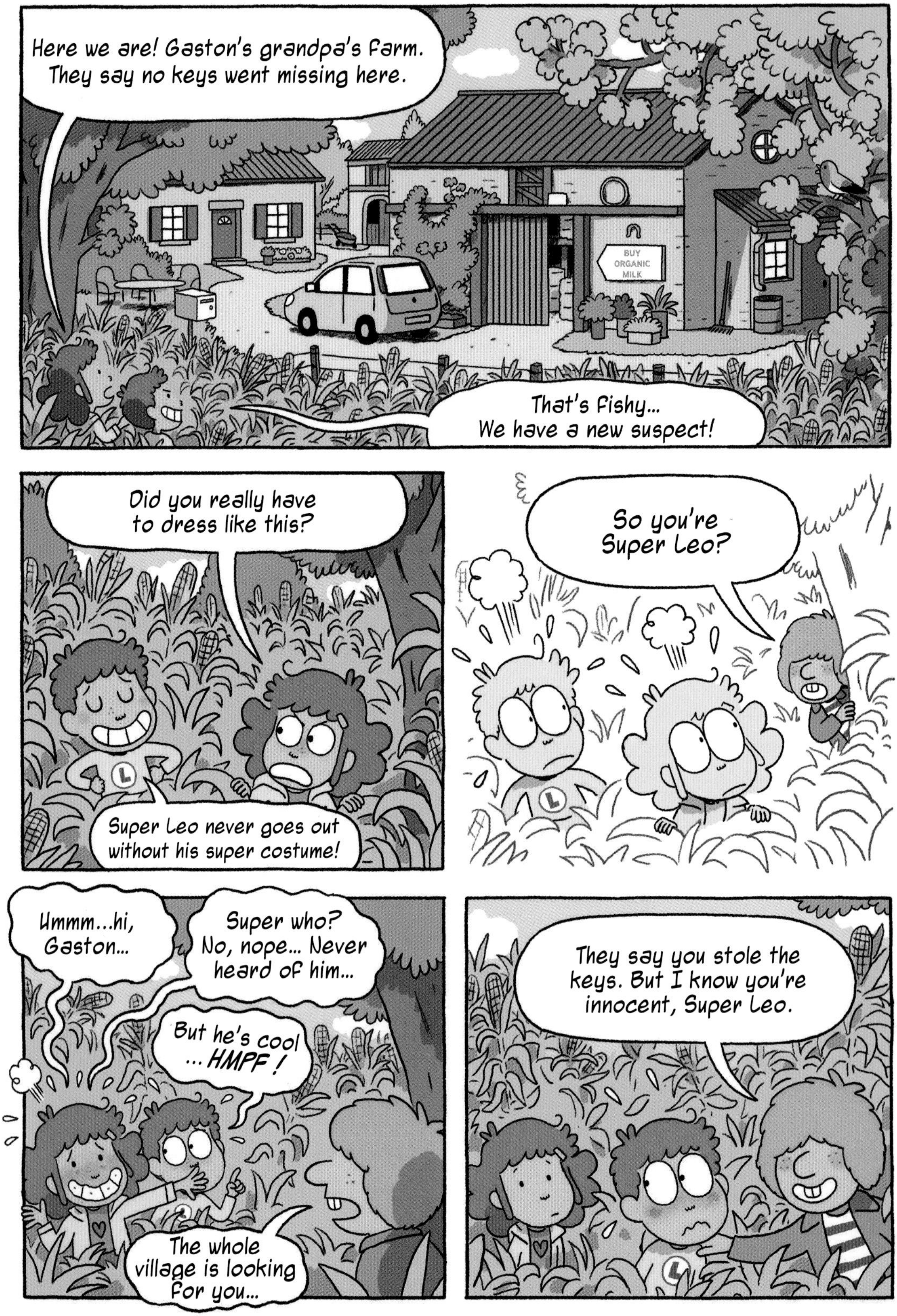
Here we are! Gaston's grandpa's farm. They say no keys went missing here.
BUY ORGANIC MILK
That's fishy... We have a new suspect!
Did you really have to dress like this?
Super Leo never goes out without his super costume!
So you're Super Leo?
Ummm...hi, Gaston...
Super who? No, nope... Never heard of him...
But he's cool ... HMPF!
The whole village is looking for you...
They say you stole the keys. But I know you're innocent, Super Leo.

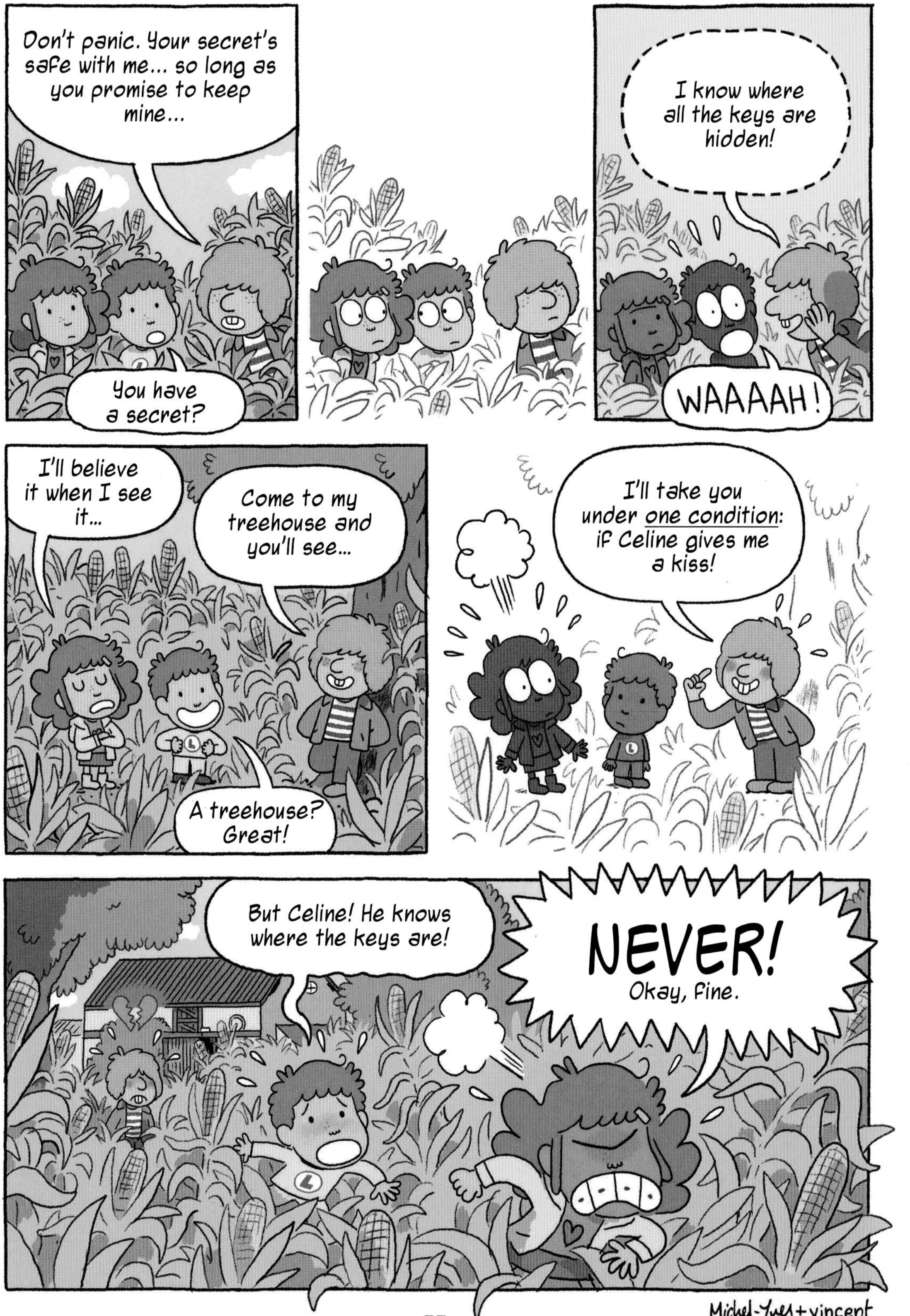
Don't panic. Your secret's safe with me... so long as you promise to keep mine...
You have a secret?
I know where all the keys are hidden!
WAAAAH!
I'll believe it when I see it...
Come to my treehouse and you'll see...
A treehouse? Great!
I'll take you under one condition: if Celine gives me a kiss!
But Celine! He knows where the keys are!
NEVER!
Okay, fine.
Michel-Yves+vincent

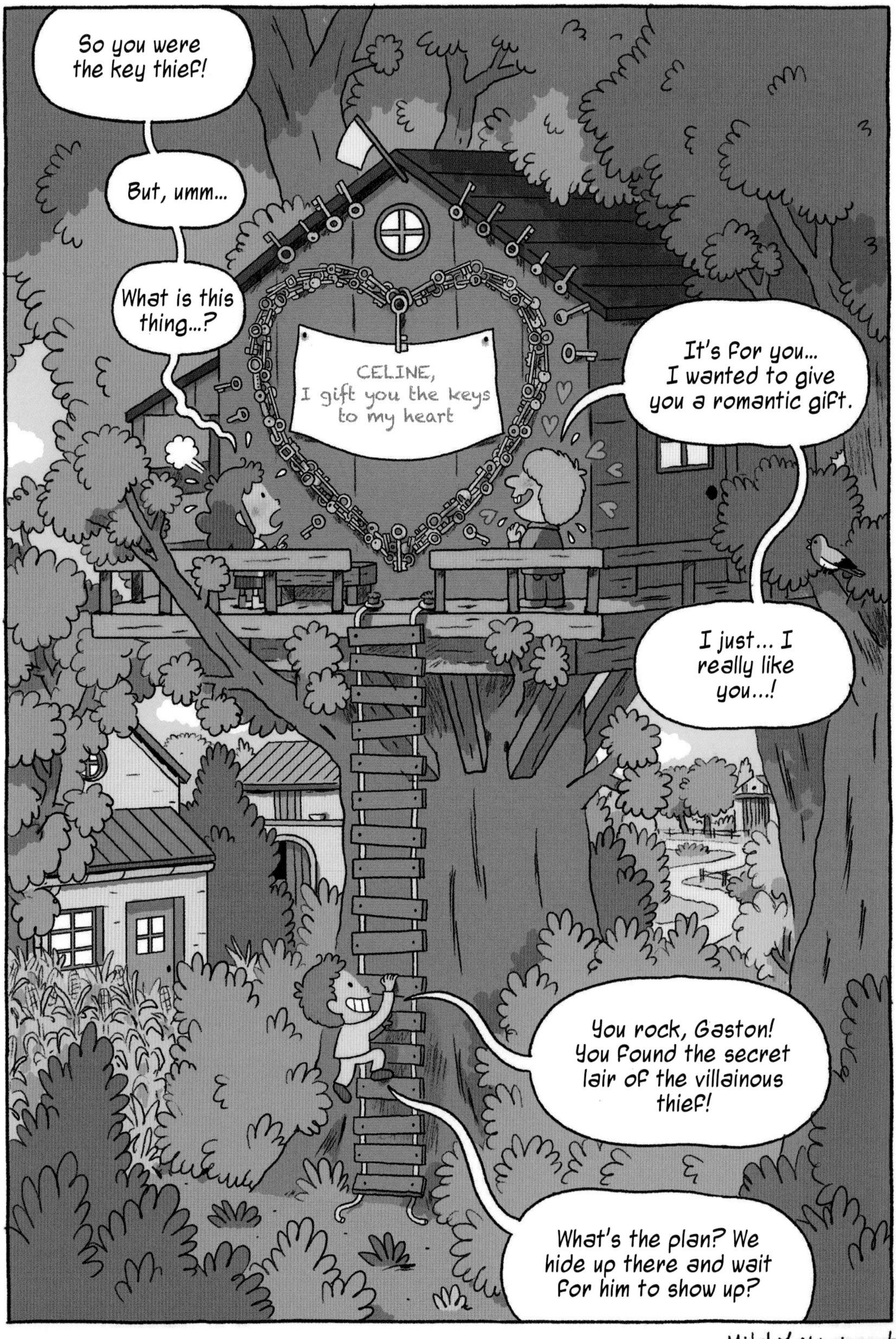
So you were the key thief!
But, umm...
What is this thing...?
CELINE, I gift you the keys to my heart
It's for you... I wanted to give you a romantic gift.
I just... I really like you...!
You rock, Gaston! You found the secret lair of the villainous thief!
What's the plan? We hide up there and wait for him to show up?

Michel-Yves + vincent

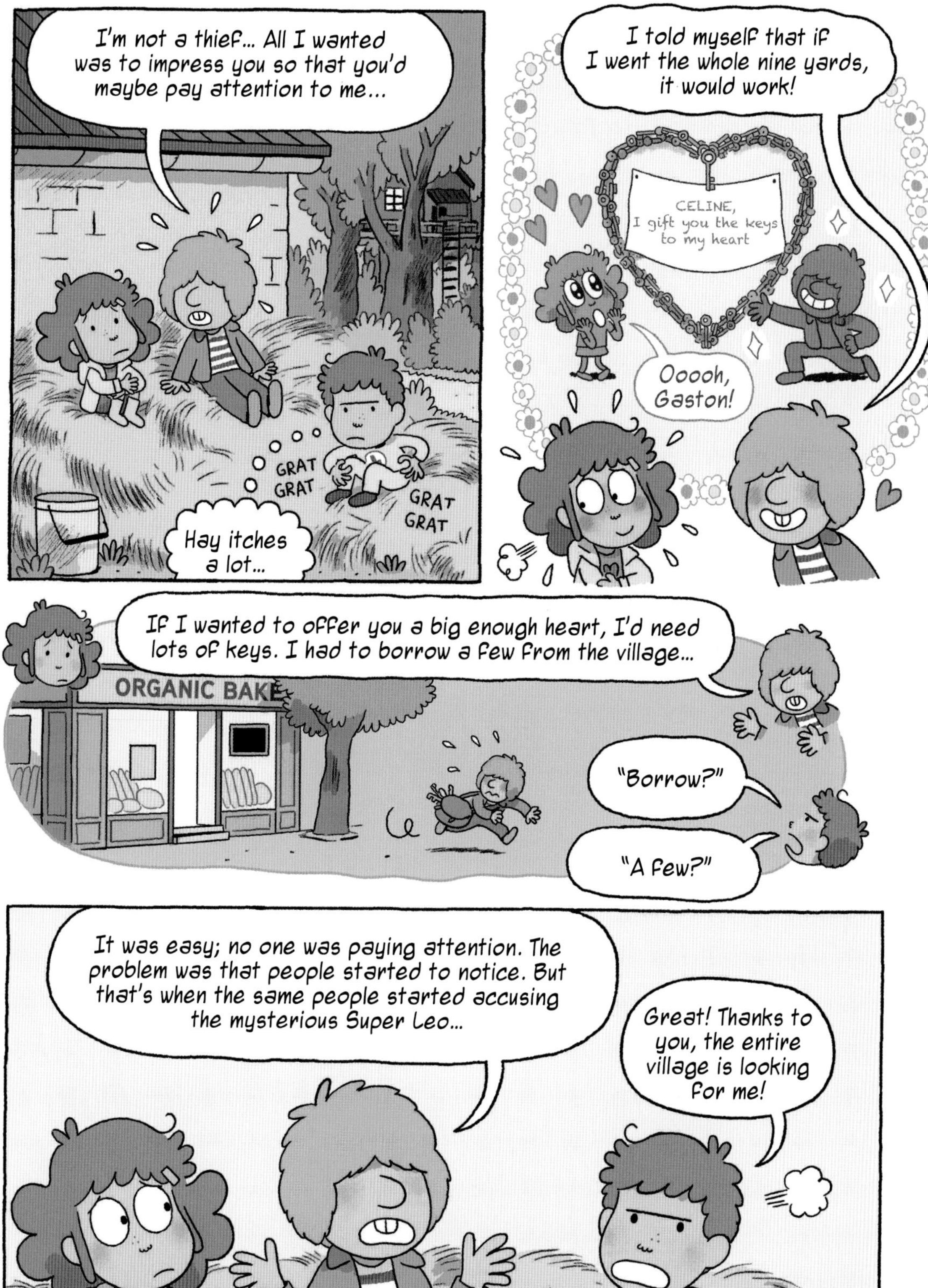
I'm not a thief... All I wanted was to impress you so that you'd maybe pay attention to me...
GRAT GRAT
GRAT GRAT
Hay itches a lot...
I told myself that if I went the whole nine yards, it would work!
CELINE, I gift you the keys to my heart
Ooooh, Gaston!
If I wanted to offer you a big enough heart, I'd need lots of keys. I had to borrow a few from the village...
ORGANIC BAKE
"Borrow?"
"A few?"
It was easy; no one was paying attention. The problem was that people started to notice. But that's when the same people started accusing the mysterious Super Leo...
Great! Thanks to you, the entire village is looking for me!

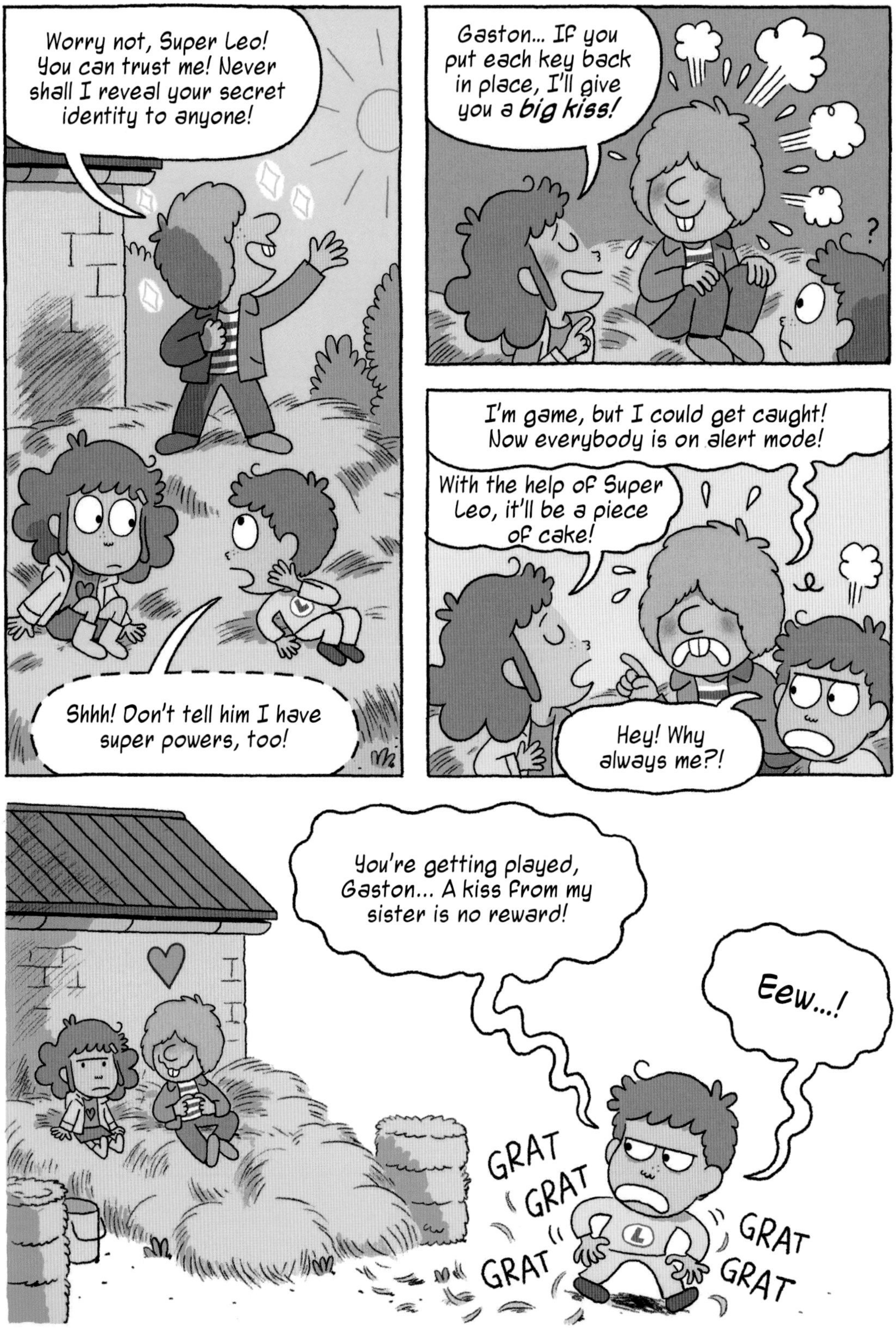
Worry not, Super Leo! You can trust me! Never shall I reveal your secret identity to anyone!
Shhh! Don't tell him I have super powers, too!
Gaston... If you put each key back in place, I'll give you a **big kiss!**
?
I'm game, but I could get caught! Now everybody is on alert mode!
With the help of Super Leo, it'll be a piece of cake!
Hey! Why always me?!
You're getting played, Gaston... A kiss from my sister is no reward!
Eew...!
GRAT
GRAT
GRAT
GRAT
GRAT

Michel-Yves+vincent

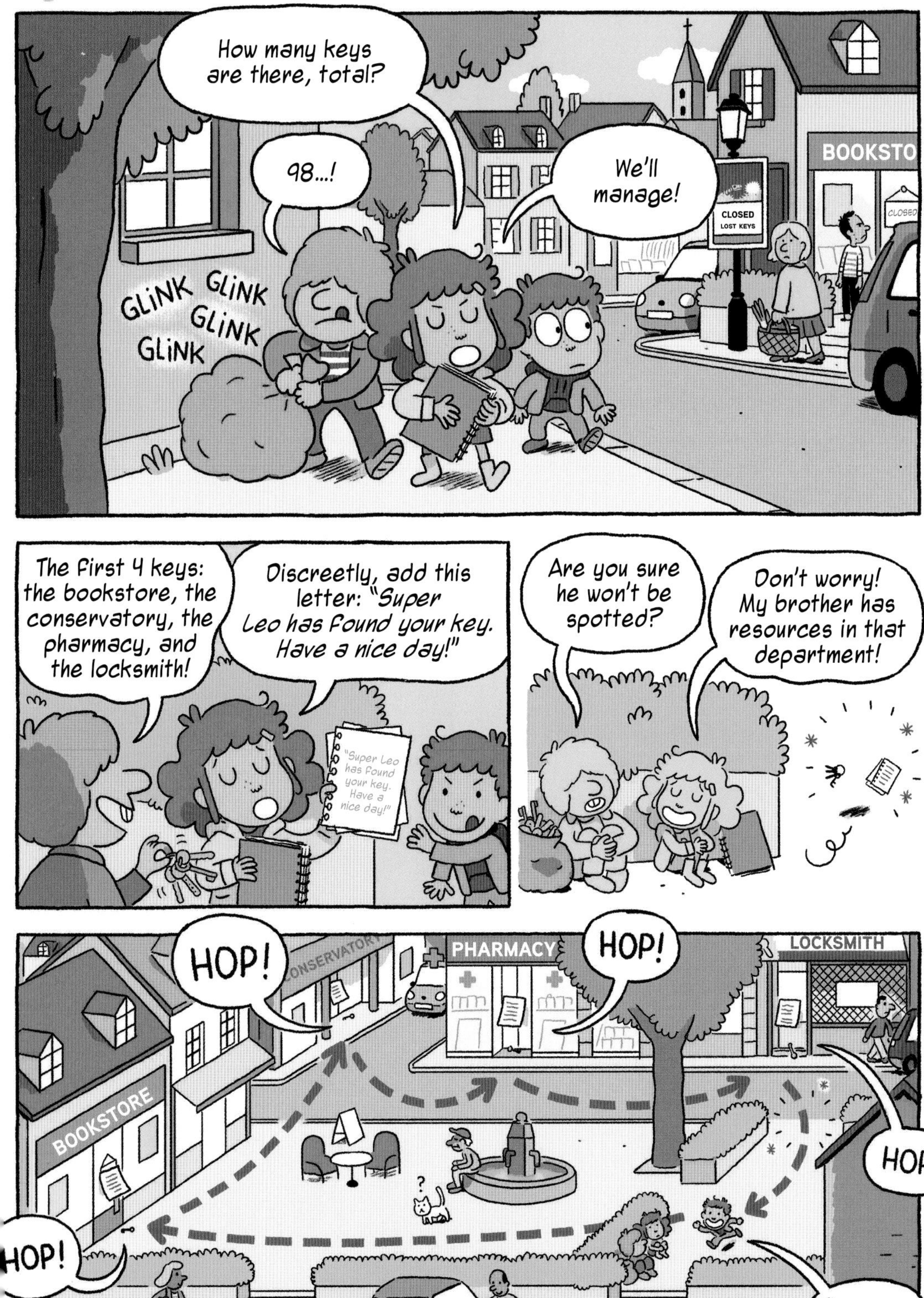
How many keys are there, total?
98...!
We'll manage!
GLINK GLINK GLINK GLINK
BOOKSTO
CLOSED
LOST KEYS
CLOSED
The first 4 keys: the bookstore, the conservatory, the pharmacy, and the locksmith!
Discreetly, add this letter: "Super Leo has found your key. Have a nice day!"
"Super Leo has found your key. Have a nice day!"
Are you sure he won't be spotted?
Don't worry! My brother has resources in that department!
HOP!
CONSERVATORY
PHARMACY
HOP!
LOCKSMITH
BOOKSTORE
HOP!
HOP!
There you go!

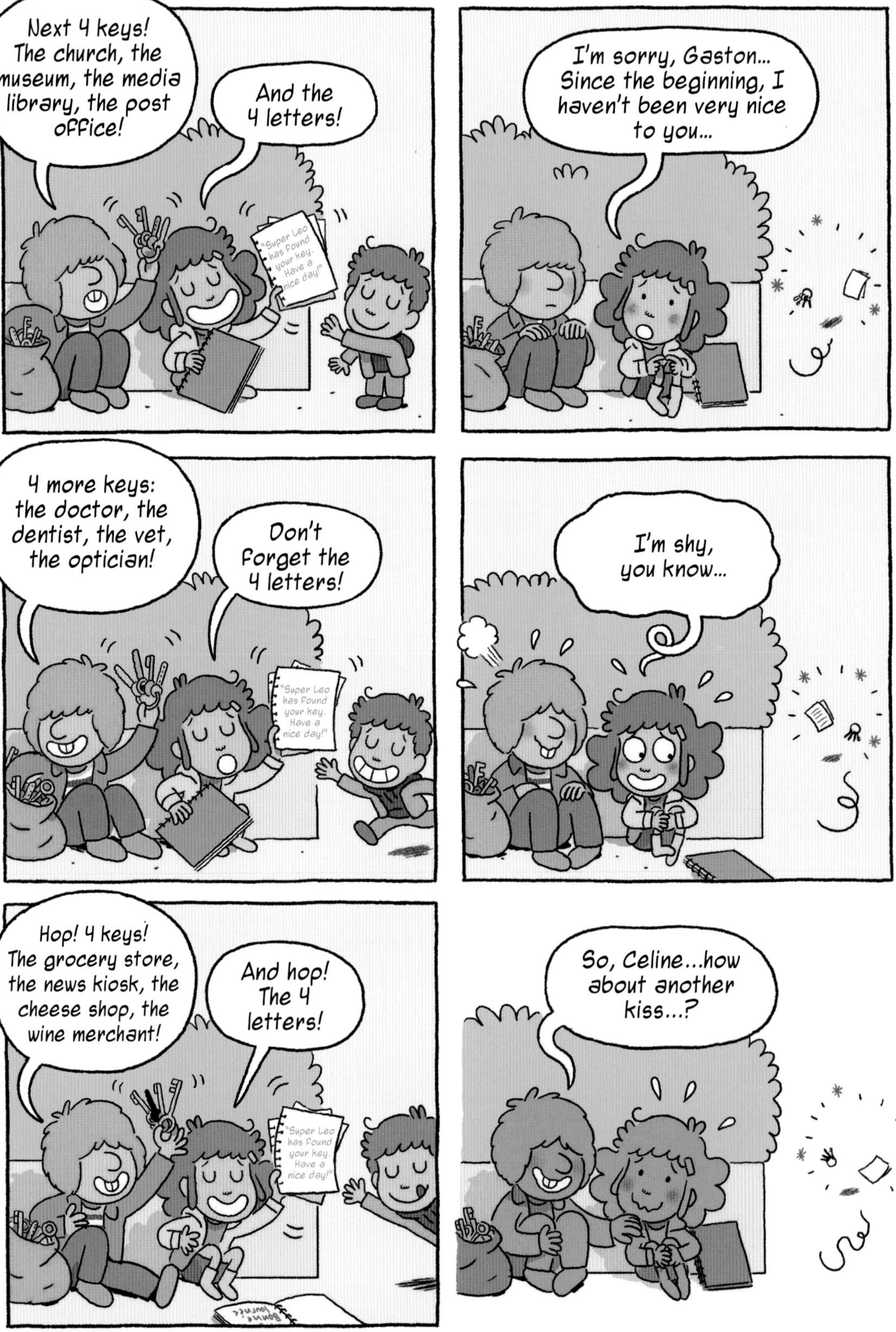
Next 4 keys! The church, the museum, the media library, the post office!
And the 4 letters!
"Super Leo has found your key. Have a nice day!"
I'm sorry, Gaston... Since the beginning, I haven't been very nice to you...
4 more keys: the doctor, the dentist, the vet, the optician!
Don't forget the 4 letters!
"Super Leo has found your key. Have a nice day!"
I'm shy, you know...
Hop! 4 keys! The grocery store, the news kiosk, the cheese shop, the wine merchant!
And hop! The 4 letters!
"Super Leo has found your key. Have a nice day!"
So, Celine...how about another kiss...?

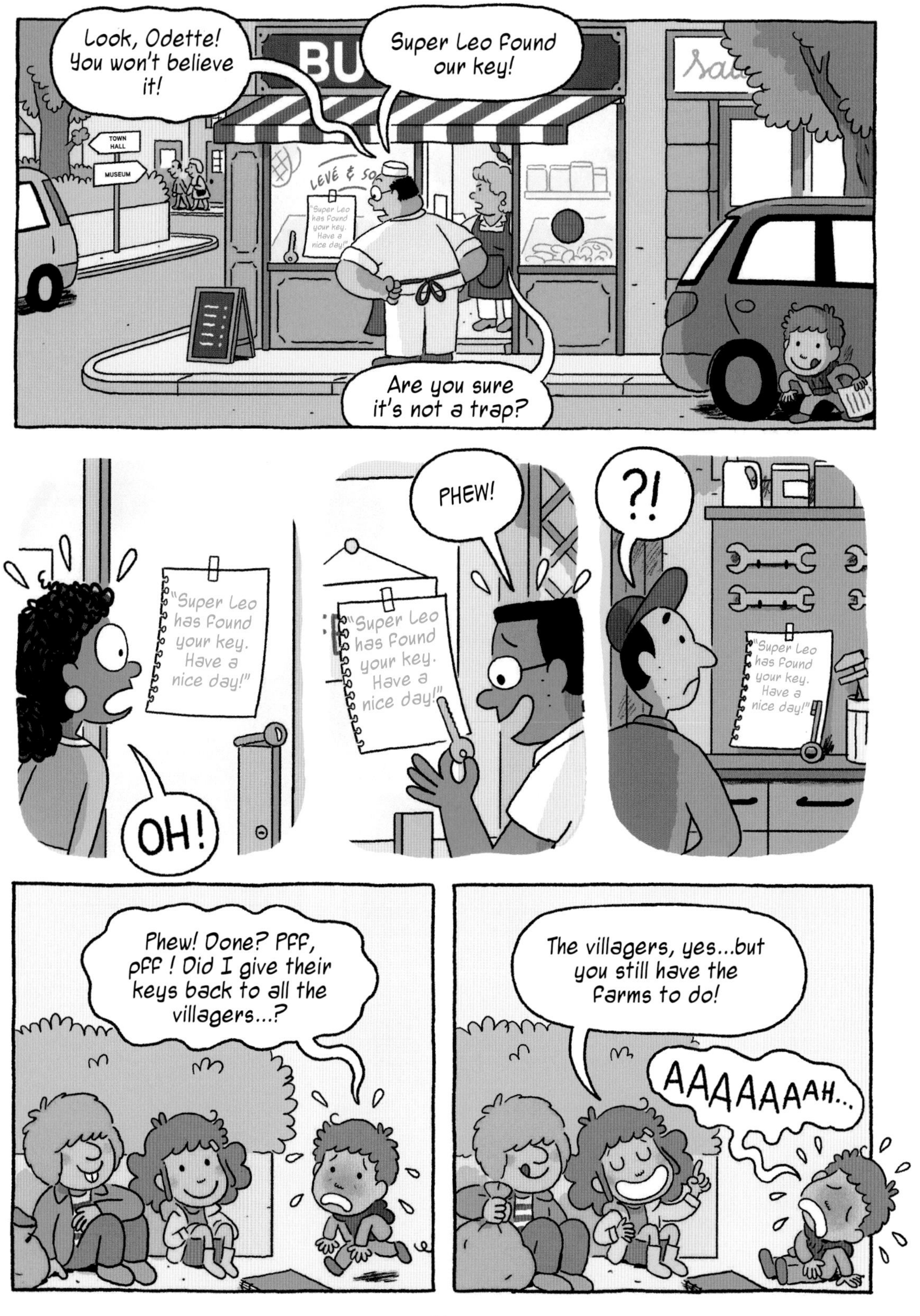
BU
TOWN HALL
MUSEUM
LEVÉ & SO
Look, Odette! You won't believe it!
Super Leo found our key!
"Super Leo has found your key. Have a nice day!"
Are you sure it's not a trap?
"Super Leo has found your key. Have a nice day!"
OH!
PHEW!
"Super Leo has found your key. Have a nice day!"
?!
"Super Leo has found your key. Have a nice day!"
Phew! Done? Pff, pff ! Did I give their keys back to all the villagers...?
The villagers, yes...but you still have the farms to do!
AAAAAAAH...

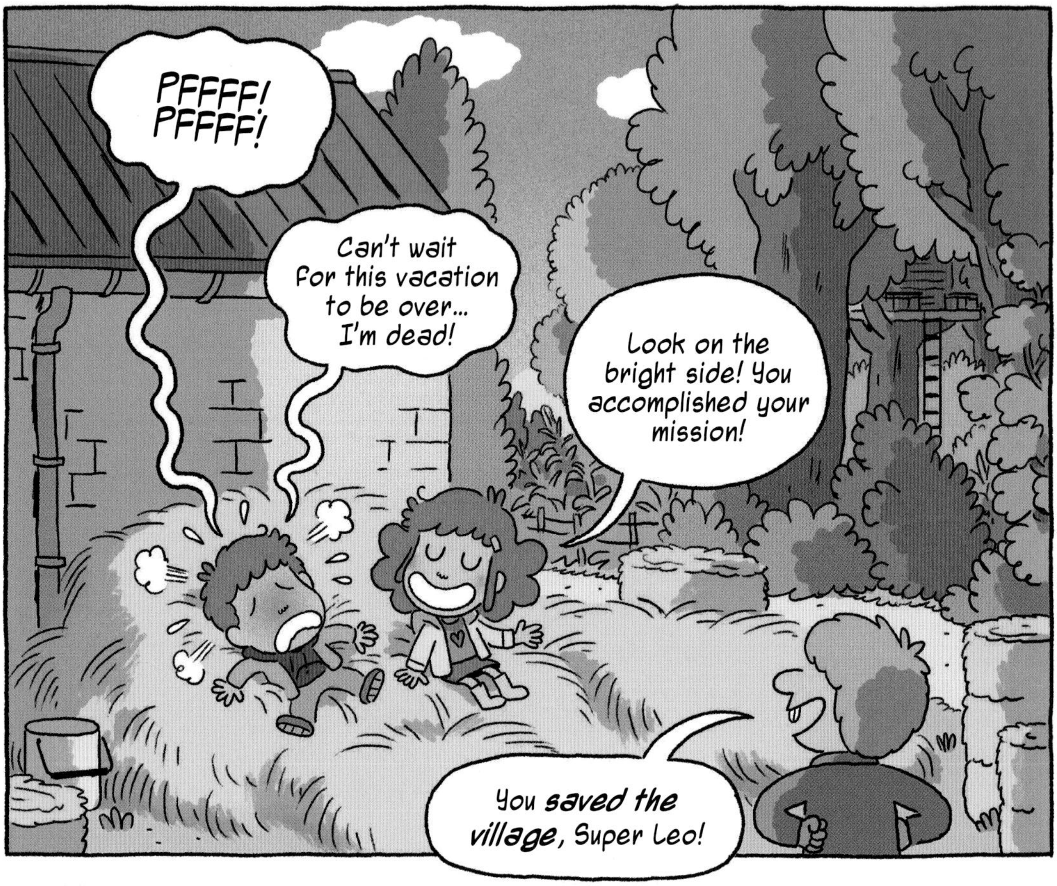
PFFFF! PFFFF!
Can't wait for this vacation to be over... I'm dead!
Look on the bright side! You accomplished your mission!
You **saved the village**, Super Leo!

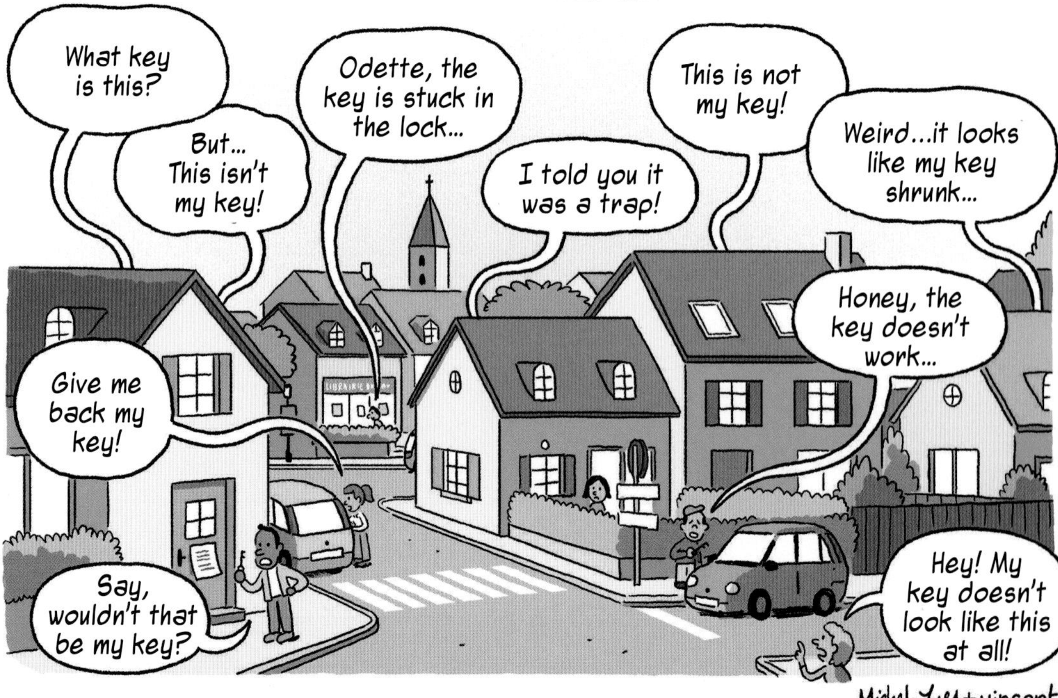
What key is this?
But... This isn't my key!
Odette, the key is stuck in the lock...
I told you it was a trap!
This is not my key!
Weird...it looks like my key shrunk...
Give me back my key!
Honey, the key doesn't work...
Say, wouldn't that be my key?
Hey! My key doesn't look like this at all!
Michel-Yves + vincent

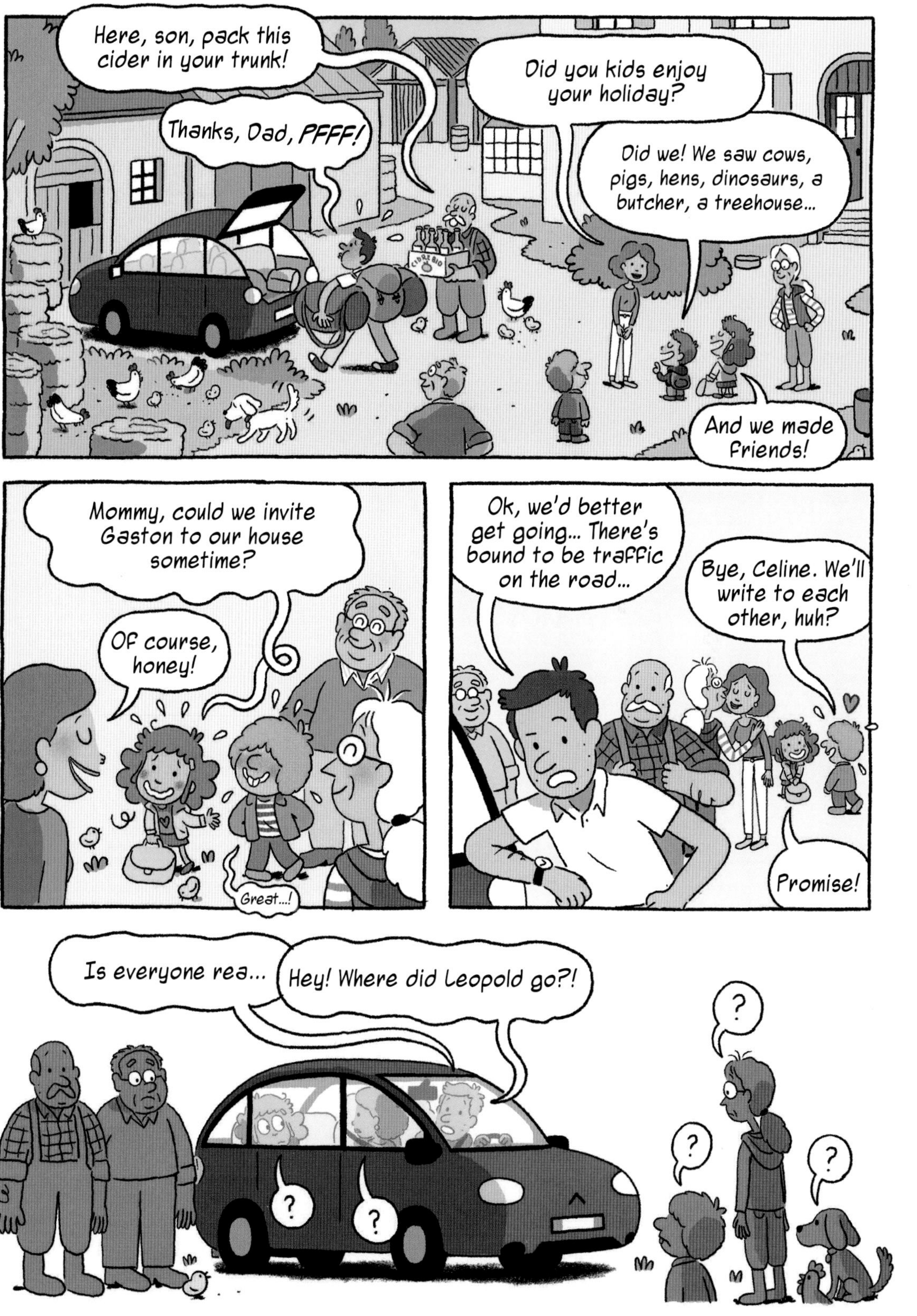
Here, son, pack this cider in your trunk!
Thanks, Dad, PFFF!
Did you kids enjoy your holiday?
Did we! We saw cows, pigs, hens, dinosaurs, a butcher, a treehouse...
And we made friends!
Mommy, could we invite Gaston to our house sometime?
Of course, honey!
Great...!
Ok, we'd better get going... There's bound to be traffic on the road...
Bye, Celine. We'll write to each other, huh?
Promise!
Is everyone rea...
Hey! Where did Leopold go?!
?
?
?
?
?

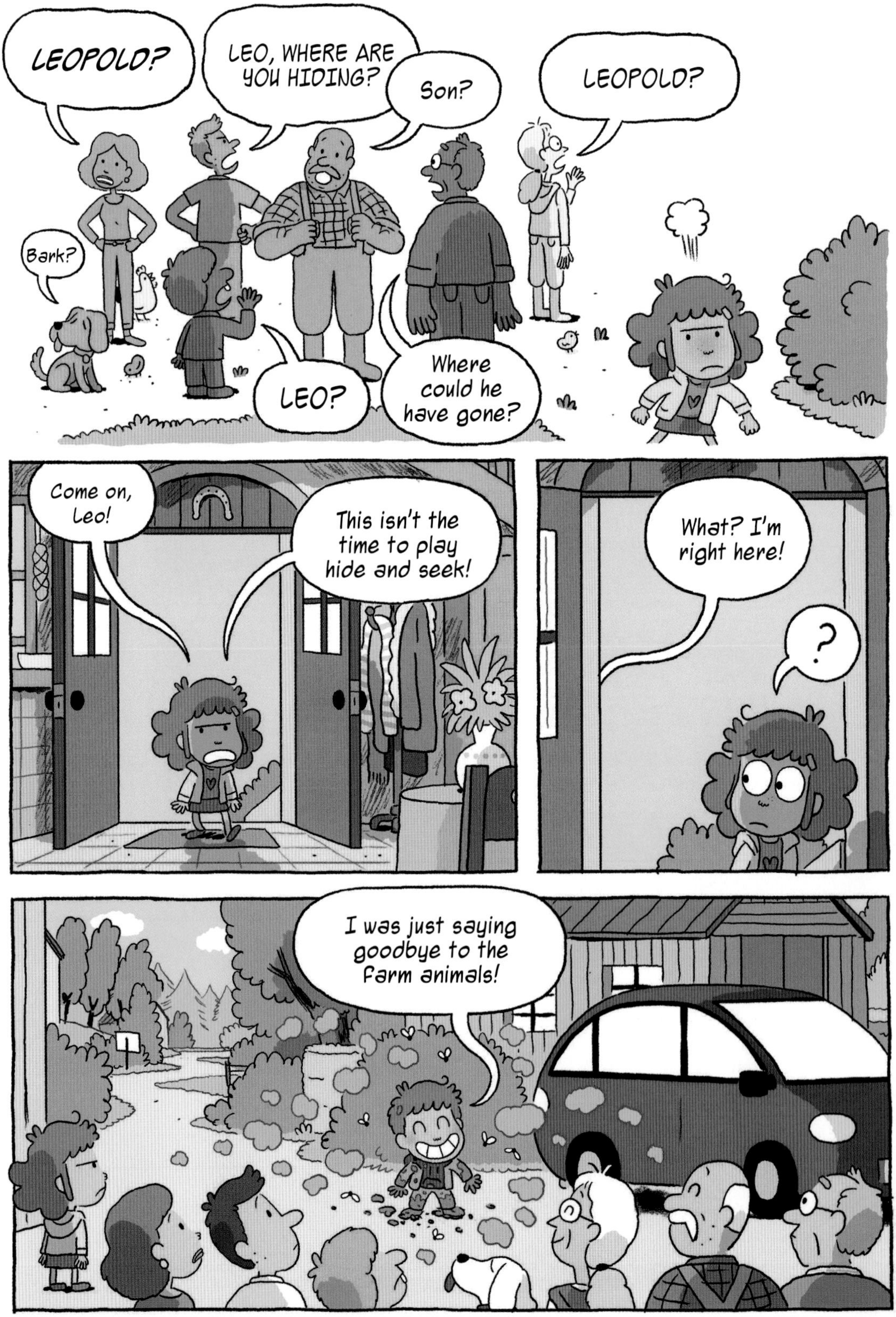
LEOPOLD?
LEO, WHERE ARE YOU HIDING?
Son?
LEOPOLD?
Bark?
LEO?
Where could he have gone?
Come on, Leo!
This isn't the time to play hide and seek!
What? I'm right here!
?
I was just saying goodbye to the farm animals!

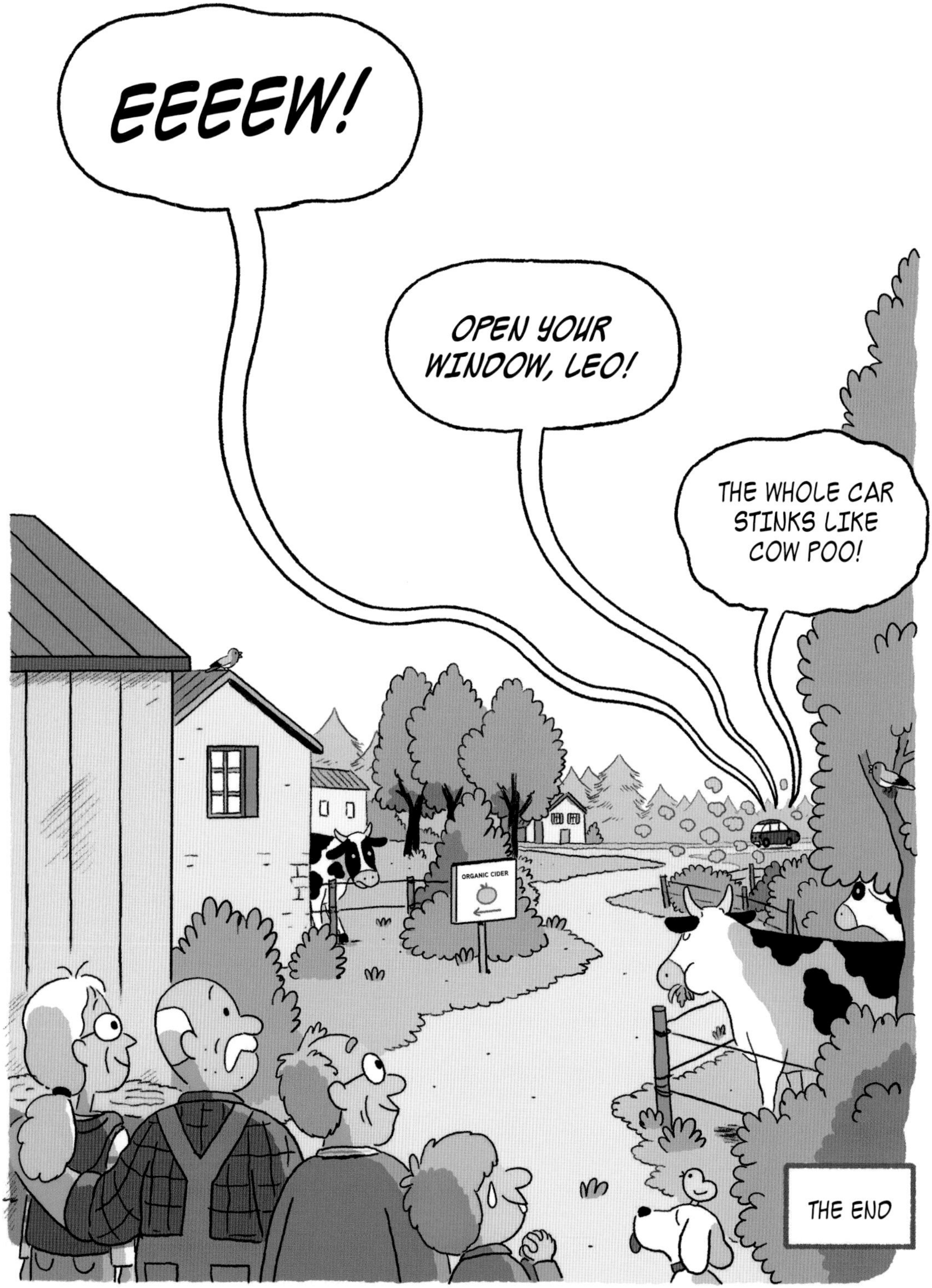
EEEEW!
OPEN YOUR WINDOW, LEO!
THE WHOLE CAR STINKS LIKE COW POO!
ORGANIC CIDER
THE END

Michel-Yves + vincent

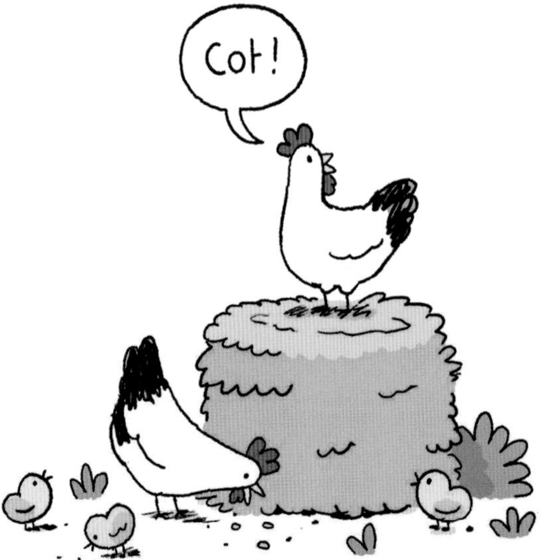
Cot!

SPOT THE DIFFERENCES

Leo and Celine are ready to hit the road! But they need help finding their belongings. Can you spot the 10 differences?

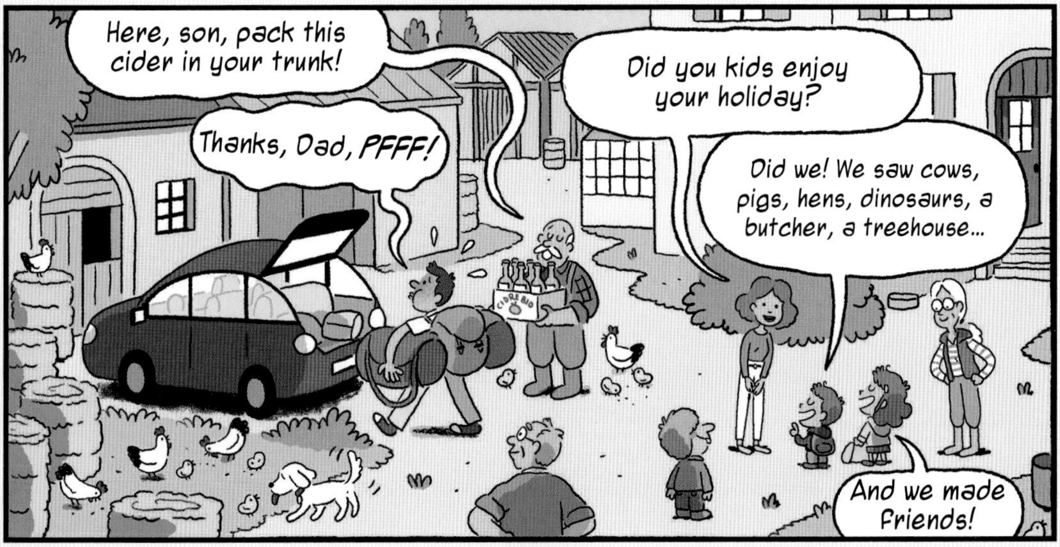
Here, son, pack this cider in your trunk!
Thanks, Dad, PFFF!
Did you kids enjoy your holiday?
Did we! We saw cows, pigs, hens, dinosaurs, a butcher, a treehouse...
And we made friends!

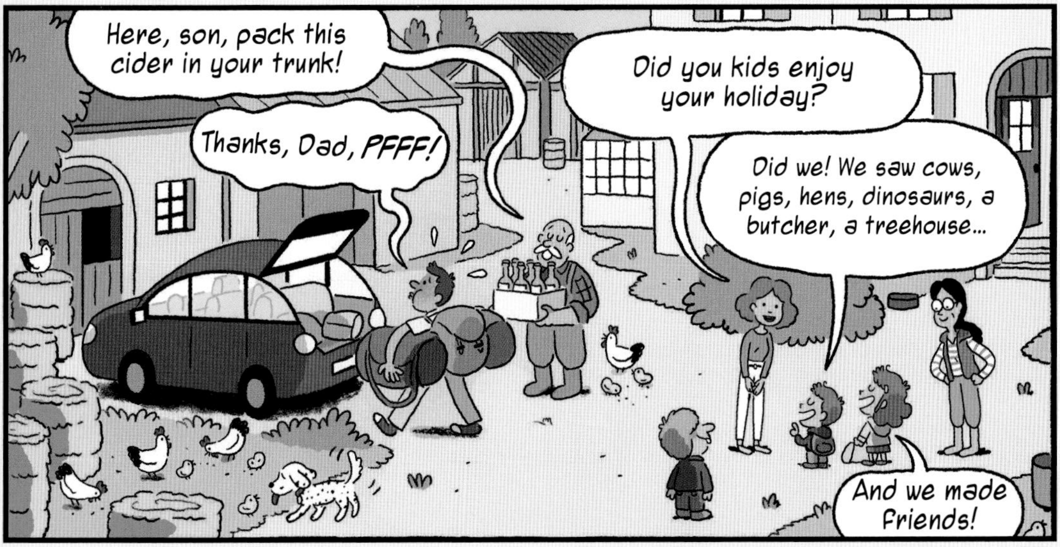
Here, son, pack this cider in your trunk!
Thanks, Dad, PFFF!
Did you kids enjoy your holiday?
Did we! We saw cows, pigs, hens, dinosaurs, a butcher, a treehouse...
And we made friends!

Answers:
Left: The green farm door -- the spots on the dog-- the purple bag dad is carrying
Center: the missing chick next to Grandpa -- the missing cider label -- the missing man below -- the red roof on the back house
Right: Gaston's green shirt -- The blue dog bowl -- Grandma's black hair

SETTINGS

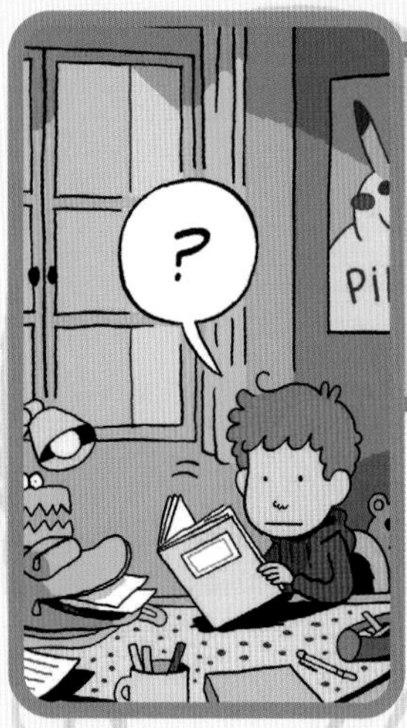

?
PI

Leopold and Celine's Home is where the main characters are most comfortable as themselves and where Leopold first discovers his power to turn invisible. Leopold and Celine are usually either conspiring or bickering in one of their bedrooms throughout the graphic novel. Their home also serves as a great space for superhero training and the occasional prank on their parents or, more often, each other.

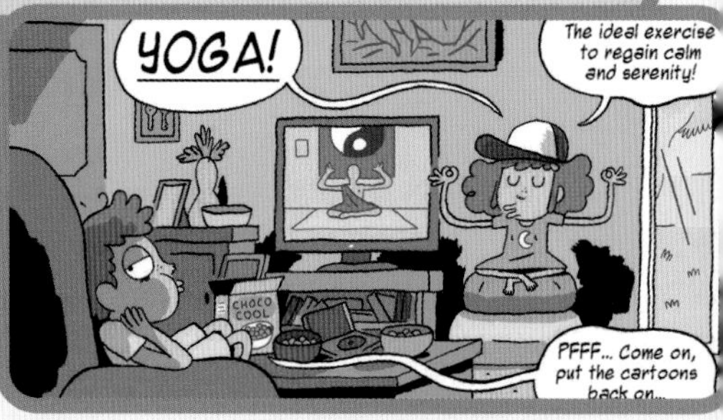

YOGA!
The ideal exercise to regain calm and serenity!
CHOCO COOL
PFFF... Come on, put the cartoons back on...

Grandma and Grandpa's Farm The farm is owned and run by Celine and Leopold's grandparents. Here Leopold and Celine learn about how a farm works, meet animals, and help their grandparents.

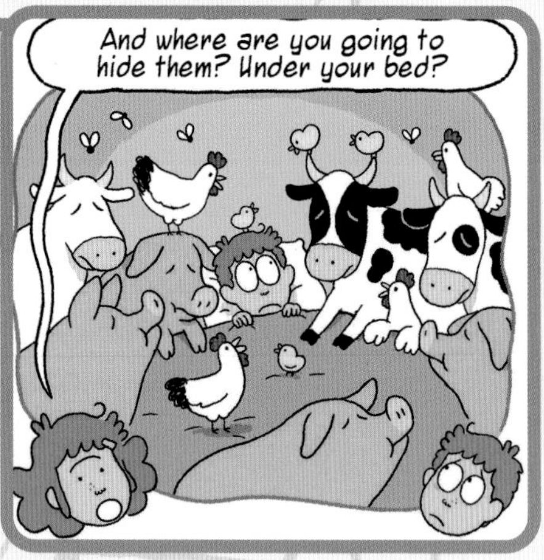

And where are you going to hide them? Under your bed?

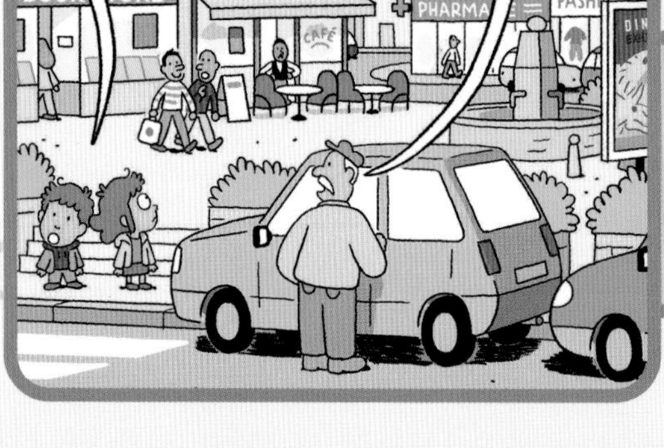

Where's the butcher's, Grandpa?
Well, it's closed. The butcher is at the market today.
BOOKSTORE
CAFÉ
PHARMA
FASHI

The town includes a collection of places that Celine and Leopold visit throughout the book while staying with their grandparents. It includes shops, grocery stores, and a museum.

THEMES

Be nice to Grandma and Grandpa.

And most of all, have fun!

Friendship and Family are core themes throughout *Where Are You, Leopold?* Even though Celine and Leopold bicker, their family ties and friendship help them overcome their problems and remain allies throughout the story. On the other hand, the way that Celine and Leopold treat each other, their friends, and their parents shows the complicated relationships friends and family can have, even when they do care about each other.

You're going to apologize to the village. Because of your dumb pranks, people will hate Super Leo, the biggest moron of all super heroes!

Right vs. Wrong is a theme that shows up in most of the stories in this graphic novel, particularly shown through the decisions of its two protagonists. While Leopold sees himself as a hero, and his sister seems to as well, their actions are often un-heroic. The graphic novel presents these actions without moral judgments, opening up interesting conversations about right vs. wrong, actions vs. consequences, and using one's powers for good.

Deception drives many of the characters and their decisions in the book. Leopold and Celine find humor and opportunity in deceiving others and each other. However, Alice seeks to reveal that they are deceiving their classmates and will do anything to find the truth.

HE'S NOWHERE TO BE FOUND!

AAAAAAAAAH! HE VANISHED!

...plus, that's a girl's power!

AHAHAHAH! WHAT A LOSER!

Peer Pressure shows up frequently as a theme, especially during scenes at the school. Often, Leopold and Celine perform pranks in order to "fit in" and impress those around them, even at the expense of their fellow classmates. In addition, many of their pranks are meant to embarrass each other or their classmates in public.

PRE-READING IDEAS

1. Have students share what superpower they wish they could have, and why. Or, have students consider what they would do if they had the power of invisibility. Have them consider the real-world benefits and downsides of the superpower. What effect might it have on them? On their friends and families? On how they view the world?

2. Have students define what a "hero" and a "villain" are before reading. Ask them to provide examples of heroes and villains, fictional and real, that embody their definitions. What do they think most distinguishes a villain and hero? Have them specify at least 3 qualities.

DISCUSSION QUESTIONS

1. On the top-left of certain pages are small images. What do you think they represent, and why were they included throughout the book?

2. Celine and her brother continually trick their friends and their parents using Leopold's powers. Do you think this is okay? Why or why not?

3. How would you feel if a friend or family member got superpowers and you didn't? How would this affect your relationship with them? How would this make you feel about yourself?

4. What do you think Leopold and Celine's relationship was like before the book begins? Do you think their relationship was changed due to his new power? How do you know this?

5. How do you think Celine might feel about her brother's newfound powers? Provide specific examples from the text as well as the images.

6. Throughout the graphic novel, the artist uses different balloon shapes and colors to represent speech or thought bubbles. Why do you think the artist does this? How does it change the reading experience? Provide specific examples.

7. Who do you think is the most "heroic" character in Where Are You, Leopold? Explain why. This can be connected back to Pre-Reading Activity #2 for further discussion.

PROJECT IDEAS

Superhero Cosplay Have students create a superhero alter ego. Have students write about their alter ego's backstory, goals, tools, and special abilities as they develop their alter ego. Using basic materials they can find at home and in the classroom, ask students to design and create a superhero costume that matches their abilities and identity and present it to the class.

Superhero Training Manual Celine attempts to train Leopold in superhero skills like speed, serenity, reflexes, and strength. For this project, have students imagine they are training Leopold or another superhero, and that they will need to build their own Superhero Training Manual. Have them consider physical, mental, and emotional essentials that they would need to include in the manual, and what steps would be needed to train a superhero in each essential. Students can use other sorts of kid-friendly procedural texts such as toy building instructions, game manuals, and how-to guides for reference.

Character Study Leopold and Celine have different motivations and goals throughout the book that drive their use of Leopold's invisibility power. Have students identify 5 examples of Celine using Leopold's power for her own gain, and 5 examples of Leopold using his power to help himself. Using a table split into two columns, identify what motivates each character in each situation. What similarities and differences do they notice? Is there a pattern for each character?

Humor vs. Humor From slapstick gags to toilet humor to one-liners, humor abounds in the text and visuals throughout *Where Are You, Leopold?* However, the writer and artist use humor in different ways to engage the reader. Have students select 5 visual examples and 5 textual examples of humor throughout the graphic novel and closely analyze them. How does the textual humor compare with the visual humor? Which one do they connect with more strongly? Do certain jokes work better in text than in image, or vice versa? Why?

Invisible Ink Have students find their own power of invisibility. By combining simple kitchen ingredients, students can create invisible ink to write secret messages. Have students watch the PBS Kids YouTube Video "Invisible Ink Crafts for Kids" for ingredients and step-by-step instructions. This activity connects with many larger themes from the book, such as Deception, and opens up the opportunity to talk about the science of turning something "invisible."

COMMON CORE CONNECTIONS

The reading of this book in combination with a thoughtful analysis through writing, presentation, or discussion (such as the projects within this guide) can promote the teaching or reinforcement of the following Common Core Standards for grades 2-4 found within the Reading: Literature strands, as well as various standards within the Reading: Foundational Skills, Writing, Speaking & Listening, and Language strands for relevant grade levels.

• CCSS.ELA-LITERACY.RL.2.1 - Ask and answer such questions as who, what, where, when, why, and how to demonstrate understanding of key details in a text.
• CCSS.ELA-LITERACY.RL.2.3 - Describe how characters in a story respond to major events and challenges.
• CCSS.ELA-LITERACY.RL.2.5 - Describe the overall structure of a story, including describing how the beginning introduces the story and the ending concludes the action.
• CCSS.ELA-LITERACY.RL.2.6 - Acknowledge differences in the points of view of characters, including by speaking in a different voice for each character when reading dialogue aloud.
• CCSS.ELA-LITERACY.RL.2.7 - Use information gained from the illustrations and words in a print or digital text to demonstrate understanding of its characters, setting, or plot.
• CCSS.ELA-LITERACY.RL.3.1 - Ask and answer questions to demonstrate understanding of a text, referring explicitly to the text as the basis for the answers.
• CCSS.ELA-LITERACY.RL.3.3 - Describe characters in a story (e.g., their traits, motivations, or feelings) and explain how their actions contribute to the sequence of events
• CCSS.ELA-LITERACY.RL.3.4 - Determine the meaning of words and phrases as they are used in a text, distinguishing literal from nonliteral language.
• CCSS.ELA-LITERACY.RL.3.5 - Refer to parts of stories, dramas, and poems when writing or speaking about a text, using terms such as chapter, scene, and stanza; describe how each successive part builds on earlier sections.
• CCSS.ELA-LITERACY.RL.3.6 - Distinguish their own point of view from that of the narrator or those of the characters.
• CCSS.ELA-LITERACY.RL.3.7 - Explain how specific aspects of a text's illustrations contribute to what is conveyed by the words in a story (e.g., create mood, emphasize aspects of a character or setting)
• CCSS.ELA-LITERACY.RL.4.1 - Refer to details and examples in a text when explaining what the text says explicitly and when drawing inferences from the text.
• CCSS.ELA-LITERACY.RL.4.2 - Determine a theme of a story, drama, or poem from details in the text; summarize the text.
• CCSS.ELA-LITERACY.RL.4.3 - Describe in depth a character, setting, or event in a story or drama, drawing on specific details in the text (e.g., a character's thoughts, words, or actions).
• CCSS.ELA-LITERACY.RL.4.4 - Determine the meaning of words and phrases as they are used in a text, including those that allude to significant characters found in mythology (e.g., Herculean).

WHERE ARE YOU
LEOPOLD?
THE INVISIBILITY GAME
8
BY SCHMITT
& CAUT

ALSO AVAILABLE: Where Are You Leopold? Book 1

FOR FURTHER QUESTIONS,

please contact
marketing@humanoids.com

CREATED BY

POP CULTURE CLASSROOM®

BiG 6+

THINK
BiG

BiG